the
House
Guest

BOOKS BY ALISON JAMES

The School Friend

The Man She Married

Her Sister's Child

The Guilty Wife

The New Couple

The Woman in Carriage 3

DETECTIVE RACHEL PRINCE SERIES

1. Lola is Missing

2. Now She's Gone

3. Perfect Girls

the House Guest

ALISON JAMES

bookouture

Published by Bookouture in 2023

An imprint of Storyfire Ltd.
Carmelite House
50 Victoria Embankment
London EC4Y 0DZ

www.bookouture.com

ISBN: 978-1-83790-762-5
eBook ISBN: 978-1-83790-761-8

PROLOGUE

The place was beautiful. All of it: the beautiful stone façade with its huge windows, the extensive grounds with tennis court and swimming pool.

Whenever she saw it, she knew deep down that it wasn't really about him; the man who owned it. It was about this house. This exceptional, unique house. In her frequent daydreams she pictured herself there, surrounded by people and laughter. After all, it was the perfect setting for parties and celebrations, like something out of a spread in a glossy magazine.

The trouble was it was another woman's house. And he was another woman's husband. That was the problem she needed to solve. But she would do it.

She would have them both.

PART ONE

JULIET

ONE

12 JUNE

It all started with that message.

The direct message I received on an already stressful morning in June, on my work Instagram account.

The profile photo is of a striking young woman, with perfect features and a lot of light red hair.

Hi, You probably don't know who I am, but I'm trying to get in touch with your husband as soon as possible.

I'm intrigued, but also a little unsettled. It looks like there's a second message, but I don't have time to read it now, or more importantly, give it my full attention. On this day in particular, there's just so much to do. The house has to be perfect. I told my husband, Hugh, as much when I set my alarm for five thirty this morning, to ensure that it would be.

'Come on now, sweetie, it's not a big deal if things are a bit rough around the edges,' he mumbled as he rolled over in bed and tried to return to his usual deep sleep. 'People come for a nose and if things aren't one hundred per cent immaculate, that's just tough. You need to learn to relax.'

He always speaks with the ease of someone for whom owning an important house is an automatic right. Because for him it always has been. This property is his family's place, his childhood home. He doesn't notice its faults the way I do. He doesn't fret like I do when things aren't perfect.

I scoop up a fragment of cellophane caught in the stems of a lavender bush and shade my eyes from the sun as I turn to look back up the drive to the house.

Mullens End. Not merely a house, but a way of life. A celebrated piece of architecture and one of the finest in the county. I think it's beautiful: of course I do. Who wouldn't want to live in such a special place, the envy of the aspiring middle class for miles around? And even more desirable since the local branch line at Benfield Holt was linked to the fast South Western service to Waterloo, giving a London commuting time of a mere forty-one minutes. That sent its already hefty value sky-rocketing still higher.

But I don't love it in the visceral way Hugh loves it. He grew up here, after all, and claims – in a way that I privately find overly sentimental – that the place is 'in his blood'. I grew up in non-descript suburbia and never formed any emotional attachment to the houses that I lived in when I was young. The idea seems a little silly to me.

Besides, living in a significant piece of property is a mixed blessing. Its Grade 1 listing means that it can't be altered without permission. Although, if Hugh and I fail to maintain it adequately, we could theoretically face criminal prosecution. Okay, so that's unlikely in practice, but it gives you an idea of the level of commitment we're looking at. There's always maintenance that needs doing, from the ancient plumbing system, to the eighteenth-century slate roof tiles to the handsome sash windows – nine at the front and ten at the back – that can only be reglazed with an approved type of pane. The window frames are crumbling and let in draughts and rain, which causes damp patches on the interior walls. It's all a lot more involved than the work you see people undertake on TV property shows.

The upkeep on the place is a burden, and a huge expense, one which is all paid for under the terms of a family trust. Because I grew up in a very ordinary home myself, I didn't have an innate feel for what was involved; I had to learn all that in ten years as Hugh's wife, as chatelaine. And then there are events like today's Garden Open Day, when gardening fanatics, village worthies and plain nosy parkers can come and wander around the grounds, stare in through the windows and ask endless questions. I find the whole thing hugely stressful; Hugh views it all as something of a laugh.

So, on balance, I don't always love Mullens End as much as I could. But Hugh loves it more than anything. Or anyone.

There's been no rain for several weeks, and beneath the blue sky, the humid air hangs heavily with dust motes and fragments of linden tree pollen. Flowers from the chestnut trees that flank the semi-circular front lawn are shedding their petals like slow-falling snow. On the horizon, distant clouds like bruises threaten that rain is finally about to arrive. Why today of all days, I think irritably. The whole point of the Open Day is just that: visitors staying outside in the open air. I don't want to have to offer them shelter. On the other hand, an imminent down-pour might put off some of the rubberneckers. I can only hope.

My phone buzzes in my pocket with a WhatsApp. Immediately I brace myself for another direct message from the unknown woman.

But no, *Message from Belle*, it tells me. Belinda Langridge, my best friend in the village. Probably my closest friend anywhere, given the amount of time we spend together.

*We're planning on bobbing up later for your garden thing.
Anything I can do to help? xxx*

I type a reply.

That's sweet, but all under control I think. See you later xx

As I finish typing, I see someone in my peripheral vision.
Pete, our gardener and handyman, approaches. He's a burly,
heavyset man in his early sixties, whose rather gruff manner
masks a kind heart. Most importantly, he's one hundred per
cent trustworthy.

'All right, Mrs M?' he enquires.

'Yes, thanks, Pete.' I smile, as though this whole thing is a
breeze. 'Everything in place with the parking arrangements?'

He gives the slightest nod of his head to confirm that it is,
and goes back to arranging the post and chain dividers.

Once I've disposed of my litter bag, I go in search of Caitlin,
the teenage daughter of our cleaner Liz, and give her the
printed guides to hand to the visitors as they arrive.

A brief history of Mullens End

*Welcome to Mullens End, a celebrated piece of Queen Anne
architecture. Described in Pevsner as 'an exquisite neoclassical gem; the eighteenth-century formal house in miniature',
the original house was built in 1701 by an unknown architect
and originally known as Benfield Manor. The great-grandfather of the current owner, Ernest Mullen, bought the estate in
1931 with his industrial fortune. He renamed the house to
signify to the residents of Nether Benfield and the rest of the
world that he was now a member of the landed gentry, despite
his money having been made in manufacturing electrical
goods.*

*Built of limestone, with a hipped slate roof and tall chim-
neys, Mullens End has three formal reception rooms, six
bedrooms and four bathrooms. A broad, elegant staircase runs
all the way up to the attic and much of the original eighteenth-
century wood panelling is still in place. An additional wing
was built by Ernest Mullen in 1932.*

*The house stands in twenty acres of flower gardens and
broadleaf woodland of beech, oak and aspen. Of particular
note are the family mausoleum (a folly modelled after an
ancient Grecian temple), the terraced garden to the south-east
and the rose maze, planted with highly scented damask and
old-fashioned tea roses.*

I didn't mention in this summary that there is also a hard
tennis court and a heated swimming pool at the rear of the
house, additions the puritanical Ernest Mullen would probably
have disdained. Or that the recent wing now houses a state-of-
the-art kitchen and utility area, plus a specially designed suite
of his and her offices. It would sound too much like showing off.

As I head into the house to change out of my dusty
gardening clothes, I get another message. This one is from my
son, Luca.

*Hi mama, hope tutti va bene, still on for next weekend? Call
me later. Baci* ☺

We always text each other like this: in a blend of English
and Italian. Luca is currently taking his Baccalaureate at the
International School of Modena. This means I only see him
briefly every few weeks, but I agreed with his father that, when
Luca was old enough, part of his upbringing and education
would take place in Italy. He was not only conceived, but born
there. I'm part-Italian myself (through my maternal grandmoth-

er), and I was studying at the University of Perugia for a year for my Modern Languages degree, when I fell hard for Massimo, then a part-time tutor in the university's engineering faculty. We embarked on an affair and, by the end of that summer, I discovered – to my horror, I can't deny it – that I was pregnant.

I ended up staying on in a rented flat in Perugia, enduring a difficult pregnancy and birth, only for it to become clear a few months later that the drudgery of domesticity and rearing an infant had dampened Massimo's desire for me. He now announced a plan to leave academia and move away from Perugia for a lucrative job in car design.

I wish I could say I was heartbroken about the relationship ending, but the truth is I didn't have the time – or the emotion – to spare to heartbreak. Every minute was taken up with caring for my newborn son, whom I adored. I had thought I couldn't love anyone more than I loved Massimo, but I was wrong; I loved Luca far more. So it was with a heavy heart but a feeling of inevitability that I decided to return to England and complete my degree as a young single mother. But the understanding I reached with Massimo was that Luca, at least, would return to Italy once he was old enough to be more independent from me. In the meantime, he paid me a modest amount of child support, but not so much that I could stop work and stay at home with Luca full time.

As I reach the front door of the house, I think I feel a single, fat raindrop fall on the bridge of my nose. I glance up at the sky for a moment before continuing round to the back entrance and into the narrow passage that flanks the kitchen. It's filled with the usual paraphernalia of country life: wellingtons, walking sticks, a trug, dog baskets. I tug off my gardening gloves and toss them into the trug.

Hugh's dogs, Pongo and Jeff, get to their feet and come towards me, tails wagging, sniffing in my pockets in case I happen to have kibble or some other treats secreted there. Pongo, ancient and arthritic, lumbers heavily, the younger Jeff skids and skitters, his claws making a scraping sound on the flagstones. I suppose, in theory, they're my dogs too, yet I always think of them as Hugh's: a pair of overweight, greedy Labradors. I pat them absently, before shooing them out of my way.

'That you, darling?' Hugh shouts from the landing as I go through into the formal hallway which still has its original Queen Anne oak doors and architraves. The carpeted staircase, with its ornate balustrade, sweeps up in front of me and round two right-angled turns before reaching the first floor.

'Yep,' I call back. 'Just going to change quickly before we're swamped.'

When I reach the landing, Hugh bends to give me a swift kiss on the cheek. He's tall – a lot taller than I am. He's put on a formal shirt and clean jeans and is struggling to insert a pair of gold cufflinks. 'Righto,' he says cheerfully. 'I'll go down and man the barricades. You take your time. And relax; it'll soon be over.'

I smile and hug him, before ducking into the huge master bedroom, decorated in shades of eau de Nil and sugar almond pink. The carpet is worn but of the highest quality, as are the heavy lined drapes at the sash windows and the mahogany Victorian four-poster bed. I tug off my T-shirt and overalls and head into the en suite bathroom.

After showering, I restyle my hair into its smooth, glossy bob, apply a full face of make-up, finishing with bright red lipstick, and then take some time selecting something to wear that says both 'lady of the manor' and 'relatable working mother'. I settle on a tomato-red linen shift dress that complements my dark colouring, and a pair of black sandals embellished with gold buckles. A gold locket at my neck and a single gold bangle are the only jewellery I add. In my opinion, it's not the right occasion to come off as flashy.

As I put the leather jewellery case back in the drawer of my dressing table, I pause briefly and run a finger over a framed photo of Luca, taken when he was six or seven. A flop of chestnut hair over his forehead, broad beaming smile, bright eyes. My beautiful boy. My son; Hugh's stepson.

Before I go downstairs, I perch on the edge of the curtained bed with my phone, and pull up my Instagram account. I rarely use the platform, other than to post content for my business: a one-woman interior design consultancy. I click on the direct message icon in the corner and begin to read.

Alexis Lambert
@lexilam

Hi, You probably don't know who I am, but I'm trying to get in touch with your husband as soon as possible.

I open the second message.

Apologies for messaging you out of the blue like that. I should explain: I recently investigated my family tree on an ancestry search site and I'm pretty sure your husband and I are distant cousins. I tried contacting him directly, but he doesn't seem to have any social media accounts so I thought I'd try you. Anyway, sorry to land this on you, but perhaps you wouldn't mind passing on this message as soon as you can. Thx, Alexis

I re-read the message, chewing on the corner of my lower lip. Then I return to the Instagram home screen, but the direct message icon still has a red digit on it. There is a third message. My heart rate quickens as I read it.

PS, sorry, I should have said... I'm a cousin on the Mullen side. Avril Lambert was my mum. Think your husband will probably know exactly who I am.

Will he? I wonder. And, more importantly, is this even true?

I start to type, my fingers trembling slightly. *Let me speak to him and get back to you.*

TWO

12 JUNE

I'm jumpy for the rest of the day.

Every time my phone buzzes in my pocket, I wonder if it's *her*, messaging me again.

'Are you okay, Jules?' Belinda asks, when she manages to find me in the garden. 'You seem a bit distracted.'

'Fine.' I force a smile. 'I always worry about whether people are enjoying themselves.'

'Oh my God, of *course* they are. And why wouldn't they be? Mullens End is the most fabulous place. I know I'm always saying it, but you're so lucky, Jules.'

I smile back at her. 'Most of the time it's lovely, yes. But sometimes I'd happily swap with you.'

The Langridges live in Birch Cottage on the far side of the village, a house as sturdy and practical as Belinda herself: but it's relatively small and, with three young children, extremely cluttered.

Belinda turns to me and gives me a broad grin, exposing the gap in between her two front teeth.

'Are you sure?' I watch the groups of people shuffling along the gravelled paths of the rose maze. The sky's clouded over, and the threat of a downpour hangs heavily in the air. One or two people are putting up the hoods on their cagoules, or unfurling rain macs. 'The weather's not really what I would have wanted,' I add, aware I sound fretful.

'Nonsense, it's amazing,' Belinda enthuses. 'All the old dears from the village are tucking into the cream tea. Trust me, it's the highlight of their year. And people appreciate the special little touches – the printed guide, and the little signposts you've put up everywhere.'

She places a comforting hand on my arm. That word sums up Belinda Langridge. Comforting. She's tall, with the big-boned build of the English countrywoman: all ample bosom and child-bearing hips. Thick straw-blonde hair is pulled back from a slightly weather-beaten face dusted with freckles. She rarely wears make-up and, despite my nagging her about it, is a stranger to SPF. Her toenails, visible in a pair of old Birken-stocks, reveal the chipped remains of nail polish that was prob-ably applied two summers ago. She's wearing cropped trousers, a Breton top and a yellow hooded jacket, which, unlike my lightweight dress, will be perfect once the rain starts. She has that very upper-middle-class trait of always having the right clothing for the British weather, the sort of woman capable of rustling up a kitchen supper or a full beach picnic at a moment's notice.

'So you think people are enjoying themselves?'

'Oh my God, of *course* they are. And why wouldn't they be? Mullens End is the most fabulous place. I know I'm always saying it, but you're so lucky, Jules.'

I smile back at her. 'Most of the time it's lovely, yes. But sometimes I'd happily swap with you.'

The Langridges live in Birch Cottage on the far side of the village, a house as sturdy and practical as Belinda herself: but it's relatively small and, with three young children, extremely cluttered.

There's a faint rumble of thunder, and heavy, earth-scented raindrops begin to fall. Visitors scatter, looking for cover, knocking over chairs and dropping their printed guides as they run. The deluge quickly turns them to patches of white pulp.

'I can stay and help you clear up if you like,' Belinda says as the two of us take shelter in the back porch.

'That would be so kind... Tell you what, why don't you and Simon stay and have supper when everyone's gone?'

Belinda pulls a face. 'Afraid we've got the kids with us.'

'That's no problem; you know they're always welcome.'

'All right, but only if Hugh's okay with it.'

'He'll be fine.'

'Of course he will; he's a darling,' she sighs enthusiastically.

I feel a frisson of irritation. Everyone always thinks Hugh's so charming. And he is, of course he is. I adore him. But there's a rigidness about him too. Hugh wants what Hugh wants. And for pretty much all of his life, he's got it.

Three hours later, Hugh and I and the five Langridges are in the kitchen. Summer rain pounds brutally on the glass of the skylights. Hugh pours wine for the adults, while I set about preparing supper trays for eight-year-old twins Daisy and Primrose and five-year-old Rufus. They're adorable children: all flaxen blonde and rosy-cheeked like something out of a Boden catalogue.

Belinda lowers the rim of her wine glass to address me. 'Don't bother giving them anything too fancy, honestly, Jules: it's not worth it. They're fussy eaters at the best of times.' She gives a self-deprecating grimace, as though acknowledging that her imperfect parenting is to blame. 'Just a sandwich and a packet of crisps will be fine.'

'Spoilt little beggars,' observes Simon Langridge, after downing half a glass of Burgundy in one swallow. 'When we were their age, we just ate what we were bloody well given, no ifs and buts. Trouble is, this lot think they're in charge of the whole shooting match.'

Simon is long-limbed and slightly stooped, with a weak chin, thinning hair and a tendency to bluster. He's wearing trousers the colour of the wine he's drinking, and his feet are bare in his yacht shoes. 'I keep telling Belle that a short, sharp spell at boarding school would straighten 'em out, but she won't have it.'

'They're too tiny,' Belinda protests, running her fingers over Primrose's curls. 'Maybe when they're teenagers.'

'Oh God, definitely,' snorts Simon. 'They're one hundred per cent going away when they hit puberty. Not having three loads of female hormones under one roof. Bad enough with one.' He slaps Belinda affectionately on her backside. 'Built for comfort, not for speed, eh, darling?'

She bats his hand away with a good-natured laugh.

'Of course you've got plenty of good options for boarding schools in this neck of the woods – you've got Dawlish House...' He tails off, and I see Belinda shoot him a look. She's warning him, as she often has to, not to embark on the sort of conversation that's staple fodder among local parents. Not in front of us Mullens. We don't have children. At least, I have Luca, but Hugh and I have none of our own. We tried; we failed. By which I mean I was the one unable to have more babies.

I fill the trays for the children with cocktail sausages, cherry tomatoes, cubes of cheese and a cupcake each, as ever feeling a pang that I have no little ones of my own to indulge. They follow me into the snug, trailed by Pongo and Jeff and the Langridges' Jack Russell, Rocket, all three sensing the probability of dropped scraps. I settle the children on the sofa in front of CBeebies, and then return to the kitchen, where Hugh and the Langridges have already embarked on a second bottle of wine. The rain is easing off, with just rhythmic, heavy drips falling on the skylight.

'Here's to adults-only time,' Belinda sighs, raising her glass in a mock toast. 'Bliss!'

'Adults only!' brays Simon. 'Sauce! Chance would be a fine thing.' He affects a rueful grin and slaps Belinda's behind again. 'Mind you, back in the day, we knew how to have a good time, didn't we, Belle? Used to be a right goer in her youth, this one, though you wouldn't think it now.'

I glance up at Belinda as I slice fennel for a salad, thinking I would be furious if Hugh treated me the way Simon treats his wife: like a familiar but worn piece of furniture. But Belinda, ever good-natured, just rolls her eyes.

By the time we sit down thirty minutes later to baked salmon with jacket potatoes and salad, a third bottle has been opened and the chatter has grown loud and boisterous.

'So, old man,' Simon grips Hugh's shoulder and leans his head on it tipsily. 'How are things in the racy world of art dealing?'

Hugh runs a business importing Ottoman artefacts from Turkey and selling them at hugely marked-up prices at a chichi little gallery near Shepherd Market. Privately, I feel a little embarrassed by his career choice, which seems to me to be no more than a glorified Etsy shop. He only earns about the same as I do from my part-time design work, and the truth is, we would never cover the bills on Mullens End if we didn't also have a private income from his family trust.

'Oh, you know; ticking over,' Hugh replies evenly, using the uncorking of a bottle of Grüner Veltliner to escape from Simon's embrace. 'To be honest, I've been spending more office hours trying to sort out this wretched Meadowbrook business.'

'That still going on?' asks Belinda, holding out her glass for some of the white wine.

'Very much so.' I lift my eyes heavenwards with a sigh. This is a conversation I'd rather avoid, so I ask, 'Shall I go and check on the kids? Maybe they'd like some pudding?'

Meadowbrook is a proposed development of forty-three new houses and twelve flats that, if built, would abut our land, and involve the building of an access road past our driveway. Hugh has been doing everything he can to prevent planning permission from being granted, including hosting meetings in the village hall, doorstopping our neighbours and getting contacts in the local press to write scare stories. Of course, I'd hardly welcome the disruption and loss of privacy if Meadow-brook were built, but I can also see the other side of the argument: that local people need affordable homes to live in. I've failed to make my darling husband see the issue from this point of view.

When I return to the kitchen after offering the children choc ices, I'm irritated to find the same topic being discussed. Belinda is asking, 'So who's the developer behind Meadowcroft? Are they at least a reputable company?'

'That's the thing,' Hugh says, 'from what I can ascertain, they seem very dodgy. The company calls itself JM Develop-ments. I researched them through Companies House and they're owned by a shell company, and that's owned by *another* shell company, and so on until I hit on a set-up owned by one Jamie Molcan. I thought it sounded familiar and then the penny dropped...' He pauses for dramatic effect. 'Molcan is the guy who bought Benfield Grange from the Bonningtons. Their land borders ours and we always had a good rapport with them. Old Arthur Bonnington was a pal of my dad's. But this Molcan chap moved here from east London, and started throwing his weight around. Knocked most of the old house down and put up an ugly modern extension. He put a lot of people's backs up, so, naturally, some of them started asking questions. Turns out he's a bit of a crook. Closed down various companies to avoid paying corporation tax. Now it looks like he's hell-bent on developing every bit of the area he can get his greedy mitts on. And he's not going to let anyone stop him.'

Simon's eyes widen and Belinda lets out a 'Gosh!' but I can't contain my scepticism any longer. 'Oh, come on, darling! That's a bit far-fetched, isn't it? You make it sound like the plot of a crime novel.'

Hugh shrugs and takes a mouthful of wine. 'These are the facts, and I'm just putting them out there... Anyway, with any luck, it'll all be irrelevant. We registered our objection with the planning people at the Borough Council within the required time frame, and if they have any sense, they won't grant the planning permission. At the very least, it will delay the building of those godawful little brick boxes. I'm going to keep putting obstacles in their way until they give up and piss off somewhere else.'

Simon, registering the uneasy expression on my face, asks, 'How about you, Jules? What's your news?'

'Well...' I spin the stem of my wine glass between my red-painted fingertips: once, twice, three times. 'Something did happen today. Something a bit weird, actually.'

Hugh turns his head sharply. 'What are you talking about?'

'I got a direct message on Instagram.'

'Someone slid into your DMs!' Simon grins with delight at his grasp of social media slang. 'That's what the kids say, isn't it?'

'Ooh,' Belinda giggles. Her hair is escaping from its ponytail in disordered tufts and her lipstick is smeared. She looks, and sounds, a little drunk. 'Some hunky man?'

'A woman, actually,' I reply coolly. 'She says she's Hugh's cousin.'

Hugh leans back in his chair and stares directly at me. 'What? Who is she?'

'I can show you.' I fetch my phone from the dresser and pull up Alexis Lambert's account. There are only about forty posts, most of them selfies. They show a confident young woman, probably not much older than thirty, with long strawberry blonde hair and perfect cheekbones. Her slightly slanting eyes are a mesmerising blend of green and smoke-grey and the shots where she is smiling reveal beautiful teeth.

'Ding dong!' says Simon wolfishly. 'She's a bit of a looker.'

'She's got the Mullen red hair,' observes Belinda. 'Bit of a tart, though, even if she is your cousin, Hugh.' She points to a shot that displays an obscene amount of cleavage.

'Why didn't you tell me about this earlier?' he asks me, taking the phone from Belinda and examining the images himself. 'You never mentioned her.'

'Because I didn't get the chance. I only just got the message as I was going downstairs to greet the Open Day visitors. I barely saw you all afternoon, and we went straight from clearing up the garden to this.' I sweep a hand around at the empty wine bottles, the half-eaten cheese board and scrunched-up napkins. 'Anyway, she says in her message that she's Avril's daughter. As if that would mean something to you.'

Hugh sets my phone down on the table, still looking at Alexis Lambert's profile. He hunches forward with his right arm encircling his ribs and the fingers of his left hand pressed over his mouth. 'She's the heir,' he says slowly, as though reading from a script. He takes a sip of wine and holds it in his mouth for a few seconds before swallowing it.

'What heir?' Belinda says, slurring slightly. 'What are you talking about?'

'She's the heir to Mullens End.'

THREE

12 JUNE

'This place is held in trust,' Hugh explains, looking at the confused faces of the Langridges. He reaches for a bottle of Scotch on the sideboard and empties his water glass before pouring a finger of the whisky. 'I'm just the life tenant. My great-grandfather wanted to place an entail on the estate which would impose certain conditions on who could inherit it. A landowner leaving his stately home to a distant male relation, for example, bypassing his own daughter if he happens to have no sons. Call it Downton Abbey syndrome if you like...' He gives a short laugh. 'I believe that was the entire basis of the plot of that show... Anyway, that was once more or less automatic with large estates and titles. Trouble is entails, or fee tails, as I think they're also called, were abolished in 1925 and my great-grandfather was making his will in the 1930s.'

'Is that the rather fierce-looking chap in the front hall?' Simon asks, referring to the oil painting depicting a man in tweeds with a bushy ginger moustache.

'Yep, that's him. Painted by Gerald Brockhurst. Next to the naff Scottish painting,' Hugh grins as he tops up his whisky and pushes the bottle across the table so the others can help themselves.

The 'naff Scottish painting' is one by an unknown nineteenth-century artist that I inherited from my own grandparents and brought with me to Mullens End. Hugh begrudgingly allowed me to hang it in the front hall, but told me loftily that landscapes are considered 'low art'. He's made endless public digs about it since.

He swallows some of the whisky and goes on: 'So, instead of entailing the estate, Ernest set up a trust that would enable his direct descendants to enjoy this place, but only if certain conditions were met.'

'Like being male?' Belinda asks. She reaches for the Scotch bottle, but Simon discreetly pushes it out of reach with a muttered, 'Come on, old girl, you've had enough.'

Hugh is shaking his head. 'No, he was happy for Mullens End to go to a woman, as long as she was directly descended from him.'

'Like this Alexis lass?' Simon interjects.

'Exactly. The life tenant has to have Mullen blood.'

'So...' Simon looks from Hugh to me and back again. 'What would happen to this place if you and Jules split up then?'

'Simon!' Belinda admonishes. 'You can't ask them that!' She glowers at her husband, and I'm grateful for her loyalty. 'That's more than a tad tactless.'

'Oh, that's all covered under the family trust too,' Hugh says airily. 'Not that that will ever happen, will it, darling?' He leans over to me and drops a kiss on my shoulder.

'Sweet!' says Belinda, undoing and redoing her messy ponytail. 'You two. Sweet, aren't they, Simon?'

'And what about this ginger bird who's just popped up on Jules' socials?' Simon frowns. 'How does she fit into all this?'

'Pretty straightforward, actually,' Hugh replies easily. 'If I die... when I die: I mean, obviously that won't be for a while yet... she'll get Mullens End. If Jules is still alive at that point, then she'll get a financial settlement, but not the house.'

'Because you don't have any kids?' Simon asks.

'Exactly.' Hugh smiles, as if to reassure the others that he doesn't mind being childless. 'I had a sister, but she was lost to a cot death at three months, so there are no nieces or nephews either. My father was an only child, so no first cousins. My grandfather had a sister, but she only had one child – my first cousin once removed – and he was killed in a boating accident. So that only leaves the line descending from Ernest's younger brother Edgar. Edgar had two sons, one of whom was killed in the Second World War. The other one produced two daughters, the oldest of which, Avril Mullen, married a man called Lambert. Avril died of cancer about five years ago, I think. This Alexis must be either her oldest or her only child. My third cousin, and just about the only remaining Mullen other than me. We're not a very prolific lot.' He stares thoughtfully into the bottom of his glass.

'Did you know all this, Jules?' Belinda gives me a look of concern.

I nod. 'Yes.'

'And you're okay with it?'

'Of course.' I smile. 'I mean, none of it really affects us right now. The trust will only revert when we're dead and gone.'

'But like Hugh just said, you might still be alive when he pops his clogs.'

'With any luck, by then I'll be old and grey and more than happy to give up the maintenance of this place.' I reach for Hugh's hand and give it a brief squeeze, and in response he bends his head and kisses my fingertips, 'Until then, we'll just go on telling ourselves we're lucky to have this place, even if it's not forever.'

. . .

My words echo what Hugh said to me when we first met.

Luca was six, and I'd been living in a flat in North Kensington and working at an interiors shop next to his gallery. In the frequent dull stretches of time between customers, I would gaze out of the front window and see a tall, handsome man coming and going, usually talking on his mobile while running a hand through his auburn hair. He brought to mind Colin Firth as Mr Darcy: not just the cleft chin and square brow, but the air of autocratic confidence. Then, one evening, as I was locking up, my back turned away from the street, I stepped backwards into his path, causing him to do a double take and leap to one side to avoid a collision.

'Bloody hell!' he'd exclaimed. 'So sorry!' Even though it hadn't been his fault.

'No, *I'm* sorry,' I'd said, and felt a curious sensation. Blood was rising up my neck in a blush, just as though I myself were a hapless virgin in a Jane Austen adaptation.

'You work here, don't you? I think I've seen you around.'

I admitted that yes, I did, and had felt my blush intensifying. He asked me if I had time for a drink, and I agreed to it, but only if it was a very quick one. 'I have a son,' I told him. 'I have to get back for the childminder.' Might as well be upfront about Luca's existence in case it put him off. It put a lot of men off.

But Hugh didn't seem at all fazed by Luca. Perhaps because he was a few years younger than me, and so the world of parenting seemed remote and exotic to him.

Eventually, after we had been dating for several months, he met Luca and was appropriately friendly, if a little disengaged. But he was quite clear that he wanted his own children, and I wanted more children too.

I was delighted – and also a little shocked – when after only a few months of dating, Hugh asked me to marry him. 'We'll be able to share Mullens End,' he told me when he proposed. 'It'll be ours for as long as I'm alive. And then it will pass to our eldest child.'

My friends had voiced misgivings. Although our age difference was only a few years, they thought that Hugh was immature, an indulged only child who'd never had to grow up. And yes, there were occasions when I found him both spoilt and selfish. But I was also infatuated and extremely flattered that he wanted me. *Me*, of all people. So I married him anyway.

Immediately, we started trying to conceive. For a long time, nothing happened, then after more than a year, we were both delighted when I became pregnant. But the pregnancy was ectopic and diagnosed too late, leading to sepsis and severe complications. I needed emergency surgery, and when I woke up from the anaesthetic, it was the surgeon rather than my husband who broke the awful news, Hugh having left the hospital in a distressed state. In order to save my life, a hysterectomy had been necessary. I would never be able to carry more children. And Hugh and I would never have a child together.

Simon and Belinda eventually remember that they have three children of their own to tend to, two of whom are asleep on the sofa in the snug, with Jeff and Rocket in a heap between them.

'So what are you going to do about this Alexis girl?' Simon asks me, as they shepherd the children and their own dog into the kitchen, then through the rear hall to the back door, scooping up coats and wellies as they go. 'Did she say what it was she wants?'

I shake my head, helping drape a jacket over the sleeping Rufus. Primrose is now sufficiently awake to walk outside under her own steam.

'We'd better get this lot home,' says Belinda. 'Text you tomorrow, okay?' She blows a kiss in my direction as she steers the girls towards the car. Rain has turned the dust on its paintwork to muddy smears. Hugh and I watch it make an arc on the gravel, waving, then we return to the kitchen to finish clearing up the dishes and leftover food.

'Do you think I should message her back?' I ask as I wash the vintage crystal wine glasses and hand each one to Hugh to dry. 'Alexis Lambert?'

'It's up to you.' Hugh smiles, but I can tell from the slight narrowing of his hazel eyes that he's feeling unsettled. 'I'll leave it to your discretion, but don't do it on my account. I mean, I have no say in what happens after I'm dead, but I certainly have no desire to meet the woman while I'm still alive.'

'Fine.' I hand Hugh the last glass and tug off my rubber gloves. 'I told Luca I'd call him ages ago; I'd better do it now, or it'll be too late.'

I head up the back staircase – the one that used to be for the domestic staff – to the first floor. Once in the bedroom, I drop into an armchair and kick off my shoes, waiting for the hammering in my chest to subside a little before picking up my phone. I don't fully understand why I feel so jumpy; so ill at ease.

As the FaceTime ringtone sounds, I draw in a long breath to calm myself. Luca takes a while to pick up, and when I see him sitting up in bed, bare-chested with his hair rumpled, I remember it's even later in Italy.

'Sorry, darling, did I wake you?'

'It's okay, I wasn't asleep yet. We had dinner out.'

'You and Papa?'

'Yeah.'

'Where did you go?'

He shrugs. 'Dunno. Some place owned by a mate of his.'

Massimo is one of those men who seems to know almost everyone, and can conjure an instant connection with all the rest.

'What did you have to eat?'

'The usual. Risotto. Some kind of meat. Gelato.' He yawns. 'How are the dogs?'

'They're fine. Missing you, of course. And I miss you too.'

'Yeah, well, you'll see me *a presto*.'

'I'll book a flight next week and text you the details... Listen, sweetie, I'm going to let you go now. You need to get to sleep. *Notte, tesoro*.'

I hang up and start undressing slowly. From downstairs, I can hear Hugh calling the dogs for their bedtime walk. Usually when I feel anxious or out of sorts, talking to Luca soothes me. This time, I can't quite dispel an ill-defined sense of dread.

FOUR

14 JUNE

'I think I'll stay in the flat tonight,' Hugh says on Monday morning, as he's downing a mug of coffee in the kitchen. He glances at his watch. 'You okay to take the dogs out? If I get going now, I'll make the 8.23.'

'Sure,' I nod. 'I'll give them a quick run, but then I need to get straight on with the Søde job. We're just at that annoying stage where everything is turning into a problem.'

I'm currently working on a redesign of a retail space: a chic Scandi-inspired boutique in Haslemere, and the client is both needy and difficult to please.

Hugh grabs his laptop bag, pausing in the doorway with Jeff's tail slapping against his thighs as he wrongly senses an outing. 'Did you decide what you were going to say to that Alexis girl?'

I hesitate for a couple of seconds. 'I haven't, no. But probably nothing.'

'I'm sure that's for the best. Okay, bye, darling, see you tomorrow night.'

Hugh and I own a one-bedroom flat near Tower Bridge, used as a pied-à-terre after late meetings or cancelled trains.

Hugh stays there several times a month; I rarely use it. If I have a meeting in London, I prefer to catch a train back to Benfield Holt, however late it is.

'I like sleeping in my own bed,' I tell Hugh simply.

'The bed in the flat *is* your own bed. Literally: we own it.'

But, to me, the mattress is too firm, the bedroom too stuffy, the traffic noise from East Smithfield Road too intrusive. I can never sleep properly there, so I prefer not to.

At my desk, I chase delivery times and phone suppliers and subcontractors before opening Instagram and re-reading the message from Alexis. Then I send a WhatsApp to Belinda.

Fancy grabbing a coffee tomorrow morning when you've dropped the kids? Meet you at Crumbles? xx

I name the coffee shop between Nether Benfield and Godalming. All the school-run mummies congregate there before and after taking their children to St Hilda's C of E – the favoured local primary school.

Belinda replies five minutes later.

Sorry, can't do tomorrow... bloody sports day.

She then sends a grimacing emoji, before a second message.

This afternoon before pickup? Xx

I check my schedule. I have a video call with the client at 2.00, but that can probably be brought forward a little. Belinda will have to be on her way to school no later than 3.10.

See you at Crumbles, 2.30ish xx

. . .

I arrive at the coffee shop before Belinda. It has a blackboard wall chalked with the menu, trailing plants and bentwood chairs painted in clashing colours: mustard yellow, teal and orange. The place is chaotic, with harassed baristas trying to respond to demands for babycinos and heated feeding bottles as well as to plate up sandwiches and foam milk. While I'm waiting awkwardly at the door for a table to become vacant, Hugh calls me.

'Listen, we'll catch up properly tomorrow, but it just occurred to me we haven't done a dinner party for ages. Why don't we have some people over on Saturday. Belinda and Simon, of course, and some others.'

I spot a couple leaving. 'Sure, why not: that's a lovely idea. Hang on...' I tell Hugh, darting between the tables to annexe the newly vacated space. I end up crammed between a Bugaboo and an elderly lady with a cohort of shopping bags at her feet.

'I've got to go, darling, see you tomorrow.' Hugh has hung up before we can discuss the plan further.

I don't want to risk leaving our precious table empty while I go to the counter to order, so I wait until Belinda arrives and ask her for a green tea.

Belinda brings it back to the table with her own cream-laden frappuccino. 'I know these things are stuffed with sugar, but I couldn't resist,' she giggles.

'You look nice,' I tell her, once we have leaned awkwardly across the table to kiss one other. Her hair has been freshly styled, and instead of looking like straw, it falls in orderly blonde waves.

Belinda pats it self-consciously. 'God, you know how desperately I was in need of a haircut... and you look immacu-late, as always. It's so unfair.' She gestures at my hair and lipstick in my signature orange-red shade, my sheer sleeveless black yoga vest and Lululemon leggings.

She always compliments my appearance in gushing terms, and it makes me feel uncomfortable, as though by being naturally petite and olive-skinned (thanks, Nonna Carmelita), I'm somehow showing off. 'You did a spot of shopping too, I see,' I deflect, pointing at the small pale yellow bag Belinda has plonked on the table. It's from Mimi's, a very expensive lingerie shop in Godalming.

'When you've been married as long as Simon and I have, you need to make a bit of an effort every now and then. And, trust me, it is only now and then.' She pulls a face. 'I'm sure you and that gorgeous husband of yours can barely keep your hands off each other.'

I give a sardonic raise of my eyebrows to indicate that this is far from the case.

'Speaking of Hugh, he wants us to have a dinner party on Saturday. Please say you and Simon are free.'

'If we can get a sitter, I'm sure we are. What's the occasion?'

'Nothing special. Just being sociable.'

'And with a house like yours, so you should.' Belinda muses. 'Show the place off... So, did you get back to her... that girl? The cousin. Alexis.'

I shake my head. 'No. To be honest, I'm just going to leave it.'

'Have you googled her?'

As I shake my head for a second time, Belinda is already reaching in her bag for her phone. 'Doing it now. Bloody hell...'

'What?'

'Thirty-eight million hits... There are loads of Alexis Lamberts.'

We scroll through dozens of images of women with the same name.

'I'll try LinkedIn,' I offer, but that draws a blank. In the end, all we find is the Twitter handle @lexilam, which has an egg avatar and a handful of tweets about TV reality shows, and the Instagram account we have already seen.

'She hasn't posted very much,' Belinda observes. 'Considering women like her are on Instagram all the time. That's a bit odd, don't you think?'

I shrug. 'Not necessarily. Maybe she's too busy having a real life.'

Belinda puts her phone down, seemingly bored of Alexis Lambert. 'So, come on, who else are you going to invite for dinner?'

'I'll ask the Dohertys, and the Kuchars. And of course you and Simon, assuming you can get a babysitter.'

'Count me in,' says Belinda, glancing at her watch before standing up and gathering her shopping. 'Now, I'd better head off and get the ankle-biters.'

I hear, before I see, what has happened.

Hear the dogs, at least. Normally too lazy to bark, they're growling and yapping frantically from the kitchen where I shut them in.

This is still my house, and yet it doesn't look how it did when I left it an hour earlier. I stare blankly during the seconds it takes for my brain to translate image into significance. What looks like several dozen eggs have been smashed against the elegant sash windows, obscuring the glass of the panes with mucousy smears and fragments of shell. Even worse, blue paint has been thrown at the front door, splashing the columns of the portico and streaking the stone steps. There is another patch on the wall to the left of the front door, and it looks as though someone has used a stick or some other primitive implement to draw a shape or a letter. It's impossible to discern what it's meant to represent.

My fingers trembling, I pull my phone from my bag and call Hugh. He doesn't pick up the first time, or the second, but I persist until he does, with a faintly irritable, 'What's up?'

I tell him exactly what I have come back to.

'Pete's there today, isn't he? Find him, and tell him what's happened. He can leave the garden and focus on starting to get things cleaned up.'

'Shouldn't we call the police first, so they can take photos and stuff?'

'No police,' Hugh says firmly. 'No bloody point. Ever since they closed the police station at Upham, there's nothing that constitutes a local constabulary anymore. They'll send some wet-behind-the-ears trainee from Guildford who doesn't know the area and who contributes absolutely nothing to the situation. When they find we're fully insured, they'll quickly lose interest.'

'But—'

'Come on now, darling, it would be a waste of time. And they'll only tell us we ought to have CCTV installed, which you know we don't want. I take it the windows aren't actually broken? Because if they are, that will be a huge pain in the backside.'

I glance up at the front of the house again. 'No, I don't think so.'

'Go inside and make yourself some tea, and put sugar in.'

With the phone still to my ear, I exhale heavily, then start walking round the side of the house to see if I can spot Pete.

'Tell Pete we'll pay him overtime if need be. And if he can't shift the paint himself he's to get that exterior masonry work guy over... What's his name?'

'Frank. Frank Reynolds.'

'That's the one. Only make sure he gets him over before Saturday, we don't want our guests seeing the place like this.'

'Who on earth would do something like this?' I ask plaintively, close to tears.

'Oh, I know exactly who,' Hugh says grimly. 'Trust me, it's all too obvious.'

He hangs up before I can ask him to explain, leaving me wondering who he is talking about.

FIVE

19 JUNE

'It has to be Molcan's lot, surely?' says Simon. 'You know, the ones whose building development you're trying to scupper.'

It's Saturday evening, and our assembled dinner guests are in the drawing room discussing Monday's vandalism incident. Vikram Kuchar, elegant and patrician in a cream linen suit, is the senior partner at Nether Benfield's GP practice. He's seated on one of the damask sofas with his wife Faith, and Patrick and Justine Doherty – both local vets – are on the sofa facing them.

'I think it's horrific,' says Justine, a tall, bony woman with cropped mousy hair and a passion for running marathons. 'What did the police have to say?'

'We didn't call them,' says Hugh airily, waving a bottle of Bollinger in the direction of his guests like a wand. 'More champagne, anyone?'

'And there's nothing on CCTV?' asks Vikram.

'I refuse to instal security cameras. Think they're an abomination. Imagine what they would look like on the façade of a Queen Anne house.'

'But they can be very discreet these days,' Faith protests.

She's short and square with an ample bosom and a fondness for skyscraper heels. 'You wouldn't necessarily be able to see them.'

Hugh makes a huffing sound. 'Well. Perhaps we'll have to think of having them now, I concede that.'

'So what are you going to do?' Vikram persists. 'What if it happens again?'

'I'm sure it won't.' Hugh stands up and places a second bottle of champagne in the ice bucket on the circular table next to the fireplace.

'If it does, I'm definitely calling the police,' I interject, giving the others a reassuring smile.

'Isn't your gardener ex-SAS or something?' Patrick asks. 'Surely he's the perfect man to have around in a situation like this?'

'Ex-special forces,' Hugh corrects him. 'Then he worked in close protection for a while before moving down here.'

'Well, I'm going to speak to him about installing a camera, at the front gates, at least, so we'll have a record of who's driving in and out,' I say firmly. 'You're right, Patrick: we should make the most of having Pete around.'

'So, you never heard any more from the cousin?' Belinda asks, holding up her champagne glass for Hugh to pour more. I notice she's made an effort with her appearance; wearing a dress and heels.

I shake my head and resist her attempts to turn the message I received into a subject of dinner-party gossip. The less said about it, the better, as far as I'm concerned. 'I'm just going to go and check on the meat,' I tell her, but she follows me into the kitchen and hovers next to the island, glass in hand, as I bend down to open the Aga and inspect the joint of lamb.

'I've always loved your kitchen units,' Belinda sighs, looking around her at the cupboards by designer Nicholas Anthony. 'So much nicer than our grotty pine ones in Birch Cottage. If I were to move somewhere else, I'd do up the kitchen exactly like this.'

I need to baste the meat, and reach awkwardly for the handle of the utensils drawer, while trying to balance the scorching-hot roasting tray, which is spitting globules of fat onto my skirt.

'Here, let me,' Belinda says, intercepting my groping left hand and finding me a large spoon. 'Jolly lucky I'm here so much I know where everything lives, isn't it?'

'It is,' I agree weakly.

Meat safely back in the Aga, we return to the drawing room, where conversation has turned to the group's working lives. For me, this is always slightly uncomfortable, as I get the impression that the others don't think my husband's trading pieces of obscure art while living off a trust fund qualifies as work. Even Simon, who is not especially bright, has a reasonably well-paid job in a City insurance firm.

'How are the kids?' I ask Justine, trying to shift the topic. The Dohertys have two boys, who are both at St Hilda's.

'Oh, you know how it is with the end of the school year coming up.' Justine flaps a hand, indicating exhaustion. 'The kids are knackered and there's so much going on. Connor's in the school play, and then we had sports day yesterday.'

'I thought that was Tuesday?' I frown, remembering Belinda's text at the start of the week about meeting at Crumbles.

'No, it's always on a Friday afternoon, just to make sure they're all especially tired...'

She's interrupted by the sound of wheels making an arc on the gravel outside the window, and a car door slamming.

I frown at Hugh, who looks equally confused.

'Were you expecting someone else?' Belinda asks, pressing her hands together in excitement. 'Oh, goody!'

I couldn't help noticing she was going in hard on the champagne, which explains why she's now acting like a giddy teenager.

All eyes swivel towards the window as we hear a suitcase

being wheeled up the front steps to the front door. It must someone who's at the wrong house. Friends all know to come round to the kitchen door.

Hugh shrugs, mystified. 'Shall I go, darling?'

'No, it's all right,' I say calmly. 'I will.'

I pull open the heavy door and find a young woman standing there with a large silver suitcase. She's of medium height and very curvaceous, with a tumble of copper hair teased into barrel curls. Her perfectly round breasts are squeezed into a cropped white broderie anglaise top, and beneath the golden skin of her midriff, there's a matching white maxi skirt with a thigh-high slit. She's artfully made up and very tanned. I immediately note the extreme slit in the skirt, and the tidemarks on her ankles that confirm the tan is fake, just as I would have expected with a redhead.

'Hi,' she says with a smile that reveals a set of perfect veneers. 'Are you Juliet Mullen?'

'I am, yes. And you are?'

'Alexis. Alexis Lambert. I thought it was time I came to see the place that's going to be mine one day.'

SIX

19 JUNE

I stare back at her, blinking.

Alexis looks past me into the hallway.

'Sorry,' I say, 'I'd invite you in, but we've got people here for dinner at the moment. Neighbours. So, it's not exactly the best time to—'

'No problem, it would be lovely to meet everyone.' She grins, flashing the improbably white teeth, and drags her suitcase into the hallway, parking it at the foot of the main staircase. It's huge: the sort of case I would use for a week's holiday. After staring at it for a few seconds in dismay, I beckon her to follow me into the drawing room. I don't want to, but strictly speaking she has a claim on this place. I can't exactly send her packing.

'Everyone, I'd like you to meet Alexis. She's Hugh's cousin.'

There's staring and widening of eyes, before people remember their manners. The men stand up and the women come forward with air kisses. Leaving Hugh to deal with the social awkwardness, I go into the kitchen, where I'm greeted enthusiastically by Pongo and Jeff. I bend and bury my face in Pongo's ruff, inhaling his doggy odour.

Why is she here? I mutter into his fur. *What does she want?*

Then, having collected myself, I take the leg of lamb from the oven and cut off a couple of scraps for the dogs. A thank you gift for their reassuring presence.

'Wow, that looks amazing,' Alexis says ten minutes later when I carry the joint into the dining room, where she is now seated with the rest of the guests.

I shoot a questioning glance at Hugh and he nods imperceptibly. So it's official. She's staying.

'Really amaaaazing.' She drags out the second syllable, then cocks her head slightly to one side. 'Thing is, I'm a vegan?'

She has the vocal tic of inflecting her sentences upwards, as though they are questions.

'No problem,' I reply calmly. 'We have plenty of vegetables.'

'But are they cooked in meat fat?'

'Only the potatoes.' I force a smile while loading carrots and green beans onto a plate. 'You can eat these.'

'I'm sure we can rustle up something else,' says Hugh quickly. 'Darling, didn't we have some veggie burgers in the freezer for situations like this?' He catches sight of my fixed smile and says, 'I'll go and investigate.'

While he's in the kitchen, and Belinda has taken advantage of the lull to use the loo, Vikram leans towards Alexis – picking sullenly at her carrots – and asks, 'Correct me if I'm wrong, but aren't you the lucky lady who's going to inherit all of this?' He waves a hand round at the formal dining room with its wood panelling and eighteenth-century oil paintings.

She pouts slightly. 'Well yeah, but only if Hugh dies childless. Which, you know, might not happen. It's not like he's old, so he's still got plenty of time to have one.' Her gaze turns to me as she says this, the look in her artificially lashed eyes faintly challenging. 'You're still young enough, right?'

'I'm thirty-nine,' I reply flatly, placing slices of lamb onto a plate and handing it to Patrick.

'Exactly, not too old at all.'

'We won't be having any children,' I say through gritted teeth. Really, the nerve of the woman to be discussing my fertility when she's only met me minutes ago. 'I can't have any more.'

Alexis shrugs. 'There are lots of ways to have kids now. Surrogacy. Or you could adopt.'

'The terms of the Mullen Trust don't allow for an adopted child to inherit,' I tell her stiffly, wishing we could change the subject from my failure to bear a Mullen heir. 'It's not a very enlightened stance, but the trust was set up last century when people looked at these issues differently.' I glance in Justine's direction, silently pleading for rescue.

'So, what do you do for a job, Alexis?' she asks, just as Hugh returns to the room with some unappetising-looking veggie sausages, heated in the microwave, which he places in front of the uninvited guest.

'I'm a model.' Alexis is smoothing her little fingers along the edges of her lashes and making little flicking movements as if to emphasise their luscious curl. She pokes one of the sausages with the tines of her fork, but doesn't eat it. 'And I've done a bit of acting.'

'Ooh, how exciting,' Faith says, turning in her direction. 'Anything we'd have seen you in?'

'I've mainly done commercials?'

Jeff, who has followed Hugh into the dining room in search of scraps, nudges against Alexis's thighs, causing her to flinch and angle her legs away. The corners of her mouth turn down and, in that moment, I notice, she does not look pretty at all. There's a hardness to her.

Eventually, I have to accept that Alexis is not going to eat and clear the plates away, as the other guests are getting restless and Justine – whose teen babysitter has a curfew – is glancing at her watch. I serve cheese (none for Alexis, of course) and then an orange and polenta cake with whipped cream.

'Does it have eggs in it?' Alexis asks. 'Only, if it does, I can't eat it, I'm afraid.'

Biting back a snort of exasperation, I confirm that, yes, it contains three large eggs. Hugh fetches a plate of cherries from the kitchen and Alexis eats a token three.

Justine and Patrick make their excuses and leave, and the remaining guests are invited to have coffee outside on the terrace, which is hung with solar-powered Moroccan lanterns in shades of green and aqua.

'Ooh, how gorgeous,' Alexis breathes, finally finding something to her liking. 'These are so pretty!' She whips out her mobile and takes a selfie with the beaded lanterns behind her.

Belinda catches my eye.

'What do you think?' I ask her later, as I escort her to the front door, while Simon goes in search of his car keys. The Langridges also have a babysitting deadline. 'Bit of a nerve inviting herself here, don't you think?'

Belinda screws up her mouth. 'Oh God, yes, total nerve. She's certainly very attractive, though. Gorgeous even.'

'But?'

Belinda drapes a reassuring arm round my shoulder. She's slightly tipsy, as she usually is on social occasions, and the front of her dress has slipped to reveal a strip of well-upholstered black lacy bra. I wonder idly what happened to the skimpy underwear she bought in Mimi's. 'Listen, my love, she seems nice enough. And it's not like you have to see her again after tonight. The day when she gets her hands on this place is so far off, it's not worth worrying about. And it's not like you'll even be here when she does.'

'You're right.' I place a kiss on her cheek, remembering as I do so the large silver suitcase in the hall. It's not the sort of packing you do for a single night's stay.

Back on the terrace, Alexis is holding court, apparently perfectly happy as long as the attention is focused on her. After another twenty minutes, Vikram and Faith have also had enough and leave. I return to the kitchen to start the clearing up. I enlist the help of Pongo and Jeff to clear the lamb scraps from the plates before stacking them in the dishwasher. A few minutes later, Hugh appears in the doorway.

'So...' he grins at me. 'What do you think?'

'About what?' I ask, deliberately obtuse.

'Alexis. Quite something, isn't she?'

I try to weigh up what this might mean. 'She seems... sweet,' I reply disingenuously.

'Good. That's good,' Hugh says. 'Only I've said she can stay. I've shown her up to the blue room.'

The 'blue room' is the nicest of the guest rooms, and has a large en suite bathroom.

'She asked if it would be okay, you know... if she stays on for a while. Gets to know the place. That is all right, isn't it?' He rubs his hands together happily.

'How long?' I demand, my heart sinking.

'Oh, I'm sure it won't be that long. Just a couple of days or so.'

SEVEN

20 JUNE

'It is okay, isn't it? Me being here for a bit?'

Alexis appears in the kitchen the next morning, dressed in a beige sweatsuit comprising joggers and matching cropped hoodie, her hair tied up in a ponytail. She lounges on one of the stools next to the kitchen island, while I make us espressos.

'Yes, of course,' I smile brightly. 'We've plenty of space.'

'Only, when I decided to come down this weekend, I thought I'd already have moved, and would be heading straight back to London.'

The excuse for her needing to stay at Mullens End has been convoluted and elaborate: something about moving out of her existing flat in Boreham Wood on Friday with the expectation of picking up keys for her new place in Muswell Hill that same afternoon, only to be told that it needed some last-minute repairs which would delay her moving in for 'a couple of days'. The exact day on which the repairs will be complete is apparently unknown, but Hugh and I have been assured that it should be before the end of the week. Possibly even Tuesday or Wednesday. Apparently it was her recent contact with me on Instagram that gave her the idea of coming here rather than crashing with a friend. 'Two birds with one stone', she called it.

'So where did you grow up?' I ask, more to fill the silence than because I'm overly interested.

'Hertfordshire, mostly. My dad left when I was little, so it was mostly just Mum and me.'

'No siblings?'

She shakes her head with a fetching smile that exposes those Persil-white teeth. 'No, just me getting all the attention.' She catches sight of her reflection in the stainless-steel side of the coffee machine and becomes distracted momentarily, rearranging her fringe.

'And you grew up knowing about this place? About the possibility that you'd inherit it?'

'Mum mentioned it, yeah, before she passed away. But, to be honest, I didn't really give it any thought. I mean, we – me and Mum – obviously we just assumed Hugh would have kids and that would be that. That I would never come into it. But then my friend Lisa got really into those ancestry websites, and she talked me into going online. And you can, like, see your whole family tree there.'

'So that's why you decided to contact me?'

When you realised that you might be closer in line than you thought to inheriting an exceptionally beautiful Queen Anne manor house in prime Surrey countryside.

'I just wanted to reach out really. See what happens. I mean, you never really know what's going to happen, do you? In life?'

Alexis smiles again. Her eyes really are the most beautiful colour, I think, bemoaning my own bog-standard dark brown ones. So beautiful that looking directly into them is a bit like looking directly into the sun: it's too much.

I prepare a fruit platter, which is picked at by Alexis, then – to kill time until Hugh gets back from playing tennis – take our guest on a tour of the house, pointing out its architectural features, filling her in on some of its history. Alexis nods occasionally, but looks bored.

'What's it worth?' she asks finally.

I blink, unnerved by the brashness of the question. 'I have no idea,' I say, although of course I do. I know that because of its excellent access to transport links it's worth somewhere in excess of ten million. 'But it's immaterial anyway, because the life tenant – whoever that is – is not allowed to sell it.'

Alexis wrinkles her neat little nose. 'The life tenant? Who's that?'

'Well, Hugh, of course. The house and grounds are owned by a family trust, and he gets to live here for the duration of his life. As you would, if you ever inherited.'

'Oh. I see,' Alexis says, furrowing her brow as she follows me back down the main stairs and out into the garden.

Although she doesn't seem interested in the house's interior, to my surprise she loves the garden. 'All these flowers,' she sighs happily as she walks through the rose garden. 'I've never seen so many in one place. Can we pick some?'

'Of course,' I reply, pleased that Alexis has found something to occupy her. I fetch the trug and secateurs and hover while she takes a long time over selecting and cutting blooms. I offer to arrange them, but Alexis is insistent on doing so herself, and does surprisingly well, producing a bold, artful arrangement.

'Wow, those look beautiful!'

Alexis seems pleased with the praise, happily accepting the offer to place them at the centre of the hall table. 'I was good at art and design at school. I've always had an eye for detail, you know?'

Although she's not in the least bit taken by the dogs, Alexis accompanies me as I walk them, and then positions herself on the velvet sofa in the kitchen, flicking through glossy magazines, exclaiming over things she sees that catch her eye. Left alone with our visitor like this, I find her agreeable enough company. But when Hugh returns, it's a different story. Alexis becomes simultaneously more guarded and more girlish.

He insists on escorting her down to the tennis court for a knock-up, and even the simple task of finding a suitable racket engenders a lot of giggling and wise-cracking from both parties.

After supper, I take myself up to bed, claiming a headache. Lying in bed, I'm prevented from sleeping by the baritone mumble of Hugh's voice from the open windows downstairs, punctuated by peals of laughter from Alexis. I wonder, irritably, what on earth can be so amusing, or even what they've found to talk about at all. Perhaps it's something to do with them being cousins.

Family.

Blood.

On Monday morning, Hugh heads into London and I retreat into my office, leaving Alexis to her own devices. She will, she has promised, be speaking to her estate agent first thing to find out the latest on her new place.

But by supper time, she is still in residence on the kitchen sofa, ignoring the dogs, and showing no sign of leaving. Did she make any progress with the agent? I enquire, when no update is forthcoming.

'Waiting for them to call me back,' Alexis says with a shrug.

The following day, she does at least make the journey into London to see the estate agent in person in an attempt to move things forward. When she returns, she claims they are now waiting for the landlord's builder to start the promised work, stating with a shrug that 'it shouldn't be long'. Then two more days pass with no apparent progress and by Thursday morning, ill at ease in my own home, I'm starting to feel a little desperate.

'This is ridiculous,' I hiss to Hugh when we're alone

upstairs. 'We're not running a hostel. Surely, she has more than one friend she can stay with?' I'm about to add 'or a family member', but stop myself as I realise Hugh will point out that he *is* a family member. 'And, anyway, why can't she be in her new flat while the work's being done? If it's a rental, it's not going to be anything that drastic, surely?'

He frowns at me. 'She's not doing any harm, is she?'

'No, of course not.' I force a smile, anxious not to make my concern look like an overreaction. Overreacting is one of the most common complaints Hugh levels at me.

He glances in the direction of the bedroom door, as if Alexis might be outside on the landing. 'I'm sure it will only be another couple of days. Come on now, sweetie, it's not like we need the room back.'

In bed that night, I consider the possibility of going up to our own flat for a night or two. Would it look odd? I wonder. And would Alexis mind being left on her own with Hugh? From the way she behaves around him, probably not. And that is the problem.

I lie awake until after one, Hugh breathing heavily next to me, running through various scenarios in my mind. None of them are good.

In the end the decision is made for me. As I come downstairs on Friday morning, the front door is open and I catch sight of Hugh, on the front steps, pressing his hands to the top of his head in a gesture of fury.

'Jesus, what the hell's going on here!'

I join him.

'Will you fucking well look at that.' He points at our cars – his black Range Rover and my more modest blue Toyota SUV parked next to one another on the gravel. Both vehicles have had their tyres slashed, and Hugh's has been daubed with paint;

green this time. 'Did you not hear anything in the night?' he demands, with a note of accusation. 'Didn't the dogs bark?'

I shake my head, staring in appalled silence at the damage.

'Maybe Alexis did.' Hugh shouts past me into the house, 'Alexis!'

'I think she's still in bed.' I walk down the steps to the cars and inspect the damage more closely. 'It's got to be the same people as before, surely. We've got to call the police.'

Reluctantly, this time Hugh agrees with me, and we're both kept from our work by waiting for a PC Dainty to arrive to take our statements. He's fiftyish, with a shock of iron-grey hair and a droll manner. He inspects the damage to the cars slowly and carefully. The dogs run out of the house and sniff his uniform boots.

'And these are your dogs?'

'Yes, obviously.' Hugh rolls his eyes behind the policeman's back. I signal back at him to stop.

'And you didn't hear them barking?'

'No. Neither did you, did you, darling?'

I shake my head.

'And would that be unusual?'

'No,' says Hugh, just as I reply with a firm 'Yes'. I'm thinking of how the dogs had been barking when the paint and eggs were thrown at the front of the house.

'Was there anyone else in the house apart from the two of you?'

'There are three of us,' Hugh admits. 'My wife and I and my cousin, who's staying with us.'

'I see.' PC Dainty thinks about this for a minute. 'And the dogs know him, your cousin? They wouldn't bark at him?'

'*Her.*' I correct him stiffly. Alexis has no interest in the dogs, avoids them even, but they in turn have become accustomed to her smell, her voice, her presence in the family home. 'No, I don't think so.' Suddenly, my brain is hijacked by images of

Alexis getting out of bed and creeping around the house in the middle of the night.

'And has anything like this happened before?'

Hugh and I glance at one another.

'Yes,' Hugh says reluctantly. He fills in PC Dainty about the eggs and paint incident. 'I suppose I should also tell you that I've been behind a campaign to get the Meadowcroft building development stopped. I'm thinking that might have made me a tad unpopular with the people who own the company.'

He goes over the details of the murky JM Developments and PC Dainty makes a note of the information with excruciating slowness, promising to look into it.

'Bet he doesn't,' Hugh scoffs when he's gone. 'Told you, it's a waste of time involving the cops.'

He stamps into the house to phone the local garage about replacing the tyres, the dogs following in his wake. I go into my office, but can't settle to work. I can hear Alexis in the kitchen, watching a morning TV show and talking on her phone. I can only hope she's arranging to take possession of her new flat.

'Taking the dogs for a walk,' I call out to her, and head into the village on foot, with Jeff streaking ahead of me and Pongo wheezing behind. It takes about twenty minutes to reach Birch Cottage.

'Hi!' says a surprised Belinda when she answers the door. It's a warm day, and she's wearing a blowsy yellow-flowered sundress, her unruly mane of hair scraped into a bun on top of her head. The three children are all at school, but Rocket races to her side and yaps at the Labradors. 'Was I expecting you?'

'Impromptu visit.' I press a cool cheek against Belinda's warm one. 'I just had to get out of the house for a bit.'

Over coffee in the Langridges' untidy kitchen, I tell her about the tyre slashing.

'And, on top of that, we've still got bloody Alexis in the

house. I'm finding it all a bit much, but if I moan to Hugh about it, he'll just say I'm overreacting as usual.'

Belinda cuts slices of carrot cake, taking a huge bite out of her own and wiping the frosting from her chin before asking. 'So does he fancy her? Is that the problem?'

I think about this for a moment. Remember the two of them talking, laughing, while I was upstairs. 'Probably. She's an attractive younger woman.'

Belinda's eyes widen. 'But there's nothing going on, I hope? I mean, they're related.'

'Only distantly... but absolutely not.' I speak with a confidence I don't entirely feel. 'As guests go, I guess she's not too bad. I'm just being oversensitive. It's just... well, three's a crowd, isn't it?'

'Yes. I suppose it is.' A concerned expression crosses my friend's face. 'How are *you* and Hugh getting on?'

I pick at the crumbs from my own slice of cake, my focus intensifying as I formulate my thoughts. Of course, I've been aware for years that Hugh feels he has to 'manage' me, to keep a lid on my anxieties and neuroses. And in turn I have to allow him to feel he has the upper hand; that he's the senior partner in the marriage, because that makes him happy. And I need him to be happy to assuage my guilt. The guilt that my inability to get pregnant means he'll never have a child. An heir to Mullens End.

'Fine,' I reply eventually, with a steadiness I don't really feel. 'Hugh and I are absolutely fine.'

But as I say this I'm wondering if we really are, or whether long-buried resentments are starting to surface.

EIGHT

26 JUNE

On Saturday morning, Hugh and Alexis announce they are heading off to play tennis. As I wave them off, a forced smile on my face, I spot a notification on my phone.

Missed call: Massimo

I don't often have direct contact with my ex, but on this occasion, with Alexis now in residence for a week and showing no sign of leaving, I'm quite grateful for the opportunity to talk to another adult. As I press the dial icon, I look out through the kitchen window. My husband and the newcomer in our lives are just passing through the box hedge that surrounds the tennis court and he is tapping her playfully on the buttocks with his racket. Alexis in turn makes a playful mock punch in the direction of his chest, laughing into his face.

'*Pronto?*' Massimo is saying in my ear.

'Hi.' I twist away from the window and face the centre of the kitchen, finding myself staring at the mess that Alexis made when preparing her daily breakfast smoothie: a dirty glass and blender goblet, with a knife and a heap of banana and kiwi skins on a chopping board, a pot of yoghurt with a spoon still inside it and a trail of milky drops over the work surface. '*Ciao. Come va?*'

Massimo sighs heavily, in a theatrical Latin manner. Luca has been suspended from school, he informs me, for being caught smoking cannabis on campus.

I drop my head, pinching my forehead. 'That doesn't sound like Luca.' Our son is spirited, but not stupid. Over the years, there have been almost no disciplinary issues, either at home or at school.

'It does not,' Massimo agrees, continuing in his excellent English. 'But, you know, he's hanging out with a crowd who are not so great. A bunch of American kids who are in the city unsupervised, without their parents.'

I exhale slowly. 'I appreciate you letting me know. And I'll speak to Luca, obviously.'

'I think it's preferable if you're here,' Massimo says with his usual bluntness. 'You are better than I am with these things. And you are coming out here soon anyway. Can you come earlier?'

My mind is spinning. 'Let me call you back,' I say, forcing a briskness that I don't really feel. I sink into one of the kitchen chairs and Pongo, sensing weakness, appears at my side, wagging his tail. I throw him one of the toast crusts that Hugh left on his plate.

Massimo is right: it would be better to deal with our son's disciplinary issue face to face, and I was due to fly to Bologna next weekend anyway. I will have to rearrange a couple of client appointments, but other than that there's nothing to stop me taking an earlier flight. In fact, it would be a relief to get away from Mullens End right now and immerse myself in the culture I love so much.

But it will also mean leaving the country with Hugh and Alexis here on their own. Belinda's question comes back to me: '*Does he fancy her?*'

And so does my unfiltered answer that, yes, he probably does. But is he *really* interested in her? She's extremely good-looking, in a contrived way, but also vapid and superficial. Hugh is thirty-five, and Alexis is twenty-nine, so the age difference between them is not huge. But he's substantial, settled in life and she's...

She's what?

That's at the heart of the problem, I decide: Alexis is still an unknown quantity. Despite mannerisms aped from reality television, she's clearly not stupid. In fact, there are occasional flashes of sharpness. But aside from earning bits and pieces of money from modelling and what she deems 'acting' (appearing recently in an online gambling commercial, for example), she doesn't seem to want much from life. She doesn't even seem especially interested in the property that she might one day inherit. It's no surprise that since discovering that it can't be sold once inherited, her questions about the place have dried up.

The latest on her own housing situation is that the work on the new flat is almost complete and she should get the keys during the following week. I calculate that by the time I return from Modena, Alexis will be gone. Allowing this thought to buoy me up, I pull up the email confirmation of my e-ticket on my phone and follow the link to change my flight to one tomorrow. Then I text Belinda.

> Got to go to Italy to deal with teen parenting crisis. Keep an eye on H and A for me xx

After Hugh and Alexis return from tennis, I wait until she's in the shower before I update my husband on my revised travel plans.

'Fine,' he says, his back turned to me as he reaches into the fridge for a cold beer. 'We'll be fine here.'

· · ·

A few hours after landing at Bologna and taking the short train ride to Modena, I find myself at a restaurant with my son and his father.

Massimo and I have agreed that we will talk to Luca together. Not to harangue or scold him, but to try to get him to see the error of his ways. Or sense, at least. His week's suspension has coincided with the last week of the school year, so he won't be returning until September, when he will begin the final year of his studies.

We are sitting outside so that Massimo can smoke, with a flimsy canvas awning overhead that gives no respite from the heat bouncing off the pavement. Massimo swivels his long legs so that he's at an angle to the small table, allowing him to blow the smoke away towards the street. As a concession to me, since my Italian is somewhat rusty, he starts off by speaking in English. 'It's not that doing weed is so bad, you know?' He glances at me, and I know he's remembering us both smoking joints at parties in Perugia when we first met. 'We're not going to be hypocritical and say you should never do that.'

Luca scowls down at his bowl of *tortellini en brodo*. Our bottle of Trebianno has been placed in a metal ice bucket, beaded with droplets of condensation. I pour myself a glass and curl my hand around it, enjoying the sensation of the cold liquid against my palm.

'It's just a question of time and place,' I urge. 'That's all we're concerned about. You're doing so well in your studies, and you don't want to put your Baccalaureate at risk. Not now, when you've worked so hard.'

Luca remains withdrawn and sulky for the rest of the evening, but the following day, alone with me, he thaws a little. After studying engineering, Massimo went on to work for Maserati, and I'm staying at the apartment of one of his colleagues who is currently abroad. It's in the Villaggio Zeta district of the city, which Luca dismisses as 'bougie', insisting on taking me into the city centre on the back of his scooter. We wander the food stalls of the Mercato Albinelli before heading to Luca's favourite gelateria to the east of the city centre, near the university. Once we've made our purchase, we stroll the covered colonnades as we eat our ice cream, passing a delightful jumble of *pasticceria*, boutique pharmacies and expensive lingerie shops.

'You always were a gelato addict,' I say with a smile as he digs into a carton heaped with four different flavours. 'Remember when Hugh and I used to take you into London to have a sundae at the Fountain at Fortnum's?'

'How is Hugh?' Luca asks politely, spooning stracciatella into his mouth. During the years that they lived under the same roof, Hugh never told Luca to call him 'Dad' and Luca never asked. Their relationship was cordial enough, but defined by a certain formality. To Luca, Massimo has always been his father, and when I visit him in Italy, I sense that my son sees himself as Italian rather than British. He was born here, after all, and since one of his parents is Italian, he qualifies as a citizen.

'Hugh's fine,' I reply blandly. I don't want to go into the attacks on the house and our cars, not because Luca will care about Hugh having a nemesis, but because he will worry about me. 'And the house is fine.'

Despite this prompt, he doesn't engage with the topic. 'I miss the dogs,' is all he says, and when I adopt a mock-offended expression, he nudges my elbow playfully and adds, 'And I miss you too. *Molte.*'

How is it possible, I ask myself the next morning, that I have forgotten how wonderful it is to be in Italy? Here I move with a freedom that's almost abandon, whereas in England it always feels as though there's something weighing me down.

I'm sitting on the little balcony of the borrowed apartment

with my book and a Bialetti of fresh espresso on the table in front of me, and a view of the ochre and amber buildings of the city. The sky is already a bright, cloudless blue, and the bells of Our Lady of the Pilgrims are chiming in the distance, punctuated by incessant complaints from car horns. Once I've finished my coffee and read for a while, I plan to go for a walk in the botanic gardens and then meet Luca for lunch in a little trattoria just off the Viale Caduti in Guerra. Then I'll do some clothes shopping before joining Luca and Massimo for a home-cooked supper at his apartment; a meal which is sure to be a treat since Massimo is an excellent cook.

The truth is, I'm enjoying myself so much that I've barely thought about the fact that Hugh and Alexis are alone together at Mullens End. After I've drained my espresso cup, I reach for my phone and call Hugh. It's only eight fifteen in the UK, and he probably won't have left for work.

'All okay?' he asks cheerily. 'How's the lad? Read him the riot act?'

'Something like that,' I murmur. 'How about you? And Alexis? Is she still there?' I can't quite keep the crispness, the touch of the headteacher from my voice.

'No, she's not here.'

'You mean she's gone?'

Hugh gives a dry laugh. 'Not as in moved out, no. Although there's movement on that front: the work on her new place is completed apparently, so she'll be gone soon. No, I mean she's out. She left early to go to an appointment at that little beauty salon on the road to the station. Getting her nails done, or her eyelashes, or some such nonsense.'

From his tone of voice, I can picture my husband's eye roll at Alexis's superficiality. How silly I was to worry that he could be attracted to her in any serious way. Vain, vapid women have never appealed to him.

'She could be gone by the time I get home tomorrow?'

'Very possibly.'

This thought cheers me through the painful business of leaving Modena. Leaving my son. The few days in Italy have been a wonderful chance to spend time with him.

'Can't you stay out here a bit longer, Mama?' he pleads as I leave Massimo's apartment after a delicious meal of homemade spinach gnocchi and zabaglione. 'I really miss you.' Luca drops his façade of teenage indifference and flings his arms around me.

I feel tears starting at this rare show of affection. Feel guilty, and not for the first time, at spending so much time away from him. 'I'll be back soon,' I promise. 'And maybe next time I'll stay for longer. Anyway, now you've finished for the summer you can fly over to London and spend some time at Mullens End. I'll speak to Papa and sort some dates.'

When he comes, there'll just be the three of us, I think happily: me, Hugh and Luca. We'll be a family again. Alexis Lambert will be gone.

NINE

30 JUNE

But Alexis hasn't gone.

When the taxi drops me at the house that afternoon, and I wheel my case round to the back door, the first thing I see is our house guest stretched out on a lounger on the terrace wearing nothing but a skimpy neon-green bikini.

'Hi.' I force my features into a tolerant expression.

Alexis waves back languidly. 'Don't worry,' she drawls, adding in her annoying up-speak: 'I honestly won't be here much longer. I'm literally picking up the keys the day after tomorrow?'

'No rush,' I lie.

Jeff appears at my side, wagging his tail vigorously and whimpering. As I bend to pat him, his whining escalates to a crescendo and he blocks my path by throwing himself on the ground, belly up. A faint chill runs through me.

'Where's Pongo?' I ask.

Alexis hesitates, chewing on her lower lip and avoiding eye contact. 'Um, Hugh's inside,' she says eventually. 'He's working from home today.'

I dump my case in the back hall and hurry into Hugh's study, which is next door to my own at-home office, Jeff still whimpering at my heels. Hugh's on the phone, but as soon as he sees me, he mutters a quick, 'Listen, I'll call you back,' and hangs up.

'Has something happened to Pongo?'

He places his palms flat on the desk and lets out a heavy sigh. 'Martin Nicholson came over this morning.'

My hand flies to my mouth. Martin Nicholson is the junior partner at the Dohertys' veterinary practice. 'You mean...'

'He had to put the poor old boy down. I didn't tell you because I didn't want to spoil your time with Luca.' Hugh's mouth twitches and he closes his eyes briefly. Remembering that my husband has had the dog almost all his adult life, I come round the desk and embrace him. 'Oh darling, I'm sorry... what happened? He seemed fine when I left.'

'You know how it is with old pets; when they go downhill, it happens fast... he was pretty ancient. He'd had a good innings.' He reaches down and fondles the ears of the quivering Jeff. 'This one's feeling it, though. We probably ought to get another dog to keep him company.'

I sigh heavily. 'Eventually. Let's not think about that just now.'

'Of course, darling.' Hugh forces a smile. 'All sorted with the prodigal son?'

'Fine. And I gather we're about to lose our guest.'

'That's right. Friday, apparently. Bit of a shame, really, I've kind of got used to her being around.'

My smile is genuine, not because I echo Hugh's sentiment, but because Friday is only a day and a half away.

The following morning, as I'm sorting the laundry from my trip, I receive a phone call from Justine Doherty.

'Just thought I'd give you a call with my condolences.' Her tone is as brisk and matter-of-fact as always, but not lacking in warmth. 'Martin just told us about poor old Pongo in the team meeting.'

'Thanks. We'll really miss him. Hugh especially.'

'And such an awful way to go, the poor old boy.'

Frowning, I set down the basket of dirty clothes on the laundry-room counter before asking 'What do you mean? I thought he was just euthanised because he was old.'

There's a beat of silence before Justine speaks. 'Martin said he'd almost certainly been poisoned. Sorry, I assumed you knew.'

'No,' I say flatly. 'I didn't know.'

As I hang up, I hear Hugh's footsteps on the gravel, then the door of his Range Rover slamming. I run outside to intercept him before he can drive to the station. He winds down the front window, irritated, but doesn't get out of the car. 'I want to catch the 9.23.'

'Justine Doherty's just told me that Pongo was poisoned. Is that right?'

'Well, yes...' He screws up his face. 'I mean, Martin thought he might have eaten something that poisoned him, yes, but they don't know for sure. They're going to run some tests.'

'But how? How could that have happened? And how come Jeff's okay? He eats everything that's within his reach.'

Hugh switches off the ignition and slumps back in his car seat. 'Jeff was ill too. He puked a few times, but Martin thinks that because he's younger he pulled through all right.'

I'm shaking my head, trying to follow this new narrative. 'So... where had the dogs been other than here in the house and the garden?'

Hugh shrugs. 'Nowhere. Martin took a sample of saliva and some of the food that was left in their bowls to analyse them.'

That same sense of unnamed dread returns. 'But, Hugh,

that means someone must have come into the house to put down the poison! How the hell could that have happened?'

'I don't know... Look, the weather was very hot, right, and on Tuesday evening Alexis and I had all the doors and windows open. It was possible that we went to bed without locking up properly. We'd both had a bit to drink.'

'In that case, I take it you've informed the police!' I hiss furiously. 'Because this has obviously been done by whoever threw the paint and slashed our tyres.'

'No, I haven't. It honestly didn't occur to me. I suppose I was just too upset about losing the old boy.'

I soften slightly at this. 'Hugh, I really think we should. You get going, and I'll phone them this morning. We've still got the number for that PC Dainty who came.'

'Okay then. I suppose you're right.' Hugh sighs again, and with a slight shake of his head switches on the ignition, puts the car into gear and drives off.

'Any chance of a lift?' Alexis sticks her head around the door of my office later that morning. She's in full make-up with resplendent brows and lashes and dressed in a short, tight dress the colour of lemon drops. 'Only I thought I'd go into Guildford and shop for a few bits for my new flat.'

I've only just started making inroads into my neglected inbox, but I smile and say, 'Of course. Why don't I drop you at Benfield Holt now, and there's a Guildford train in...' I glance at my watch. 'About twenty minutes.' The truth is, I know I'll concentrate better and therefore be more productive if I'm not half-listening to doors opening and closing as Alexis drifts aimlessly around the house.

After I've deposited her at the station entrance, and turned onto the main road, I decide that I should take Jeff for a long walk at some point. He seems to be needing more attention now that he's the only canine member of the household. I think with a pang about poor Pongo's suffering, and wonder again who could be so cruel and so callous as to poison a dumb animal. And how they managed to get into the house without the dogs barking. What was it Hugh said? 'We'd both had a bit to drink.' I'd assumed he meant they had been drinking separately; Hugh with his buddies at the golf club, and perhaps Alexis with friends in town, or at the village pub. But now, suddenly, I picture them sitting on the terrace as the sun was setting behind the copse, downing a special bottle of champagne retrieved from the cellar. Or cocktails, perhaps. Hugh fancies himself as something of a mixologist. If it was hot, as Hugh said, perhaps Alexis was still in her bikini, her improbably pneumatic breasts shiny with suntan oil. Perhaps Hugh was sitting close enough to smell that sweet, musky scent she favours and wasn't able to resist reaching out and touching her. Perhaps someone had easily been able to break in because the two of them had been upstairs, in a sweaty tangle on her bed...

The mental image becomes so vivid and present that I temporarily take my eyes off the road and almost turn my Toyota into the ditch. I pull over, breathing heavily, and dial Belinda using the car's Bluetooth. I had, after all, asked her to keep an eye on Hugh and Alexis, even though I'd been semi-joking when I made the request.

'Hi,' Belinda's voice is distant, a little echoey, as though she has put the call on speaker and carried on with whatever task she was in the middle of. 'How was *la bella Italia*?'

'Can you come over? I need to talk to you.'

'Are you okay, Jules? Only you sound a little—'

'I'm in the car, just on my way back to the house. Can you come over for a coffee?'

'Bit tricky today, got a lot on.'

'Or lunch; I could make us some lunch.'

Belinda makes a breathy sound, as though she's stifling a sigh. 'Okay. I suppose I could pop by quickly. I'll be there in around an hour.'

In the end, it's nearly two hours before Belinda shows up, by which time the salad I've prepared is limp and the bread going hard at the edges. She has at least brought Rocket with her, which sends Jeff into paroxysms of delight.

'I heard about Pongo.' Belinda pulls a sad face as she embraces me. She's make-up-free and wearing one of Simon's old shirts with the sleeves rolled up and a pair of capri pants that cling tightly to her ample hips. 'Patrick bumped into Simon at The Crown and Cushion and told him. Have you called the police?'

'Not yet, but I'm going to.' I carry the food out to the table on the terrace, fetching a jug of water, glasses and a chilled bottle of wine from the fridge. 'Wine? This is a rather nice Sancerre.'

'I'd better not. Got a bloody ton of stuff to do before the school run.' When she sees my sceptical expression, Belinda adds, with a tinge of impatience, 'I actually have. It's our tenth wedding anniversary next month, remember? And I've got to plan the party.'

'Oh yes.' I hand her a plate of salad.

'Anyway, how was Italy?' She tucks a hank of wheat-coloured hair behind her ear and begins slathering butter on her bread.

'Pretty good. It was wonderful to see Luca...'

'I'll bet.' Belinda keeps her eyes down on her plate.

'But also pretty weird to come back and find another woman in my house.'

Belinda does look up now. 'She's still there? Mind you, I did hear she was still around.' Despite having turned down wine, she now grabs the bottle and slops some into her water tumbler. 'Actually, I heard something a bit more specific, but wasn't sure if I should tell you.'

I keep my gaze level. 'Tell me.'

'Well,' Belinda wipes the butter off her mouth with a piece of paper towel. 'Hannah – you know, Hannah Whitehead, who cleans for me a couple of hours a week? Well, she was with me this week, and she knows you and I are friendly.'

I draw in my breath. 'Go on.'

'She'd just done a shift behind the bar at The Crown and Cushion, she said that Hugh had been in there with someone. From the description it was *her*.' Belinda's lip curls in distaste. 'And she said they looked pretty cosy.'

'What does cosy mean? You mean they were kissing?'

'I don't think they went that far, but, apparently, she was leaning in pretty close. They seemed "intimate", I think is the word Hannah used.'

'Oh God.' I breathe out hard and drop my head.

'Look, I'm sorry, Jules, maybe I should have said something sooner, but I've been so stressed trying to find somewhere to hold this bloody party.'

'I don't see why it should be a big deal,' I say, trying to adopt a soothing tone while my mind is in overdrive. 'Why don't you just bung up a marquee in the garden and get some caterers in. That's what Hugh and I always do.'

Belinda swallows down more wine, staring straight at me as she does so. 'Because there isn't space in our tiny little garden for fifty people.' There's a coldness in her voice that I've never heard before. 'We don't all have a mini stately home to hold our events in, you know!'

Belinda's freckled cheeks are flushed pink, and she's still staring straight at me.

'I know, I wasn't suggesting...' I'm becoming flustered,

which is not like me at all. 'I just meant... I mean, why don't you and Simon have the party here? Mullens End is the perfect venue. I'm sorry, Belle, I should have suggested it earlier, I just didn't think—'

'"The perfect venue"... Have you any idea how smug you sound, Juliet?' The flush on Belinda's face and neck is deepening. 'And you'd just love that, wouldn't you? Another excuse to flounce about playing the lady of the manor. When we all know you're not exactly to the manor born. God knows how, but you really struck lucky when you managed to snare the most eligible man in the county.'

I stare in shock. 'Belinda, I don't understand where this is coming from,' I say eventually. 'I've no idea what I've done to upset you, but if I have done something without realising, then I'm sorry.'

I reach across the table to touch her arm, but she shakes my hand off, knocking over the tumbler of wine, which drips through the wooden slats of the table. Before I've had time to react, she's pushed her chair back and snatched up her bag, shoving the table forward so that I'm pinioned awkwardly between it and my own chair.

'I'm sorry,' Belinda mutters, grabbing Rocket's collar with her other hand. 'I think I'd better go.'

I'm still feeling shaken a couple of hours later when I hear Alexis coming in through the kitchen. I'd been so blindsided by the argument with Belinda I'd all but forgotten about our long-term house guest.

'Good shopping trip?' I call.

'Great thanks,' Alexis calls back. 'Bought literally tons of stuff.' I can hear the tap running into the kettle. 'I'm gasping for a cup of tea; d'you want one?'

'No thank you.'

My mobile rings and I reach across the desk and grab it. I'm hoping it might be Belinda, but it's Patrick Doherty.

'Hi, Juliet... I've just tried Hugh but he's not picking up, so I thought I'd speak to you. We've just had the results back from the path lab.'

I'm silent, so he goes on.

'The place where we sent the dog food sample. And the...' He clears his throat. 'The stomach contents.'

'What did it show?'

'Looks like the poor old boy ingested antifreeze.'

'Antifreeze?' I repeat dumbly.

'Afraid so. As little as a teaspoon can kill a dog. It was in the food sample, so it looks like it was definitely done deliberately.'

Only then do I remember that I haven't yet phoned PC Dainty. At least I will now have proof of foul play rather than just a wild theory.

After Patrick has hung up, promising to email the formal report, I hunt around for the card with the police officer's number. Once I've found it, I pick up my mobile again, about to dial, then hesitate. Instead, I try Belinda's number. The call is rejected instantly.

I replay our argument again in my mind, still shocked by it. The ill-disguised and ugly resentment Belinda voiced had come out of nowhere. Or had it? Now I stop to analyse it, there have been hints of it over the years, some subtle, some less so. Little digs at me for having landed so squarely on my feet, deprecating comparisons between the grandeur of Mullens End and the Langridges' own more modest but perfectly comfortable residence.

I send a WhatsApp to Belinda.

Are we okay? xxx

I decide to put off phoning PC Dainty and instead head to

bed alone, because Hugh's at some parish council thing to discuss the Meadowcroft planning permission issue. I check my phone before I turn out the light, but there are no message notifications.

After struggling to sleep for an hour and a half, I check again. Still nothing.

TEN

2 JULY

The first thing I do when I wake up is check my phone again.

Nothing from Belinda. I sigh heavily and let my head fall back on the pillows.

Hugh eyes me warily, and I can see him weighing up whether to ask me what's wrong. Yet again feeling he needs to manage me. 'Everything okay?' he asks eventually.

I, in turn, weigh up the wisdom of telling him about my fight with Belinda. He's always telling me how lucky I am to have her friendship, that although Belinda is a little younger than me, she's mature and decent; 'good people'. And he's right, I know he is. I also know that he's likely to dismiss the argument as a silly hormonal spat, when it's more than that. A lot more. It felt like the sort of falling out you can't come back from. And for that reason, I need my husband's support.

'Belinda and I had a massive row yesterday, out of nowhere.'

Hugh pauses as he's about to get up off the four-poster bed, swivels his head and looks at me intently. 'You did? What on earth was that about?' Far from trivialising the situation, he seems genuinely alarmed.

'Oh, something and nothing.' I reach for the hairbrush on

my nightstand and tug it through my hair, restoring it to its neat, jaw-hugging bob.

'Come on now, darling, it can't have been nothing. Not if you're so upset.'

I hesitate. 'It was about the house.'

'The house? Which house?'

'This place.' I wave a hand in the direction of the impressive sash windows and the view of the rose garden beyond. 'Belle accused me of being smug about living here. Of playing lady of the manor.' I decide it would be better to omit the bit about him being the most eligible man in the county. In the past, Belinda's mock-swooning over Hugh's looks seemed funny; now it seems it was just part of her suppressed resentment of me.

'You *are* the lady of the manor,' Hugh says reasonably. 'How else does she expect you to act?'

I reach for his hand and give it a grateful squeeze.

'Would you like me to talk to her for you?'

'You?' I frown. Hugh's manner towards Belinda has always been joshing, playful, almost brotherly, but he's never been her confidant.

'Okay, to Simon then. I could have a word with him, see what's going on.'

'No, it's okay. I expect it will blow over soon enough.'

Hugh gets up off the bed, still in his boxers, and heads for the bathroom. 'I've got an early-evening drink with a broker today... if it runs on late, I might stay up in the flat tonight. On the other hand, I might decide to come back. I'll try to let you know either way before supper time, okay?'

'Fine.' I look up briefly in his direction, then return my attention to my phone. I check the WhatsApp thread with Belinda and there are now two blue ticks on the message I sent last night. But still no reply.

I get out of bed, pull on my robe and walk over to the windows that look over the front of the property. The sun is on the ascendant through thin, hazy clouds that promise another hot day and the gardens are at their midsummer peak. A faint breeze stirs the rich crimson leaves of the Japanese maples and the searingly yellow foliage of the Indian bean tree. But instead of focusing on nature's perfection, all I notice is the flapping of a shard of metallic blue in the topiary: an ice cream wrapper that someone must have discarded during the Open Day. I'll have to go down and retrieve it. Or ask Pete to, when he arrives.

There's a tap at the door and Alexis sticks her head round it. She's wearing tiny white shorts and a frilled gingham off-the-shoulder top, her hair and make-up immaculate, as always. 'I'm just about to get a lift to the station with Hugh... I'm on my way to pick up my keys.'

'Great,' I say, arranging my features into a smile. 'Good luck.'

'Only, is it okay if I put a wash on? You know, get a few things clean before I pack them.'

I furrow my brow slightly. 'I thought you were going today?'

'Hundred per cent, I am literally getting the keys, but the thing is, my removal men can't move my stuff until tomorrow. So...'

'So you're actually leaving tomorrow?'

Alexis wrinkles her pretty nose. 'Is that okay? I'm meeting up with a friend after I've been to the agents for the keys, so I probably won't be back 'til late, anyway. If you're in bed when I get back, I'll make sure I'm super quiet.'

'Of course,' I say, aware my tone is begrudging.

'You're the best.' For once, there is genuine warmth in the flashing white smile. 'And I really will be gone tomorrow, I promise.'

I wait for a thank you for her prolonged stay, but she's already left the room.

. . .

After I've showered and dressed, I come downstairs to a silent, empty house.

I'm alone apart from Jeff, who now follows me mournfully everywhere, missing his companion. I make a cup of coffee to take into the office with me, then hesitate and leave it on the countertop, instead going up the back stairs to the first floor. On the landing, I turn right into the blue guest room, which I now think of as Alexis's room. I'm met by the faintest whiff of marijuana and the oversized silver suitcase lying open on the floor in the centre of the room. Most of her clothes have been folded into it with a precision and neatness that surprises me, given the state Alexis leaves the kitchen in. I lift out a top and hold it against my face, inhaling the younger woman's scent, before dropping it again.

In the bathroom, I find a bottle of her perfume and spray a little on my wrist, then quickly run my hand under the tap to rinse off the sickly musk-heavy smell. The surface of the vanity unit is cluttered with beauty products, hair extensions and make-up. There, in the jumble of serums, strobe creams and highlighters is an unopened box of hair dye. I pick it up and examine it, slightly surprised. 'Organic toner in Hint of Copper', it tells me on the outside of the pack, underneath a photo of a model with flame-coloured locks of a cartoonish intensity. Why would Alexis want to dye her hair such an unnatural shade when her own shade of red is so much prettier? Perhaps it's for an acting job?

Back in the bedroom, I stare for a few seconds at the open suitcase, puzzled by something else. There is just the one case, which seemed huge for an overnight stay but perhaps not so big for one that has extended into nearly three weeks. So where is all the other stuff? The recent purchases Alexis claimed she had bought for her new flat, on her trip into Guildford? I check in the wardrobe. There is nothing extra. Just the clothes she brought with her that she hasn't yet packed.

As I head back down the stairs towards a whimpering Jeff and my cooling cup of coffee, something else occurs to me. Hugh has gone into London, saying he might be back late, or not at all. Alexis has gone into London, also claiming she'll be back late. Have the two of them made a plan to meet up somewhere? At the flat? The possibility plays on my mind while I'm phoning clients and emailing suppliers. But at around 4 p.m., as the heat of the afternoon is reaching its peak, the sound of car tyres on gravel makes Jeff bark and whine to go to the front door. I stand up from my desk chair and see Alexis getting out of a taxi.

'Ta-da!' she shrieks triumphantly, as she struts into the front hall. She brandishes a large set of keys in my face, a gesture which seems a little aggressive. 'And I bought this. Thought we could celebrate.' She pulls a bottle of supermarket-brand prosecco from her bag.

'Well done,' I respond faintly. 'I was just thinking about finishing work for the day and having a swim.'

'Count me in,' says Alexis with a buoyant grin. She tosses her bag and the keys onto the highly polished walnut console table. 'It was sweaty as fuck on that train.'

She takes the bottle into the kitchen and goes upstairs, appearing on the pool terrace ten minutes later, dressed in one of her barely-there bikinis which exposes the lower contour of her breasts. I'm in a flattering but conservative navy one-piece covered up with a floaty kaftan. I carry out a tray with a jug of homemade cordial, two tumblers and a bucket of ice.

'Ooh, fab,' sighs Alexis. 'We can start in on the prosecco once we've drunk that lot.' She holds her phone at an angle high above her head and snaps an artful selfie on the lounger, lips pursed in a pout.

I slip off my kaftan and dip a tentative toe in the shallow end. In contrast to the air temperature, the water feels chilly.

Alexis eyes me over the top of her glass. 'You should really wear a bikini, you know, Juliet. You've got a fab figure.'

'Thanks,' I say, with a smile. 'But I think my bikini days are probably behind me.'

'Oh, come on, forty isn't that old! Seriously, though, you're hot. Hugh should appreciate you more.'

This strikes me as an inappropriate thing to say, but I push it from my mind as the refreshingly cool water ripples over my arms. I complete ten lengths of breaststroke, then Alexis swims for a few minutes before trailing pool water into the kitchen to fetch the prosecco and two of my best champagne flutes. We stretch out on the loungers in companionable silence for a while, sipping the fizzy wine, which privately I find a little too sweet.

My phone buzzes with a text.

Will be back later tonight but not in time for supper, so go ahead w/o me. H x

'Is that from Hugh?' Alexis twists her head in my direction, but her huge sunglasses make her expression unreadable.

'Yes. He won't be back until late, so it's just us for your last supper, I'm afraid.'

'The two of us can have a girly night in then. Shall I open some more wine?'

'Not for me, thank you.' I repress a shudder at the thought of a twenty-something 'girly night', and find myself thinking, with a pang, of Belinda. She would have winced in sympathy at the idea.

I prepare a simple avocado, bacon and walnut salad for supper, having learned by now about my guest's tastes and food preferences. Alexis claims that although she's a vegan, it's okay to eat bacon 'as a seasoning', a contradiction that I'm quite happy to ignore. We eat at the kitchen table, with a slightly tipsy Alexis rambling about nothing much in particular.

'So, when you were growing up...' I'm aware that I'm going over old ground, but persist, in what could be my final chance to get answers. 'Surely your mother must have made you aware that you stood to inherit Mullens End at some point? I mean, she will have known the family history, possibly even have been here...' Has Hugh told me whether Avril Lambert ever visited the house? I can't remember, but make a mental note to ask him. 'It's such a special place and such an incredible privilege to be heir to it; did she not talk to you about what that meant?'

Alexis shrugs. 'Not really. I mean, you know what it's like when you're a kid? You don't really listen. It all seemed a bit unreal.'

'And what about your father? What was he like? You never talk about him.'

'I don't remember him.'

'But didn't you try to make contact with him when you grew up? Weren't you at least curious about him?'

'Not really.'

Alexis evades further questioning by making a fuss of Jeff, and giving him bacon despite the injunction against feeding dogs at the table. I watch her, puzzled. Her lack of interest in her own recent past seems at odds with someone who set about reconstructing her family tree on a genealogy website.

Once the meal is over, I open Instagram and check the @lexilamb account. I expect to see the poolside selfie, or the one from the dinner party on her first night, but they're not there. In fact, there have been no posts or updates since before Alexis arrived at Mullens End. Nothing about the house or, indeed, about her imminent flat move. While I'm still on Instagram, the screen displays a WhatsApp from Hugh.

On the 7.59. See you in a bit x

It's now 8.25, which means he should be back from Benfield Holt in no more than half an hour. I leave Alexis watching reels of elaborate make-up routines in the snug and set about cleaning the kitchen to my satisfaction. This involves throwing away the remains of the prosecco and returning a tub of half-melted ice cream to the freezer, before scrubbing down all the work surfaces with a solution of bleach and disinfectant. Only once the room is pristine do I check my watch. It's nine fifteen, but there's no sign of Hugh. A little concerned, I try phoning him, but it goes straight to voicemail. I try a few more times over the next half-hour, but I'm still unable to reach him. He must have bumped into someone he knows on the train, I reason, and gone for a drink at The Crown and Cushion. It's happened before.

As the ormolu clock in the drawing room strikes ten, it starts to rain; one of those sudden summer showers that electrifies the air and fills it with the intense scent of wet earth and damp roses. I was about to capitulate and join Alexis for a dose of mindless reality TV, but instead race outside and rescue the lounger cushions, stowing them away in the pool house. I double back for the towels, holding one aloft to try to keep the rain off my hair.

I'm in the utility room about twenty minutes later, shoving the sodden heap into the washing machine when I hear Jeff barking.

'Silly creature!' I follow him into the front hall and grab his collar to pull him back from the door. 'It's just your papa.'

But instead of a key in the lock, there's a sonorous ringing on the Victorian butler's bell that's connected to the brass doorbell push outside. Puzzled, I open the door. Standing on the stone step are a man and a woman, the rain falling in the beam of the porch light behind them. The sun is just sinking to the horizon, so I can still clearly see the car they came in: a non-descript silver saloon.

'Mrs Mullen?'

I frown. 'Yes.'

'I'm DS Hightower, and this is DC Carter. May we come in please?'

Because of the unmarked car and the absence of uniform, it takes me a few seconds to understand that these are police officers. Detectives. The man is tall, with wavy hair and a goatee and looks to be about forty; the woman is younger and wearing glasses.

'Did PC Dainty send you?' I wave them into the hall. They're both wearing beige raincoats over their dark suits, giving off a faint odour of damp fabric. 'Is this about the vandalism we reported?'

They exchange glances.

'Mrs Mullen,' the female officer says carefully. 'Are you here on your own?'

My stomach contracts, and I feel an icy trickle of fear shoot down the back of my legs. 'We've got a family member staying. Why?'

Again, that look passes between them.

'Is there somewhere we can sit down?' DS Hightower asks.

I lead them into the drawing room. I'm trembling visibly now, but I can't sit, hanging on to the back of an armchair instead.

The detectives both sit down, their eyes moving round the room to take in the beautiful original fireplace, the expensive drapes, the exquisite antique furniture. DC Carter points to the sofa, indicating that I should make use of it, but I shake my head, paralysed with fear.

'Just tell me what's happened.'

'It's your husband,' DS Hightower says, looking down at his own hands. 'He's been in a serious traffic accident. He ran his car off the road.'

'Where is he?' I demand. 'Is he okay?' But I know even as I

ask this that it's not a possibility. Not with the two of them here, in my drawing room, trying to make me sit down.

DC Carter lets out a little sigh and pauses a beat, as if reluctant to let the words pass her lips. 'Mrs Mullen, I'm afraid he's been killed.'

ELEVEN

3 JULY

I can't remember what time it was when I went to bed.

Anyway, I didn't really 'go to bed', not in the conventional sense. I collapsed at an angle across it, fully clothed. Alexis, who had hovered at my elbow since the police officers' visit and – somewhat surprisingly – been calm and supportive, brought me a small pale blue tablet and some water. I waved it away, but Alexis was insistent.

'It's a Xanax. It'll just take the edge off a bit, help your body relax. You need to rest.'

I took the pill and eventually – my body still rigid from suppressing wave after wave of shock – fell into a light doze.

When I wake, it's just after five and starting to get light. As I sit up, I'm hit by a jolt of shock like an electric current as I remember what happened the night before. Hugh is dead. I fall back on the pillow and close my eyes, scalding tears trickling over my cheeks and down the sides of my neck, soaking the pillowcase. After a few minutes, I slow my breathing and manage to collect myself. I fumble for my phone and try again to call Belinda. I tried at least half a dozen times last night after DS Hightower and DC Carter left. But Belinda is still not

taking my calls. She will at least know by now what's happened,
I reassure myself, so surely she'll have to get in touch soon.
Alexis gave the police detectives Simon Langridge's number
when they left, and they said they would contact him straightaway, and ask him to tell anyone he thought needed to know the
news. It will be a shock for everyone, the loss of Hugh Mullen at
the age of thirty-five. Still a young man,

Shivering, even though it's not cold, I stumble onto the landing. There's no sound from Alexis's room, and it doesn't seem
fair to wake her. From downstairs, there's a familiar clicking
sound and Jeff appears, his tail drooping between his legs and
his head hung. I tiptoe downstairs and kneel down next to him,
grateful to be able to bury my face in his fur. My tears sink into
his ruff and he whines plaintively.

After a few seconds, I gather myself, and Jeff follows me
into the kitchen, where I fill his bowl with kibble and put the
kettle on. I stand with a mug of tea in my hands, staring blankly
out of the window as the sun rises over the garden. I can hear
the drawing-room clock strike six, Jeff licking vainly at his
empty bowl, blackbirds singing enthusiastically in the honey-
suckle that grows up the kitchen garden wall. Everything
sounds normal; and that is what feels so strange.

I take my tea into the drawing room and hunt around for the
business card that DS Hightower left. Eventually, I find it on
the fireplace, next to the clock. There's a Surrey Police logo and
beneath it 'Derek J. Hightower, Detective Sergeant' and a mobile
number. 'Call any time,' he'd told me as he left. 'Anything at all
that you need, any questions that you have… I'll try to help.'

I phone DS Hightower and leave a message asking him to
return to the house at his earliest convenience, then walk slowly
upstairs with my tea. I look around the elegant bedroom, a place
where, for several years at least, Hugh and I were very happy
together. His bathrobe still hangs on the back of the bathroom
door and I bury my face in it, giving way to tears again as I

inhale the familiar scent of him: Trumper's shaving cream and sandalwood aftershave.

After a shower, I dry and style my hair and apply make-up, managing to disguise the worst of the puffiness. I deliberate over what to wear, eventually choosing a lightweight grey cashmere hoodie and black cigarette pants. I will not be broken by this, I tell myself fiercely. I may be disintegrating on the inside, but on the outside I'm going to at least try to keep myself together. Maintain appearances.

By the time I've finished, there's a tap at the door and Alexis sticks her head round it. 'Oh,' she says, so surprised that she takes a step backwards. 'You're up. And... dressed and everything. I was just coming to ask if I could make you some tea.'

My answer is to raise the empty mug.

'Ah, okay, you've already had... Well, how are you feeling? Do you need another Xanax?'

I shake my head. 'No. I'm okay.'

'So, I looked up the number of the Dohertys' practice online?' Alexis goes on, with her irritating upward cadence. 'And I spoke to the veterinary nurse, who said she'd contact Justine.'

Sure enough, Justine's car draws up half an hour later and she barrels into the front hall, still dressed in her running gear, and envelops me in a hug. 'My God, you poor girl... what a terrible thing!'

I don't really feel like being pawed by everyone, but I allow her to hug me briefly before leading her into the kitchen, where Alexis makes coffee.

'We found out late last night... Simon messaged Patrick... it was a car crash, is that right?' Justine reads my expression and adds hurriedly, 'Listen, if you're not up to talking about it, that's all right. You must still be in shock. I'm just here to offer any support I can.'

'No, it's okay.' I pretend to brush a speck of fluff off my cashmere top, my fingers trembling as the terrible image floods my brain again. 'He was driving back from Benfield Holt after being in London all day and he took a bend too quickly... you know, that treacherous one just past the riding school... and his car came off the road and into the ditch.'

'My God...' repeats Justine, her face pale under her wiry mouse-coloured hair. 'But, look, you mustn't worry about telling people, Jules. Patrick and I will help take care of it.'

'Massimo,' I say quietly. 'Someone should phone him, so he can tell Luca... tell him what's happened.'

'Leave it with me. I spoke to Faith and Vik this morning. Vik wants to come by and check on you, see how you're holding up.'

'And Belinda?' I ask. 'I've tried phoning her.'

'Yes, the police went round and spoke to Simon last night. So she knows.'

The unmarked silver car returns an hour later, but DC Carter is alone this time.

'I'm so sorry, Mrs Mullen,' she says, as soon as she's inside the hallway. She has the faintest Irish brogue. 'DS Hightower has been called away on another case. But I hope I'll be able to help.'

The expression on her freckled face is earnest. She's a tall, slim young woman with lank pale blonde hair. Her watery grey eyes, behind the steel-rimmed glasses, have fair lashes.

'Do you need me to stay?' Alexis is still hovering at my elbow.

'No,' I say firmly. 'Perhaps you could make DC Carter some tea or coffee?'

'Do please call me Niamh. And that would be lovely, yes. A white coffee, one sugar.'

The policewoman follows me into the drawing room.

'I must say, you seem very...' Her gaze travels over my

immaculate outfit, and my expertly applied make-up. 'You seem to be handling things very well.'

There's almost an accusatory tone, as though in her line of work she can only deal with people who are tearstained wrecks. I let it pass.

'When you and your DS came, I thought it was something to do with the campaign of harassment we've been going through. Our cars and the house were vandalised, and one of our dogs was killed. Did you know about that?'

'We do, yes. The case came up on the system when we found out your husband's identity.'

'And you don't think it's suspicious? The timing of the crash?' My voice is surprisingly firm. I need answers. 'You don't think he was somehow... run off the road?'

'Trust me, Mrs Mullen, we will be looking into that, and reporting our findings to the coroner. And also the post-mortem will show if...' Niamh Carter's pale face flushes slightly. 'It will give a blood alcohol measurement.'

I inhale deeply, steadying myself again. 'What's happened to his car?'

She looks startled, gives a little cough. 'It's been taken to our forensic vehicle assessment unit.'

I look down at my hands, examining the red polish on my nails. 'I want to see him,' I say eventually.

She's silent a beat, looking pained.

'I want to see Hugh. See his body.'

'Yes, Mrs Mullen, I understood what you meant, it's just that...' She leans forwards, her forearms resting across her knees in an expression of professional sympathy. 'Your husband's car came off the road at speed, and obviously he was badly injured. He's not... he may not be...'

I keep my gaze steady, and the younger woman becomes flustered.

'...in the ideal condition to be viewed. I wouldn't want that to be your lasting memory of your loved one. Look...' She gently pulls a zipped black folder from her bag and reaches into it. 'These are the crash scene photos. After Mr Mullen had been extracted from the vehicle,' she adds hurriedly. She hands me a set of 8' x 10' colour prints.

And there is the black Range Rover, nose down on a steep embankment with the front driver's side badly dented. There's tape around it saying 'POLICE LINE DO NOT CROSS' and each shot shows the car from a different angle. I pause longest on a close-up of the registration plate. *For the avoidance of doubt*, I think, and an icy shiver runs through me. Because there is no doubt. This is Hugh's car.

I nod stiffly, and hand the photos back to Niamh Carter, just as Alexis comes in with a mug of coffee.

'I still want to see him.' I speak quietly, but firmly. 'Even if he's... damaged. For my own peace of mind. If I don't, none of this will ever seem real.'

Alexis and the police officer exchange a look of concern.

'Juliet, are you sure?' Alexis asks. Her voice is tight with anxiety, coming out as a strange squeak.

'Yes.'

'Well, all right then...' Niamh Carter nods. 'I'll make a few calls and get that arranged. Just so I don't disturb you with phone calls while you're going through this, is it alright if I liaise with your cousin here?'

'My husband's cousin,' I correct her formally. 'Yes, yes that's fine. But please, make it soon. It's important for me.'

The front doorbell jangles, and I walk out into the hall, leaving Alexis and DC Carter talking in low voices. Jeff has already rushed to the door, wagging his tail and giving little whimpers of pleasure. I open it to Rocket and Belinda, holding a large casserole dish. The puffiness of her face betrays that she has recently been crying. She also seems taken aback to be greeted by Hugh's widow in person.

'My God, it's you!' She shuttles sideways awkwardly so she can place the casserole on the hallstand and pull me into her arms in an enveloping embrace. 'I mean, goodness, Jules, should you be answering the door yourself?'

I submit willingly to the embrace, then pull back and say drily, 'Did you think I'd be locked in my bedroom with the curtains drawn, *Gone With the Wind*-style?'

'No, of course not... Bloody hell, Jules, how *are* you? I mean, you poor darling, you must be devastated!'

Is she, like DC Carter, implying that I don't seem upset enough? I wonder.

'I am. Of course I am. But I've got to keep going somehow.'

'I've brought you a beef stroganoff...' She rummages in the carrier bag she's holding for a Tupperware. 'And I've done some rice to go with it, you know, so you don't need to faff with that. You can heat them up for your lunch.'

'I don't think I can manage lunch,' I say faintly. In fact, I feel queasy, suddenly overwhelmed again.

'Well, supper then.' Belinda now strides towards the kitchen with the food, very much in charge, and the dogs and I follow. 'You need to make sure you eat something. That Alexis one won't eat the beef, of course, but that's just tough luck... Justine said she was still here, is that right?'

I nod, and sit down at the kitchen table, feeling completely exhausted. Out in the hall, I can hear Alexis showing DC Carter out and closing the front door behind her.

'And look – I've got fresh bread here, and milk and a few other bits to just tide you over the next couple of days, until I can come back and stock you up.' Belinda bustles around the kitchen putting the food away, rearranging the fridge contents as she does so.

'That's very kind, Belle,' I say weakly.

'Of *course*, my darling, that's what friends are for.' She bends and gives me another awkward hug, adding quickly, 'And

I'm really so sorry about before. About the argument. I didn't really mean those nasty things I said, it's just... well, Simon and I haven't been getting along very well, and the house is a mess: we need a new roof and we haven't got the money for it. Your life seemed so problem-free in comparison; I suppose I was a bit jealous.'

I give a wry smile. 'Problem-free; that's me.'

'Oh God, Jules, I didn't mean... I feel so awful now, of course. I hope I didn't tempt fate. Coffee?'

I shake my head, but Belinda, who knows where to find everything in the Mullens End kitchen, makes some anyway and pours herself a mug. Her hands tremble as she does so.

'So, have you told your folks?'

I nod.

'And are they coming? Would you want them to anyway?' She knows that I'm not particularly close to either of my parents.

'They'll come for the funeral.'

'Gosh, I didn't want to ask about that, but... have you made a start on the arrangements? I suppose having your own mausoleum makes things a bit more straightforward.' She gives a strange little laugh, that I can't quite interpret.

'Not yet.' I reach down and dig my fingers into Jeff's coat. 'There are a few things that have to be sorted first.'

And I have to see Hugh for myself.

TWELVE

6 JULY

'Are you sure this is right?' I ask.

My car, with Alexis driving, draws up outside a building on the outskirts of Woking, where the old town merges into bland suburban sprawl. The shopfront sign, with gold letters picked out against black, reads: 'Ellesmere & Daughters Funeral Directors'.

'This is the address I was given.' Alexis climbs out of the driver's seat and closes the door.

After sitting for a couple of seconds in a catatonic silence, I climb out too. I'm wearing a black crepe dress with a pleated skirt and black court shoes. Open-toed sandals seemed a little flippant.

'No, what I mean is, it's not the right firm. The Mullens have used the same undertakers for decades. Drewers, just outside Cranleigh.'

Alexis's expression is unreadable behind her massive Chanel shades. She's wearing a long black cheesecloth wrap-around dress and trainers. She bunches her cheeks slightly.

'Ah, you see, that's the thing... the Irish police lady – what's her name?'

'DC Carter.'

'Yeah, she explained it to me. They had to arrange to move...
him... Hugh from the hospital morgue at short notice yesterday
because they don't have, like, viewing facilities there?'

Again, the irritating upward cadence of her sentences. Still,
I'm grateful she's stuck around after originally planning to leave
on Saturday. Better than being in the house alone.

'And this was the only company they could find within a
reasonable distance who could, you know, accommodate us at
short notice. But, look, don't worry, yeah? Apparently, they're
perfectly good.'

I look doubtfully at the shop frontage. The windows are
discreetly screened with gathered curtains, in front of which are
artificial flowers and a few examples of urns and monumental
stoneware.

'DC Carter said they seemed very nice on the phone,'
Alexis adds by way of encouragement.

I sigh and give a little shrug of resignation. Once you're dead,
I think, what difference does the name of the undertaker make?
'He has to be laid to rest in the mausoleum though,' I say firmly.
'That's where all the Mullens are. His parents are there. As long
as they can accommodate that, then I don't suppose it matters.'

Alexis nods and places a hand briefly on my shoulder. 'Let
ask them, shall we? Afterwards. And if they can't, well then, I
guess we'll have to think again about using them for the funeral.'

We. I flinch at the word. 'We' used to be me and Hugh

We're greeted at the door by a young man whose formal suit
and black tie are at odds with his trendy fade haircut. He introduces himself as Tom Ellesmere, shaking my hand with a little
bow and asking if I'm ready, or if I need a little more time. A
cup of tea, perhaps?

'No need. I'm ready,' I say calmly, adding, 'Thank you.'

We're led through a narrow, carpeted passageway to a door,

which Tom opens, bowing his head reverentially as I walk past him and into the room beyond it. 'I'll leave you alone, but I'll be outside if you need me.'

Alexis is standing a couple of metres behind me, but I'm barely aware of her. Because there he is. Hugh.

He's lying on a purple-draped plinth that's been made to look like a bed, with a sheet pulled up to the top of his naked chest, his thick auburn hair swept back from his forehead. Two large flower arrangements on pedestal stands are at the head and foot of the plinth. The light in the room is extremely dim and, after a few seconds, I realise that its only source is a handful of flickering church candles.

Some sort of cosmetic work has been done on his face, but there's no mistaking the bruises and abrasions. Even so, it's him. It's Hugh. There's no doubt.

'Do you think I'm allowed to touch him?' I ask.

'I wouldn't,' Alexis says quickly. 'I mean, is it really a good idea?'

I shake my head. 'No. No, I don't think I want to. I don't want to feel...' My voice has dropped to little more than a whisper. 'How cold he is.' My throat closes with suppressed sobs, and after taking one last look, I turn on my heel and walk out of the room, back into the brightly lit corridor.

'Thank you,' I say to the waiting Tom. No sign of the Ellesmere daughters in the company's name, which strikes me as odd.

'Are you sure you're all right?' he asks kindly. 'Can I get you some water?'

I shake my head. 'No, thanks.'

'If you'd like to take this opportunity to discuss caskets?'

'Just go with the best-quality oak you have, solid, not veneer. And it will need to be ventilated correctly for an above-ground mausoleum.'

He gives another of his reverential bows. 'In that case, your loved one will also need to be embalmed.'

'Please just do what you need to do. I'm sorry...'

I push past him and Alexis and hurry out of the building, yanking open the door of my car and climbing inside. Only then, when I'm alone, do I give way to weeping.

That afternoon, I'm paid a visit by Roger Banborough.

Banborough is a senior partner in the City law firm used by the Mullen family for generations, and chief trustee of the Mullen Trust. He arrives in a sleek Mercedes, not quite in funeral garb but soberly dressed in a dark blue suit and club tie. By then, I've changed out of my black dress into jeans and a shirt ready to walk Jeff. I lead him out onto the back terrace.

'Terrible business, terrible business,' he murmurs, clasping both of my hands. He's a tall, well-built man with a shiny pink face and heavy jowls. 'How are you holding up, my dear?'

I ignore this question. 'How did you hear about it?' I ask. 'Only, the death notice isn't appearing in the papers until Friday. That way, I could add details of the funeral arrangements, so people will know when it's happening.'

'I had a visit from two police officers at my office yesterday morning.' He rummages in his jacket pocket and pulls out a familiar-looking card. 'A Detective Sergeant Derek Hightower, and a young lady detective.'

I blink in surprise. 'They're the officers investigating the crash, but how would they know to inform the trustees? How would they even know of the existence of the family trust? It has no bearing on what happened.'

Banborough folds his hands across his stomach, his gold signet ring catching the sunlight and reflecting it like a miniature flare. 'As I understand it, the beneficiary informed them.'

'The beneficiary?'

'Ms Lambert. The cousin of your late husband, who will become the new life tenant. I understand that she's been living here? That she was here when the police called to inform you of... the accident.'

Jeff, impatient for his walk, crashes against my legs and thrusts his nose into my lap. I push him away. 'Yes, but only temporarily until her new...' My voice trails off. It only now occurs to me that the flat Alexis had been due to move into will no longer be needed. That this place, Mullens End, is now her home. And, clearly, she had wasted no time in making sure the executor of the trust knew about Hugh's death. I had no idea Alexis even knew who that was, but Hugh must have spoken to her about it.

'DS Hightower told me that they'd requested the coroner to issue an interim death certificate, so that you can hold the funeral without needing to wait for an inquest. You do understand that an inquest is mandatory in the case of accidental death, even if no third party is involved?'

I nod.

'Good.' Banborough reaches forward and pats Jeff. 'And the death certificate will be passed directly to the funeral director to allow them to make the... arrangements. The police officers said they'd make sure I received a copy of the certificate too, which I'll need to apply for the grant of probate.'

'I appreciate you letting me know. Alexis has very kindly taken care of most of the paperwork.' As I say this, I can't help wondering now whether this was the right decision.

'So I understand.' He manages a faint smile of acknowledgement. 'I'm glad you've had some help with the bureaucracy at such a difficult time.' He hesitates a beat. 'And I'm only too aware that this is a delicate matter, but I thought it was important that we speak about it before the funeral, when people might start asking you awkward questions. About the future of Mullens End.'

I manage a faint smile. 'You're here to chuck me out.'

'No, no, goodness no.' Banborough steeples his fingers and presses them briefly to his face. 'It doesn't work quite like that. Your income from the trust will start being paid immediately, but under the terms set out by Ernest Mullen, there is a grace period of six months, during which you can stay here and set your own affairs in order. After that...'

'Alexis Lambert gets all of this.' I wave my hand in a circle, taking in the swimming pool, the tennis court, the rose garden.

'She is the next surviving Mullen, so yes.' Banborough speaks slowly, heavily. 'She becomes the life tenant with immediate effect after the six months.'

'And tell me,' I lean forward, my hand still on Jeff's collar. 'Who's the lucky jackpot winner who gets it after her?'

'As I understand it, Ms Lambert is still young enough to marry and have a family. So one hopes there will be an heir via that route.'

Ah yes, that word again. An heir. The thing that I failed to supply.

Banborough pushes back his chair and stands up. 'I'll leave you in peace for now, but, of course, I'll be back for the funeral. And if, in the meantime, there is anything I can help you with... I know this transition can be very difficult.'

This transition, I think bitterly. I've become a widow just shy of my fortieth birthday. I'll never see Hugh again, never again get to share his boundless enthusiasm for the house we both loved so much, for the life we built together here. My life has been completely destroyed, forcing me to leave my home of the last ten years. And this pompous man calls it a 'transition'.

'Thank you.' I also get to my feet and force a gracious smile. 'I'm sure I'll be perfectly all right.'

THIRTEEN

12 JULY

The thing about funerals, I think, as I dress for my husband's, is that you'd quite enjoy them if it wasn't for the reason they're being held. A chance to catch up with family and old friends, good food and drink.

The day has dawned heavy and very humid, with a sky obscured by a layer of yellowish-grey cloud. My parents will be coming, along with some of the friends from my London days that I haven't seen for ages. And all of Hugh's and my Benfield circle will be there, plus a few of Hugh's closest work associates, along with Banborough and the other three trustees of the Mullen estate: a cousin from his mother's side of the family, an old friend of the family called Venetia Swindell and William Lawson, his late father's stockbroker. The number of mourners has to be kept small in order to fit inside the mausoleum, which houses a tiny chapel. The Roman Catholic Ernest Mullen, unwilling to attend Benfield's Anglican St Peter's Church, built his own place of worship above the crypt.

Roman Catholic priests are thin on the ground in the Surrey Hills, but Alexis has arranged for one from St Augustine's in Chilworth to take the service. Despite my own lack of religious affiliation, I know it's what Hugh would have wanted. I've made vague verbal promises to Hugh's wider circle of friends and acquaintances that a full memorial service will be held in London at a later date, but, to be honest, my heart isn't really in the idea.

The one saving grace is that Luca is here, asleep now in his childhood bedroom on the top floor of the house. Massimo put him on a flight from Bologna and arranged for a car to pick him up at Heathrow and drive him to Mullens End. His presence has been such a balm for me; the only thing that is providing me with any real comfort. Around Alexis he is bashful and tongue-tied, his skin turning bright pink when she speaks to him; Alexis predictably delights in flirting with him, despite the fact he's only a teenager.

'What about her boyfriend?' Luca asked me when we were alone in the snug a couple of days ago.

'I don't think she has one.'

'Don't be stupid, Mum, girls who look like that always have a boyfriend. Or a girlfriend.'

'Alexis is not exactly a girl,' I corrected him mildly. 'She's almost thirty.'

Luca flushed again. 'Whatever.'

Privately, I wondered why I had never thought to ask Alexis about a significant other. Luca was right: someone as stunningly attractive as Alexis is likely to have someone. She's always been oddly silent on the matter of her private life. Perhaps she confided that sort of stuff to Hugh.

The day before, I overheard her talking with Luca as they both stood at the big mezzanine window on the landing, looking out at the sweep of the drive below.

'It must have been lush growing up here?' Alexis was saying with her infuriating millennial up-speak. 'You must have had, like, amazing parties?'

'Yeah, kind of,' Luca mumbled. 'I mean, I had, like, kids'

parties and stuff. By the time I was old enough to have proper house parties, I'd moved to Italy.'

'This must be tough for you, you know, losing your dad? I never knew mine, but I was devastated when my mum died. Like, destroyed.'

'Hugh wasn't my dad,' Luca said gruffly. 'I was seven when I moved here. Massimo's my dad, and, you know, not gunna lie, I think of Italy as home now. But yeah, it's sad, I guess.'

'This is the perfect house for parties,' Alexis sighed dreamily.

Is that what she plans for Hugh's beloved family home? I thought, my stomach twisting, with despair. Redecorating it in silver and pale pink and filling it with her vacuous prosecco-drinking friends?

I put on a sleeveless black linen dress and heels, deciding to leave my legs bare. As I head for the main staircase, I can already hear Belinda's strident tones floating up from the kitchen. She's offered to provide food for the wake, and despite my assurances that I'm bringing in caterers, she's turned up to help anyway.

'Put those canapés on the table over there,' I hear her saying as she comes into the kitchen, 'and you should find ice buckets on the bottom shelf of the pantry, there. No, that door over there.' She's wearing a rather matronly black shirt dress and thick black tights, and her freckled face is beaded with sweat despite the inexpertly applied face powder.

'I'm so sorry for the loss of your husband,' one of the caterers murmurs, as her colleagues scuttle around the room obeying Belinda's directions.

'Oh, my goodness, it's not me that's been widowed,' Belinda corrects her. 'Although he was a very close friend, obviously.'

She starts slightly as I come into the room, and has the good grace to look embarrassed.

'Everything's going to plan, I think.' She leans in to kiss me on the cheek. 'You just concentrate on getting through the day.'

'I'll be all right.'

'I'm sure you will, Jules.' Belinda takes the cling film off a platter of cheeses. 'I must say, you look terrific.'

There it is again. That faint suggestion that I am *too* all right. Ignoring it, I ask 'Has Alexis surfaced yet?'

'You mean she's still here?' Belinda's eyebrows shoot up. 'Even after...'

'Well, yes,' I counter matter-of-factly. 'Technically, this is her house now.' Seeing Belinda's frown, I go on, 'Or it's about to be. Obviously, it's a bit awkward, having her under the same roof at the moment, but then everything's been so wretched anyway, her being here could hardly make it worse.'

'So she's coming to the funeral? Even though she barely knew Hugh?'

She's either forgotten confiding to me that Hugh and Alexis were seen in a clinch, or is tactfully choosing to pretend it didn't happen.

I give a small shrug. 'I thought she should be there. And she said she wanted to be, so...' My voice trails off at the sound of a vehicle's slow approach over the gravelled drive.

'Oh God, is that...?' Belinda instinctively smooths her hair and the skirt of her dress.

'That must be the hearse, yes. Pete's getting everyone else to park in the paddock.'

Simon appears at the kitchen doorway, looking older than usual in his dark suit. 'They're ready, Jules. Shall I fetch Luca?'

I nod, closing my eyes briefly and fingering the antique emerald cross I'm wearing round my neck: a Mullen heirloom that Hugh gave me for our first anniversary. A few minutes later, I hear the clack of Alexis's five-inch Louboutins in the hall, followed by Luca thumping down the main staircase and greeting my parents, who must have just arrived. I go to embrace them too, then, with a deep intake of breath, head onto the front steps, in time to see the pallbearers – a group of Hugh's closest friends – shouldering the heavy oak coffin.

Tom, the young undertaker, is there, with an older colleague. His fade has been freshly shaved, and the neck tattoos just visible above his white shirt collar. I let my eyes focus on them to try to calm the thumping of my heart, and the uncontrollable shaking in my limbs. Luca, wearing one of Massimo's suits that's slightly too large for him, hooks his arm through mine and I lean on him. We fall in step behind the pallbearers, my parents behind us, then Alexis, followed by and Belinda and Simon.

The vestibule of the mausoleum has marble pillars and a small, stained window depicting the Virgin Mary. Folding chairs have been set in rows on either side of a makeshift aisle, at the top of which is a trestle where the pallbearers place the coffin. Belinda told me that the village ladies who do the flowers at St Peter's would take care of floral arrangements, and the small space is filled with lilies, delphiniums and hydrangeas, their perfume mingling with the cool, dusty scent of the building. Behind the trestle is the door leading down to the crypt, with twelve burial vaults built into its walls. Ernest Mullen's remains lie there, along with Hugh's grandparents and parents.

I take my seat on the front row, still clutching Luca's hand. My head drops and I close my eyes. Behind me, there's a lot of scraping of chair legs as people squeeze along the rows and settle into their seats.

The Catholic priest, in soutane and lace surplice, starts to speak. 'May the Father of mercies, the God of all consolation, be with you.'

'And with your spirit,' some of the congregation murmur.

There's a hymn, then more of the mass, then a friend of Hugh's who I barely recognise reads something from the Bible.

'Are you okay, Mama?' Luca whispers.

I nod slowly, but don't open my eyes. I just want this to be over.

Forty minutes later it is, and we all emerge into the sultry July humidity, the guests chatting in that tension-relieving way people do at the end of funerals, knowing that alcohol is in the offing.

Tom Ellesmere and his fellow funeral director remain either side of the mausoleum door, hands respectfully clasped in front of them. Once everyone is in the house, they will seal the coffin in a plastic covering and place it in one of the unused vaults. I push this thought roughly from my mind. I hate the thought of Hugh lying there a couple of hundred yards from the house, stored like a carcase of meat. That's one reason I would never want to remain here at Mullens End, even if the term of the trust didn't prevent me from doing so.

The caterers' waitstaff are at the ready with champagne and canapés, and the guests spill through the French windows of the drawing room and onto the lawn outside, with the exception of Alexis, who's nowhere to be seen. Perhaps she thinks it would be more tactful if she absents herself.

I circulate through them, forcing a smile. At first, I'm greeted with people pulling sorrowful faces, their heads tilted slightly to one side, but as the vintage Krug flows and the mood lifts, they move on to telling amusing anecdotes about Hugh and telling me what a 'terrific bloke' my husband was. I smile some more, nod, agree. It's exhausting.

After a couple of hours, the volume of the laughter is rising and the stories getting raucous. My mother looks up from her conversation with Vikram Kuchar, then materialises at my side. She's worn a black felt hat, bless her, and is clearly uncomfortable in it.

'Dad and I thought we'd get going, love, and then maybe people will follow.'

I smile gratefully, then make a show of kissing both my parents goodbye and walking them out to the front of the house.

As Mum predicted, people take the hint, and the crowd starts to thin until it's just Luca and me and a few people from the village, chatting in the garden.

'Is it okay if I go and watch TV?' he asks, tugging off his tie.

'Of course, darling. You've been brilliant.' I kiss him and go alone to the kitchen, where the caterers are packing up their glasses.

Alexis appears, changed from her funeral black into one of her leggings and crop top ensembles, her perfectly pedicured feet bare. The two of us face each other awkwardly.

'I was thinking...' Alexis starts. 'Maybe I should go to London, to my flat, for a bit. You know, to allow you to get stuff sorted out?'

'That's really not necessary,' I reply stiffly.

'I know, but Roger Banborough told me the house is still yours for another six months? So perhaps if you stay 'til the New Year? Then you can have one last Christmas here?'

She doesn't understand, I think bitterly. She doesn't realise that Christmas at Mullens End was always about Hugh. Everything was done the way Hugh said it should be done, the way it always had been done, for decades. The ritual choosing of a tree from a nearby farm, the delivery of the turkey by the family butcher, the Christmas Eve drinks party with the neighbours and annual visit from the village carol singers. It was Hugh's Christmas, never mine. I try and fail to imagine what Alexis's Christmas would be like. Something involving a takeaway and ready-mixed cocktails perhaps.

'Thank you, Alexis, but I've already decided. I'll hire someone to pack up my stuff and put it in storage then I'm going to fly out to Italy with Luca. It should only take a few days.'

Alexis looks confused. 'You mean, like, for a holiday?'

'No.' My voice is flat. 'Not a holiday. But obviously before I book a flight, I need to speak to DS Hightower about the date of the inquest. I've still got the card with his number.'

Alexis startles slightly, her eyes widening. 'God, no, Juliet, you don't need to do that. Way too upsetting for you. I'll phone Hightower, okay? And I'll make sure you know what's happening on that score. He told me it would probably be months before it's held though, so...'

So I may as well get going, I think bitterly.

'Thank you,' I say in a tight little voice, turning on my heel and heading into the library. I sit down at the huge partner's desk, which neither Hugh or I ever really used. Then I pull out Hightower's card from my wallet, tapping it absently on the edge of the desk. I hesitate for a few minutes before putting it away again. But I do pull out my mobile and after a brief Google search, make some phone calls.

There's a tap on the door, and Justine Doherty sticks her head round it. Her tall, wiry frame looks unusually elegant in a burgundy crepe dress, and she's had her boyish crop styled specially; a gesture which I find touching. She's a very decent sort, Justine, for all her brusqueness.

'Jules? Are you okay? Only I saw you heading in here on your own and thought I'd check up on you.'

I smile up at her. 'Fine. Just trying to sort out my travel back to Italy.'

'So soon? Are you sure you're ready?'

I nod. 'To be honest, I can't face staying here a day longer than I have to.'

She comes over to the desk and places a hand on my shoulder. 'Is there anything Patrick and I can help with? You will tell me if there is?'

'I'll let you know. And thanks, Justine, that's very kind.'

She gives my hand a squeeze, then turns and heads back to the door.

'Wait... Justine, can I ask you something?'

She hesitates, her hand on the door handle.

'D'you think it's possible...' My voice tails off. 'No; it's nothing. Forget it.'

'Okay then. But listen, you know you can phone me any time.' Justine opens the library door. 'And maybe we'll see you when you come back for the inquest?'

I look down at the wedding ring, still on my left hand. 'I'm not sure. I haven't decided if I'm going to attend or not.'

'But we'll see you when you get back from Italy anyway?'

I shake my head. 'I don't plan on coming back. I'm moving there for good.'

PART TWO

SUMMER

FOURTEEN

19 JUNE

The house is amazing; there's no doubt about that.

I climb out of the taxi and stand there taking it in for a few seconds before approaching the front door. It's like something from *Downton Abbey*. Nowhere near as large in scale; it's not a massively big house. But it has such an air of grandeur and self-importance. Of belonging in its surroundings. And something like this being so close to London; it's crazy.

Even crazier is the idea that it could one day be mine.

I decided to time my arrival for mid-evening, so as to make the maximum possible impact. I'm delighted when I discover there's a formal dinner party going on. Even better. Usually at a social occasion, I'd be looking stylish but understated. One of my favourite outfits is a narrow navy blue dress, midi length with a black and white stripe up the side. I wear it with trainers, and perhaps a denim jacket slung over the top. That's my usual vibe: quite low-key. But today I need my clothes to work twofold: they need to imply that I'm a bit of an airhead and also give Hugh Mullen the hots for me. So I've chosen a skimpy white top that shows an indecent amount of boob, and a clinging skirt with a thigh slit. *Only Way is Essex* vibes. Trashy.

It's Juliet who answers the door. She's shocked, I can tell, and definitely not pleased. But what did she expect when she blanked me on social media? That I'd just melt away into the ether? She's slight and dark; attractive in an expensive, carefully curated way, with Mediterranean colouring and aggressively angular bobbed dark hair. The smile of greeting on her face definitely doesn't extend to her eyes.

Despite her displeasure, she remembers her manners and leads me through a massive hall and into a grand drawing room, where she introduces me to a handful of middle-aged neighbours. And her husband, Hugh. My distant cousin.

I've seen photos of him, of course, and I'm relieved to find that he's even more attractive in the flesh. He's tall, with dark red hair swept back from a patrician forehead, and the sort of good looks typical of British movie stars of the 1940s.

'Alexis. Great to meet you.' He grins wolfishly, and as his eyes take in my outfit, I see the flicker of interest in his eyes.

Juliet has already excused herself to go and take care of the meal, leaving her husband flirting with me shamelessly, and not even trying to hide it. I imagine that in the bedroom his tastes are predictable, but I get enough of a vibe from him to be confident that sex with him could be raunchy once we've got past the public-schoolboy cheesiness. I don't hold back on the flirtation either. If he thinks I'm already interested in him, so much the better. I need him to be interested in me.

I ask him to show me where the bathroom is, and he takes me out into the grand hallway and points me in the direction of a downstairs guest cloakroom. He sees the suitcase, of course, as I had intended him to. This allows me to give him the spiel about how I'm between flats as the new one needs some unexpected work doing to it.

'But you can stay here,' he says immediately. 'Of course. You must. After all' – he's looking straight at my cleavage when he says this – 'you're extended family. Stay as long as you need to.'

'Don't you need to check with Juliet? That it's okay?'

'Leave it to me to square it with the trouble and strife,' he says, with a wink. 'It won't be a problem.'

When I emerge from using the cloakroom, the others are already seated in the dining room. As I take my place between the doctor, Vikram, and the vet, Patrick, Juliet comes in carrying a platter of roast lamb. It smells garlicky and delicious, and elicits admiring sighs from the assembled guests. I hold up a hand as I'm offered a slice.

'Thing is, I'm a vegan.'

I'm not, obviously, but this has the desired effect of driving Hugh off in search of a veggie option and making Juliet irritated with him, as well as with me for my unscheduled arrival. From what I can see, there's little, if any, chemistry between the two Mullens. Juliet is uptight, cold and a little mechanical, while Hugh seems extrovert and spontaneous, unruffled by petty problems.

And then there are the friends. I set to work flirting with Vikram, aware that the others are covertly scrutinising me, assessing me. The woman called Belinda, in particular – buxom, blonde and outdoorsy-looking – has resting bitch face, and there's a patronising undertone to her questions.

But, so far, so good. I'm in, and apparently accepted. The seed of a plan, planted over a year ago, is working.

The truth is, it started even longer ago, during my first term at the Guildhall School of Music and Drama.

A tall, striking redhead approached me in the lunch break of my first day, and introduced herself.

'Hi, I'm Alexis Lambert.'

'Summer Willetts.'

We shook hands, straight-faced, then both burst into spontaneous laughter. And that was the start of a friendship that lasted through the whole of our drama course, despite me being gregarious and outgoing and Alexis quiet and sometimes withdrawn. And the fact that I grew up on a council estate in Bromley while Alexis was due to inherit a country estate one day.

After graduation, we drifted apart and lost touch, until that day just over a year ago, when I had a tiny part in a late-night Channel 4 sitcom. A crew member bounded up to me, red hair cut longish on top and a fade at the sides, and a tight T-shirt revealing a lot of hours put in at the gym.

'Summer, hi!'

I squinted at the face that was familiar and yet not familiar.

'It's Alexis.'

I couldn't help but stare. The short hair, the clothes, all so dramatically different.

'Wow... Alexis. How are you?'

'Good, pretty good. I go by Alex now.'

'You look fantastic,' I said, and my enthusiasm was genuine. This version of Alexis seemed so much more confident and at ease.

We went for a coffee together and exchanged our news. And Alex had *big* news. Having given up acting to work on the technical side of television production, she – or I should really say 'they', because they had become gender-neutral – had scored a contract working as a lighting director on a hit US show, and was moving to Los Angeles permanently.

'But what about the house?' I demanded.

'The house?'

'You know, the amazing country place you're in line to inherit.' Alex had spoken to me several times about her distant family's amazing home.

'Oh that... well, I only get Mullens End if my cousin Hugh

dies childless, and he's not that old, so he's bound to have kids. Anyway, even if it did pass to me, I wouldn't want it.'

'You don't want it?' I was incredulous. 'But it's your family home. It's not like it's just some two-up, two-down either.'

'Not really; I've never even met that part of the family, and Mum barely did. I'm only a distant cousin, and it's not like I've ever been to the place.' Alex shrugged.

'Even so... I mean, it must be worth loads.'

'Probably. But that's a part of my old life. I want to start fresh somewhere new. To be honest, Summer, now my mum's dead, there's nothing to keep me in this country. I'm starting over with a new identity in a new country, and I don't plan on ever coming back.'

And there it was. Alexis Lambert was never coming back. The seed was planted.

After that chance meeting with Alexis, the next step was me looking up Mullens End online.

Just idle curiosity, I told myself.

There were a lot of photos of a handsome stone house with huge windows and tall chimneys, lots of descriptions of its importance on architectural and historical sites. There was a Wikipedia page for the industrialist Ernest Mullen, describing the complex family trust he had created to secure the future of the house. Then I found a picture of Hugh Mullen, who was as handsome as the house he owned. And that started me thinking.

Okay, so he wasn't my type, but that didn't need to be an issue. He was just the means to an end. After I'd done the research, I registered on a genealogy website as Alexis Lambert and, sure enough, there was the link to the Mullen family, via Alex's mother Avril Mullen. And despite Alex's assumption, it looked as though Hugh Mullen – Ernest's direct heir – did not have any children.

For months, I kept revisiting those online images, kept thinking about that beautiful house. My acting career was going nowhere, my boyfriend Marc and I were in the process of a messy break-up. What was to stop me becoming Alexis Lambert? Alex said they'd never visited the house, never met the family. So the Mullen family would have no reason to know that the real Alexis Lambert was now Alex, and living on another continent. Ernest Mullen famously had vivid red hair, as did Hugh Mullen and Alexis. But that was no problem; I could dye my own ash-blonde hair red easily enough. I was the right age, and with my acting experience, I could inhabit Alexis as if she was just another role. I could make Alexis whatever I needed her to be.

To render her believable, Alexis Lambert had to exist in the online world. So, once I had dyed my own blonde hair a pretty shade of pale red, I created an Instagram account and started uploading selfies to it, following the sort of accounts I think this new Alexis will be interested in. I had to be patient and let several months' worth of posts accrue to lend some credibility to my new identity. Then, eventually, when a potentially lucrative spot on a reality series fell through, I decided I couldn't be patient any longer. I ended things definitively with Marc. And then I messaged Juliet Mullen.

'I'll show you up to your room,' Hugh says, when the interminably dull dinner party has finally ended. 'We're putting you in the blue guest room.'

'Great, thanks,' I drawl. I use the voice I've practised for my Alexis character, thick with Generation Y vocal fry and up-speak.

I follow Hugh as he carries my case up the beautiful carved oak staircase and into a large square room, with a pale cream carpet and blue and white *toile de jouy* wallpaper and drapes.

'Bathroom's through there,' he says, pointing to the door to an en suite. 'And Jules and I are just over the landing if you need anything.'

I thrust my boobs provocatively and look up at him from under my fringe. 'What... anything?'

He gives a little laugh and lets his gaze linger a fraction too long on the exposed flesh. 'Well... within reason.'

'So, if I get scared in the middle of the night... because I am literally scared of the dark, you know?'

'If it gets really bad, I suppose you could just come and give a little knock on the door.'

God, he believes me; he really believes me.

'Not sure about that. I literally sleep naked.'

Hugh makes a strange little coughing noise. 'How about if I keep my phone on, and you can send me a quick message. Here' – he points to the mobile in my hand – 'let me put in my number.'

'And will you come and rescue me?' I ask, as he types his number into my Contacts.

The expression that crosses his face, the slight twitch of his mouth betray that he is thinking of this very possibility. Of crossing the landing on tiptoe, late at night. And I'm meant to be his distant cousin, I think: is that weird? But then the Queen married one of her cousins, and nobody thought that was weird.

Bingo, I think. *Only four hours in, and I've got him.*

FIFTEEN

20 JUNE

I wake up stupidly early, but stay in bed for ages. I decide that is what 'Alexis' would do.

After dressing in the sort of revealing athleisure wear my new persona favours, I go down to the kitchen, where I find the icily immaculate Juliet tidying up. Hugh, apparently, is playing tennis. I fancy nothing more than a fry-up with bacon and sausages but, since I'm now a vegan, accept a plate of fruit, and then a tour of the house. Anything to stop the endless questions about my background. I'm able to offer up what I know of Alex Lambert's upbringing, but the truth is, it's not all that much.

The place is stuffed with incredible furniture and artefacts, which presumably have always been here and are intended to remain in situ forever. But I have other ideas, and while feigning boredom, I make a mental inventory of what I see. There are Japanese screens, Ming dynasty Chinese lacquer-ware, eighteenth-century French silver, a lot of velvet-covered Georgian chairs, a Napoleon III marquetry table. My grand-mother used to have a dealership in Grays antiques market and when I helped out there in my school holidays, I learned a whole lot about which pieces were collectable and what they would fetch. The contents of Mullens End must run into many hundreds of thousands.

'Hugh's great-grandfather was a bit of a collector,' Juliet tells me. 'We probably ought to look at getting some valuations done so we can update our contents insurance.'

Reminding myself that I need Hugh's wife on side in order for this to work, I make a big show of admiring the garden. I then insist on picking some flowers and arranging them, finding I quite enjoy having something to do other than scroll through my phone and read glossy magazines. The enforced idleness when I'm being watched is frustrating. There's so much I need to do.

When Hugh returns from whatever *he's* been doing, I agree to go and have a game of tennis with him. I have zero interest in playing, and he's far too good for there to be a competitive match, but neither of us is really thinking about the sport. It's just an opportunity for some heavy flirting. Hugh stands behind me to teach me to serve, and I'm gratified to feel the beginnings of an erection as he presses himself against my backside. I giggle and deliberately arch my back during the ball toss so my buttocks are on obvious display.

Later, once tedious Juliet has gone upstairs to bed, we sit outside on the terrace and Hugh fetches an ice bucket and a bottle of Chablis.

'A question for you...' I run a fingertip over my glass, streaking a trail through the icy condensation. 'Juliet said something about the house belonging to a trust. But I thought it belonged to you?'

'Well, it does, and it doesn't.' Hugh positions himself so that our knees are just touching. 'I get to behave as if I own it, and to enjoy it, and so does my spouse, obviously. I also get to make decisions about upkeep and to worry about the bloody place falling to pieces.' He adopts a hangdog 'poor me' expression, which I decide to ignore. 'But because of a restrictive covenant created by the trust, I can't sell it, I can only pass it on to the next Mullen in line. And, as you know, because Juliet and I don't have kids and I don't have any siblings or first cousins, that happens to be you. So, as far as I'm concerned, you have a stake in the place. And everything in it.' He gives me a faintly suggestive smile.

I press two fingers to my lips. 'Still not sure I get it... If the trust owns it, then who's in the trust?'

'There are five trustees.' Hugh tops up my glass. 'I'm one of them, obviously, and the chief trustee – who basically does all the admin – is the senior partner at the law firm we use. But you don't need to worry about any of this, not yet, at least. Hopefully not for a good long while. Enjoy your wine.'

I giggle. 'Are you trying to get me drunk?'

'Maybe.' He takes my wine glass, dips a finger in it and holds it up to my lips, a gesture that makes his intentions crystal clear.

I respond in kind, sucking his finger into my mouth and swirling my tongue around it. And that's it: after the briefest of preambles, we've crossed the Rubicon. Hugh is on me swiftly, ruthlessly, kissing me and kneading my breasts.

'I'd better go upstairs to Juliet,' he whispers, once we've broken apart. 'But later... yes?'

And, sure enough, just after midnight, there's the faintest tap on the door of the blue guest room. In the moonlight, from the half-open curtains, I can just see him hold a finger up to his lips as he comes into the room.

I'm naked, as I promised, and Hugh draws in his breath when he sees me stretched out on the bed, my back arched so that the curves of my expensive silicon boobs are lit with silver. He wastes no time tugging off his checked pyjama bottoms and T-shirt. His body isn't bad, I note, with detachment.

'Jeee-sus,' I drawl, drawing out the word. 'Is this what you call toeing the marital line?'

'Trust me, sweetheart, you have no idea.'

There's just enough light for me to make out a sardonic grin, before his mouth is on mine, kissing me roughly, and pushing me back onto the pillows. The sex is brutish and unimaginative, but at least it's over quickly. I summon my acting skills to fake pleasure convincingly. I need to ensure that Hugh will be back for more.

The next morning, once he has headed into London, and Juliet is ensconced in her office, I creep into Hugh's study.

The wretched dogs try to follow me and I have to drag them back by their collars and shut them in the kitchen. Once I'm alone, it doesn't take me long to find what I'm looking for. The spines of the box files on the shelves are labelled by hand with thick black marker, and there are several with 'Mullen Trust' on them, followed by the relevant year. I select the most recent one and thumb through the contents. There's information about various investments, some bank statements showing the sort of healthy balance I've only ever been able to dream about, and a lot of correspondence with the letterhead Slater & Watkins. Most of this is signed by a Roger Banborough, 'On behalf of the Ernest Mullen Trust'. He must be the chief trustee Hugh was talking about. I take a photo of the address on the letterhead and tiptoe back to the kitchen to release the dogs, who have started to bark at their confinement.

On Tuesday, I tell Juliet I'm catching the train to London to visit the estate agents about my new flat. Only there is no estate agent. No new flat either, for that matter. At this moment in time, my things are in boxes in the spare room of my friend Lisa's house in Catford, just as they have been since I broke up with Marc. Instead, I head to Victoria Embankment, to the offices of Slater & Watkins.

I want to be taken seriously, but also for this man to notice me, so I'm dressed in a pair of cropped black trousers, a man's white cotton shirt and a pair of bright pink heels, with my newly dyed red hair tied up in a high ponytail. No, I inform the snotty receptionist, I don't have an appointment, but I'm Alexis Lambert, and I'm here on Mullen Trust business.

After being made to wait in the reception area for fifteen minutes, I'm told that Roger Banborough will see me.

'Miss Lambert.' A large, balding man in a pinstripe suit stands up to greet me when I come into the room. 'It's a pleasure to meet you.' His gaze roams over the tight trousers and vertiginous heels. 'A very great pleasure.'

'You know who I am?' I ask, my modesty as false as the red of my hair.

'Indeed, I do.' He gives a formal little nod, then sits, indicating that I should sit opposite him.

I make a show of rummaging in my bag. 'I've got my ID here.'

'No need,' he says pleasantly. 'Not for an informal chat. Let me see now... your mother's great-uncle was Ernest Mullen, which makes you a third cousin of the current beneficiary of the Mullen Trust.' He leans back and swivels his chair from side to side, tapping his Montblanc pen on the legal pad in front of him, 'And what can I do for you, Miss Lambert? Is there something specific that you needed?'

'I've recently made contact with my cousin... with Hugh... for the first time. And after speaking to him, I thought I ought to find out more about the trust.' I smile what I hope is a trustworthy smile. 'About how it works. Keeping this chat confidential, of course.' I've decided it's not a good idea for either Hugh or Juliet to know I'm here.

Banborough nods. 'Of course.' He hesitates for a few

seconds, as though wondering the best way to be rude without seeming rude. 'But forgive me, Miss Lambert; I really don't think you need to worry about the workings of the trust. Not for the time being, at least. Or, indeed, for quite some time, bearing in mind that Hugh Mullen is only thirty-five. And even then, for you to be directly affected, he would have to remain child-less at his death. There's still time for that to change.'

'What happens if he sells it? The house.'

His voice takes on that edge that important men use when talking to someone they privately think is of limited intelli-gence. 'With respect,' he begins, demonstrating that he has no respect for me whatsoever, 'that's the whole point of property being held in trust. The beneficiary can't sell it without the approval of the trustees. And they would never approve, since it would contradict the intention outlined in Ernest Mullen's will, which is how the trust was established. The life tenant could rent it out, as long as they informed the other trustees, but there's no reason I can think of that Mr and Mrs Mullen would want to do that.'

I'm remembering the conversation Hugh and I had over the bottle of Chablis, and our subsequent adulterous bunk up. 'What about if they divorce though?'

'Ah, well... this is where the trust is a little unusual. Ernest Mullen had a bit of a bee in his bonnet about divorce, you see. His parents divorced when he was very young, leaving his mother virtually penniless. And he was also a staunch Catholic, believing marriage was for life. So, in the event of a divorce, the life tenant would be in a very difficult position. He or she would still be unable to sell, but their spouse would be able to go after them for the equivalent of half the value of the house. Which would be several million.'

I think about this for a few seconds. 'So, what would he... they... do then?'

Banborough gives a dry little laugh. 'They'd have to either

make the best of it and stay married, or find a way of getting their hands on a very large chunk of cash.'

'Even if it was the wife who wanted a divorce?'

'Yes, that's right. As I said, Ernest had a certain sympathy for wronged female spouses. Even though he took steps to ensure the house couldn't be sold and the proceeds split between the divorcing partners.'

Interesting, I think. Because it looks as though whatever happens, Hugh can't divorce Juliet. Not unless he finds a money tree in the back garden, because it doesn't look as though he earns very much from his antiquities business, and wasn't he just moaning about how expensive it was to run the place? So, if he pisses off Juliet, he has a big problem. Basically, he can't afford to get rid of her. My mind goes back again to his corridor-creeping on Sunday night. One thing's clear: the man certainly likes to take risks.

'Another thing,' I add, thinking on my feet, as this scenario has just occurred to me. 'You say the trust only affects me if Hugh remains childless... what if he went on to have a child or children with someone else? They would be Mullens, wouldn't they?'

'Indeed they would. That child would supersede your claim. But I think we can agree that scenario is highly unlikely.'

I'm now very glad I've made this trip and learned what Roger Banborough has just revealed to me. Because if Hugh and I are caught, Juliet would be able to bankrupt him if she chose to divorce him. I'll have to make sure we're much more discreet, for the time being at least.

Banborough taps his pen and gives me a professional smile, but there's a coldness to it. 'As I've said, there's no immediate need for you to be concerned with any of this.'

The message is loud and clear: you won't be getting your grubby hands on the place, so don't even bother asking.

Well, we'll see about that.

SIXTEEN

27 JUNE

After my visit to London, I'm forced to spin my wheels for a few days, until Juliet conveniently flies to Italy to take care of some parenting issue, leaving Hugh to worry about the car vandalising incident.

But I'm not entirely idle. While Juliet thinks I'm watching YouTube make-up tutorials or reality TV shows, I'm emailing and phoning my contacts, lining up potential allies. Hugh knocked on my bedroom door on Tuesday evening, and again on Thursday, but I ignored him, pretending to be sleeping. After my conversation with Roger Banborough, there's no way I'm going to risk exposing Hugh's dalliance with me. Not now that I know about the divorce problem generated by Ernest Mullen's will. But it seems he's not willing to give up, and as soon as Juliet has left, he saunters into my room in broad daylight.

'While the cat's away...' he murmurs, bending to kiss the back of my neck. I'm sitting at the dressing table, contouring my face with a brush.

'Hiiiiii,' I drawl in my Alexis voice, and lift my hands up over my shoulders to wrap my arms around his waist.

'What have you been up to today, young lady?'

'Nothing much.' I smile at my reflection, thinking how much I'm longing to go back to my natural hair colour. 'Just passing the time until we're alone, you know?'

'It's good, isn't it?' He's already reached down and cupped my boobs, before lifting my vest top and unclipping my bra. 'Come here, you gorgeous creature.'

This time, the sex is pretty good. Not great, per se, but definitely a level up from the first hurried wham-bam effort. I've slept with plenty of men, enough by now to know the difference between a physical relationship that's going nowhere and one that's got real potential. And this... now that we're alone in this amazing house, this actually feels pretty good. Juliet's absence has removed her husband's inhibitions, and he's making the most of it. He gives himself a holiday from work, and we frolic like teenagers. For the three days that she's gone, we wander round the house in our underwear working our way through the contents of Hugh's cellar, we swim naked in the pool and play drum and bass music at full volume on the drawing-room speakers. We even pay a visit to the local pub. And at night, of course, we give way to our mutual desire.

'Just as well we're only third cousins, eh?' Hugh murmurs, after one particularly pornographic episode.

Not even that, I think, burying my face in the pillow so he can't see me smirking. *We're not related at all.*

'No wait, it's okay,' he goes on, 'You're legally allowed to marry a first cousin, so I don't think it's an issue. Still feels a bit... transgressive, though, doesn't it?'

'It does,' I agree, with sincerity.

'Hell of a lot of fun, though,' he says, kissing my naked backside.

And I have to admit, it *is* fun. I could actually do this, I tell myself, on Tuesday night. I could live here like this. It would work.

But life isn't all cupcakes and butterflies, and on Tuesday night, with Juliet's return imminent, I have to get back to business. While we're sprawled out on loungers after fucking in the pool – making sure we wait until Pete's gone home – I initiate a serious conversation. It's another hot evening, the sun just kissing the horizon, and I've fetched us orange ice lollies from the freezer.

'Are you happy with Juliet?' I've decided to be blunt. I can't reveal that I know about the divorce issue caused by the trust, so I'll have to get Hugh to raise it. I run my tongue purposefully over the tip of the lolly, going slowly although the sticky liquid is already trickling down my wrist.

He gives a little snort and waves his own ice lolly at the empty champagne bottle, our discarded clothes, our naked bodies, gleaming in the twilight. 'What do *you* think?'

'Yeah, like, obviously! I mean, the two of you are so mismatched... you're fun and relaxed, she's uptight and boring. But you don't have kids together, so why don't you guys split up? Don't tell me you've never thought about it.'

'Christ, of course I have.' He lets out a long, slow breath, then throws me a bitter little smile. 'The thing is, I can't afford to.'

I shrug, licking the orange-flavoured syrup from my palm. 'Juliet doesn't strike me as the sort of chick who'd take her ex to the cleaners. She's got too much pride.'

'It's not that...' Hugh sighs again, looking out over the box hedge that surrounds the pool and towards the copse, the sun a rose and tangerine orb in the distance. 'You know I told you about the trust that controls this place?'

I nod.

'Well, if I get divorced, Juliet could sue me for half of what this place is worth, even though I can't sell it or even mortgage it. I'd have to somehow borrow an amount, which would take every penny I have and then some to repay. I'd be screwed.'

'What?' I widen my eyes with faux shock. 'That's really rough.'

Hugh gives me a wry smile. 'Tell me about it. But Great-Uncle Ernest's mother was left in dire poverty after a divorce, and he felt extremely strongly about it being a sin. That it was wrong and victimised women. He set up the trust to try to prevent it. But, of course, divorce law has changed a fair bit since Ernest set up the trust eighty years ago, and rather than standing by their men, wronged wives now get a crack divorce lawyer and go after their share of the pie.'

'So Jules is really sitting pretty,' I muse, standing up from my lounger to rinse my sticky hands in the pool. 'She knows you can never afford to leave her.'

'I suppose she is, unless I pop my clogs,' Hugh says, with another bitter laugh. 'Then she gets pensioned off and you get this place.'

We stare at each other for a long beat, and later I wonder if the same idea that had been swirling in my mind crossed his at that moment. But, for now, I decide not to push it further. Instead, I reach for his arm and pull him down on top of me, pressing the length of my body lasciviously against his.

We spend the night together in my bed.

'This is the last time we're going to be able to do this,' Hugh says sadly, twirling a lock of hair between his fingers as we lie sated by the latest bout of athletic sex. 'It's been fun. I'm sorry it's got to end.'

'Does it have to, though?' I prop myself up on one elbow so we're facing each other.

'What d'you mean?'

And that's when I outline the plan.

He stares at me for what feels like minutes. 'No,' he says eventually, shaking his head. 'Come on now, Alexis, that's insane. It would never work. Too many people could get suspicious.'

'But think about it,' I remind him. 'You've already told people that these property thugs are out to hurt you. By doing that, you've already laid the groundwork.'

'I suppose so.' He still looks doubtful.

'What else are you going to do? Stay here miserably with Juliet until you're both old and grey? And you're how old now?'

'Thirty-five. Anyway, she might leave. She's always banging on about wanting to spend more time in Italy.'

'But she might not.'

There's another long silence.

'All right,' he says eventually. 'If we're in this together, then it might just work.'

'So we're doing it?'

He runs a finger down my side, tracing the line from shoulder to hip. 'We're doing it.'

SEVENTEEN

30 JUNE

I'm familiar with Hugh's routine by now.

If he's not heading into London, he gets up around eight to let the dogs out for a pee, then heads back upstairs to shower and dress before feeding and walking them, usually with a mug of tea in his hand. After that, he eats toast and drinks coffee and mooches into his home office to make phone calls.

On Wednesday morning, I wait until he's in the shower – in his own en suite so that unused towels don't make Juliet suspicious – and walk quietly and quickly downstairs. The dogs, eager for their breakfast, greet me with whines and frantically wagging tales. I brush them aside and head out to the garage block.

Pete, the gardener, has already started work, and the doors are unlocked and open. There's a wooden shelf on the back wall that stores various cans and bottles, and eventually I find a bottle of antifreeze. The liquid is dyed blue to discourage humans from ingesting it, but dogs are far too stupid and greedy to notice what they're being given. They inhale their food so fast, they can barely taste the stuff.

When I get back into the house, I can no longer hear the

sound of the power shower coming from the master en suite.
Hugh must be getting dressed. I grab the dogs' bowls from the
utility-room floor and open the large tub of kibble

'Jeff! Pongo! Brekkie!'

There's a scrabbling of claws on stone floor tiles and the
stupid creatures appear at my side, looking up at me hopefully. I
tip kibble into the bowls, then sprinkle a liberal amount of the
antifreeze on top. It's consumed before I've got back from
replacing the bottle in the garage.

'Oh, you've fed them,' Hugh comes into the kitchen, his hair
wet from the shower. 'I was just about to.'

'Thought I'd save you some time,' I say, and in an attempt to
distract him, I wind my arms round his neck and press myself
against him. 'What shall we do with that time?'

'Steady on, Alexis, Juliet's due back in a few hours.'

He's interested though, I can sense it.

'Exactly. So we need to make the most of the time we've
got.'

He needs no further persuasion. I lead him back upstairs
and engage him in a final shag, which I neither need or want,
but which at least gets him away from the wretched dogs. By
the time we come downstairs again, the stuff seems to have
worked. Both of them have been sick, and the older one – Pongo
I think, I find it hard to tell them apart – is lying on its side,
panting. Flecks of foam seep from its mouth.

'Oh fuck!' Hugh drops to his knees beside the dog, running
his hand through his hair. 'What the hell's up with the dogs?
They must have eaten something they shouldn't.' He turns and
snaps at me, 'Fuck's sake, don't just stand there! Go and phone
the vet. The number's on the pad by the phone.' He points to
the kitchen landline. Jesus, who even uses a landline these
days?

The vet comes, but the older dog is dead by then. Which I
have to stress wasn't at all what I intended. I just wanted them

to get ill, like the younger one. The vet gave it a fluid drip and by the afternoon it's fine.

'Martin Nicholson thinks they've been deliberately poisoned,' Hugh says after the vet has left and Pete has taken the old dog out to the wood to bury it. 'Who the hell would have it in for us enough to want to kill an innocent animal?'

'It's obvious, isn't it?' I say, without meeting his eye.

'You mean Jamie Molcan and his mob again?'

'They went for your house and your cars, why not your pets?'

At first, he seems to accept this explanation, and then, of course, he's distracted by Juliet returning from Italy and having to go over the whole saga with her, taking care to play it down and let her think the dog's old age was responsible. Now that he and I are locked in to our pact, he can't afford to let Juliet look too closely into what's been going on in her absence, and he certainly doesn't want the police involved. She's not as soppy over the dogs as Hugh is, and fortunately doesn't seem overly upset.

The next day, I cadge a lift with her to the station, telling her I'm going to do some shopping in Guildford for the new flat.

But, of course, there is no new flat. Instead, I take the train into London.

Alan Golding wants us to meet in North London where he lives, and suggests a café at the bottom end of Swain's Lane, in Highgate.

He always had a bit of a thing for me, even though he's over a decade older. We appeared in Alan Ayckbourn's 'A Small Family Business' together at the Chichester Theatre not long after I graduated from Guildhall. He played my father, something I reminded him of if he ever tried getting handsy. It's not really an age issue with Alan: I've just never fancied him.

I haven't seen Alan for several years, but I have heard from mutual friends that he's been out of work for ages. In other words, he needs the money.

'Bit surprised to hear from you, Summs, I have to admit,' he says, once I've brought two cappuccinos to our table. 'You look terrific.' He gives my tight orange sundress an admiring look. 'Didn't I hear you'd signed a deal for a TV series? Is that what this is for?' He indicates my dyed strawberry blonde locks.

I shake my head. 'It fell through,' I tell him coolly. 'But I have another project on the go. Something you'd be perfect for, if you're interested.'

He takes a sip of his coffee, looking at me over the rim of his cup. 'Could be.'

'It pays well.'

He raises an eyebrow. 'In that case, tell me more.'

So I do, omitting the whys and wherefores as I see fit, and explaining that I need him to rope in an actress friend he thinks might also be interested.

'I'm not sure,' he says eventually. 'It sounds pretty dodgy, Summer.'

Then I tell him how much I'm prepared to pay and his expression changes.

'Okay, leave it with me. I think I know someone I can ask.'

'I need to know by tomorrow: the timing's critical. And, you'll need a car too.'

Alan frowns. 'I don't have one.'

'Hire one then, and I'll add the expense onto what I owe you. You'll get the money tomorrow, and we'll fine-tune the details then.'

At Mullens End that evening, I can tell from Hugh's body language that he's in a mood with me.

He pretends in front of Juliet, of course, but as soon as she's out of the way, he grabs me by my elbow and yanks me into the library.

'What did you do that for?' he hisses. 'Patrick Doherty just phoned Juliet.'

'And?' I counter, yanking my arm free.

'The dogs were poisoned with antifreeze. And since they were perfectly okay up 'til they ate their breakfast, they could only have been given it first thing yesterday morning.'

'So?'

'So, it was you who gave them their breakfast. You must have done it. There were no gangsters letting themselves into the kitchen at eight in the morning. The only people around apart from me were you and Pete, and I know for a fact that Pete would never do anything so vile.'

'Okay,' I say, sounding calmer than I feel. 'I did do it.'

'You killed Pongo! For fuck's sake, I've had that dog most of my adult life. How could you do something so callous?'

'Look, I didn't mean for him to die, okay?' I'm sweating slightly now, genuinely disturbed by the expression of intense disgust on Hugh's face. 'I just thought he'd be ill, like... like the other one was.'

'But why was it necessary to do it at all?'

Now it's my turn to get angry. 'Don't you get it, Hugh? We need to escalate the perceived threat from Jamie Molcan's heavies!' I'm snarling at him, momentarily forgetting my ditsy Alexis act. 'It's important for people to think they're still out to get you for our plan to be believable. That's why I slashed the tyres.'

'You did that too?'

'Of course. I'd have thought it was obvious.'

He stares at me for a few seconds and I can't quite read the look that passes over his face. 'No,' he says quietly but firmly. 'No. There is no plan, Alexis. Not anymore. If you could do something as horrendous as killing my dog, then there's no way I can trust you in this.' He turns back towards the library door.

'You need to forget it and clear off to where you came from: it's not going to happen.'

'Oh, but it is,' I say coolly, and there's no pretence any longer. 'I'm not going to let you back out now. If you do, I'm going to tell Juliet everything.'

I pull out my phone, and show him a picture of him lying stark naked next to the pool, my bikini draped over his lounger. Then another of him asleep in my bed, also naked.

'If she finds out what's been going on, she's going to end your marriage before you can say "family trust". You'll have to find half the value of all this to pay her off.' I wave my hand at the beautifully hand-built oak bookcases lined with leather-bound classics, the oil paintings on the walls. 'You'll be living with crippling debt for the rest of your life.'

He seems temporarily stunned, but quickly gathers himself. 'For all Juliet knows, you could have faked them. I could just be passed out drunk.'

I shrug. 'True. But I got talking to someone when we were at the pub the other day and you were in the loo, and they told me a rumour that this isn't the first time you've played around on your wife...'

He stands stock-still, as if he's frozen.

'And that the lucky lady is someone pretty close to home. Someone Juliet would definitely not want you going near.'

He doesn't reply, but his face has gone pale.

I realise I've pushed things too far, and I'll need to rein it in a bit. The fact is, it doesn't really serve me to have Juliet running to the divorce lawyers. I reach out for him, wrapping a hand round his wrist. 'Come on, Hugh, we're good together, you know it. And I'm genuinely sorry about poor Pongo. Truly, I am.'

'All right.' He gives a shrug, and then a smile that doesn't quite reach his eyes. 'You're right: we have to see this through. We've come this far.'

'Exactly.' I run a finger up the inside of his arm. 'Also, for the next stage I'm going to need some cash. To cover our costs. And I'll need it by tomorrow.'

'How much?'

I tell him. His eyes widen at the amount, but he nods his agreement.

'I'll get some out of the safe later, once Juliet's gone to bed.'

I lie awake in bed for a long time that night. It's a still, moonlit night and somewhere in the distance I can hear an owl screech, and dog foxes fighting. I've never slept well in this place, too used to the sounds of a city. I can also hear low voices from the master bedroom. Is that Hugh confessing all to Juliet, making sure I'm stopped in my tracks, that this is indeed all over?

I hear footsteps on the main stairs, and ten minutes later there's the faintest thudding noise as something is wedged against my door. I get out of bed and pull the door open to find an envelope far too thick to slide underneath it. Inside it is a thick bundle of fifty-pound notes, secured with a rubber band.

He's doing it. It's happening.

EIGHTEEN

2 JULY

It's not really convenient to have to flog all the way to Highgate again, but for the sake of simplicity I agree to meet Alan in the same coffee shop as before.

There's a girl with him. This is good; it means he's taking the job seriously. She's a bit young for what I have in mind, but there are ways of ageing her up a bit to make her look around thirty, at least.

'Summer, this is Naomi.' I reach across the table and give the girl an awkward half hug, since nobody our age shakes hands. 'We did the Edinburgh Festival together a couple of years ago.'

'But you're out of work?' I ask as I sit down, and I'm unable to mask my concern.

'Oh, don't worry, she's good,' Alan assures me. 'Very good. She'll be convincing.'

'Can you do accents?'

She nods.

'And you've got people for the second part?'

'Yeah, my mate Phil, and Tom Gutteridge. You remember

Matt Gutteridge at Guildhall? Well, Tom's his kid brother.' He catches my eye and grins. 'Don't panic, Summs, they'll be good too.'

After we've ordered coffees, we go over what's going to happen next, and I treat it as if we're running lines, rehearsing what they're going to say, and when.

'We don't want it to be too scripted though,' Naomi says. 'We'll need to riff a bit, to make it sound natural.'

'That's true,' I agree. 'As long as you've got the key bits of information memorised, it doesn't matter which order you say them in.' I suck my iced latte through a straw and address my next question at Alan. 'What about the car?'

'I've lined up a car-hire place that has something suitable, but I'll need the cash to pay for it. Also, I'll have to show them my real driving licence. Unless you've got a handy forged one? Now that you're a criminal mastermind.'

I leave that last comment hanging. Alan didn't ask too many questions about why I was doing all this, but you'd have to be extremely stupid not to realise that it was probably illegal. I'd had to work quite hard to dress it up as a huge practical joke, and convince him that he'd be able to walk away with no consequences to him personally. Even now, I don't think he believes me, but I've offered an eye-wateringly large fee to sweeten the deal. It's fortunate that Hugh buys some of the oriental artefacts he trades for cash and keeps plenty of the stuff in the safe in his office at home.

'This will cover the car hire, and any other props you need, plus your payment is in there too.' I glance over my shoulder and, when I'm sure the barista is looking the other way, pull out the fat envelope from my bag and put it on the table a few inches from Alan's cappuccino. 'I'll text you a map in a bit,' I say, standing up. 'Are you both completely clear about what you need to do?'

Alan glances into the envelope and checks the contents before answering. 'Yep. Got it.'

'Good.' I give them both an Alexis-style finger wave and sashay out of the café as if none of this is a big deal. But beneath the nonchalance, my heart is pounding.

Back at Mullens End, I wave a set of keys at Juliet (the ones to Lisa's house, which I still have) and present her with a bottle of prosecco I picked up at Waterloo. I can't stand the stuff personally, but reckon it's a very Alexis drink. Then, as it's sweltering, I go upstairs to change for a swim.

It's obvious straightaway that she's been in my room. A top which I had folded neatly and put in my suitcase is lying draped over the edge of the case, unfolded. In the bathroom, my bottle of Bvlgari Allegra has been moved from where I left it and, from the faint scent in the air, sprayed. Is she just being nosy, or is she starting to get suspicious? I'm suddenly overwhelmed with dislike for her, and don't feel sorry at all about how her husband treats her. Of course, I'm going to have to be nice for this wretched 'girly' evening I've proposed, but not for much longer after that. Not if Hugh goes through with what we've agreed.

Over supper, Juliet starts questioning me about my childhood. So she's definitely suspicious then. I pretend I want to watch *Love Island*, staying out of her way. When I hear voices in the hall, I realise it's not Hugh, but someone else. I go to investigate and find Juliet with two police officers. She's as white as a sheet, her eyes glassy with shock. When she is finally able to speak, it's to tell me that Hugh has run his car off the road on his way home. He's been killed.

Juliet as a widow is exactly how you would imagine she'd be.

After the initial shock has worn off and she's managed a few hours' sleep, thanks to one of my Xanax, she's perfectly together. Even down to the bright red lipstick she favours, which in combination with her glossy dark hair makes her look a little like someone from a Bob Fosse musical.

She doesn't slob about the house in a bathrobe or sweats, crying, but gets dressed in the sort of clothes she normally favours: bland but elegant. I can't help but wonder how much she cared about Hugh after all. He was keen to stress their incompatibility – for obvious reasons – but now, in the wake of his death, she seems so cold and unemotional. Forget the dodgy property developer wanting rid of Hugh Mullen; maybe his wife did too.

Her insistence on seeing Hugh's dead body comes as a bit of a surprise, I have to admit. I do everything I can to discourage her, but she won't be put off.

The actual viewing is a bit of a nightmare. My knees are shaking and my palms are sweating and all I want is for it to be over. Somehow, we get through it, and Juliet seems calmer, more accepting when it's done, so perhaps it is for the best.

Her son Luca arrives from Italy a couple of days later, and the reality of him throws me a bit. Because Mullens End is where he did most of his growing up. It's his home. He's still a teenager but with the sort of looks that mean he'll be hot as hell in a few years. I flirt with him a bit, just to wind up Juliet. Roger Banborough visits too, and pretends not to have met me before. I'm quite impressed with his acting skills, although I wonder what's going on behind his impassive demeanour. Whether he has his own suspicions.

Then there's the funeral. Juliet dresses like a Mafia widow, so I trump her with a pair of black Louboutins and a gauzy black fascinator. The Catholic service in the mausoleum is actually super moving, but it's hot and muggy and the men are sweating in their suits, the women fidgeting with their hats. Like me, they probably can't wait to get back into the house and lay into the vintage champers.

I can feel a pair of eyes boring into my neck and look round to see Juliet's horsey pal Belinda giving me filthy looks, just as she did at the dinner party that first night. Earlier, she was in the kitchen organising the food and bossing everyone around as though she owned the place.

In the house afterwards, I head to go upstairs to take off the fascinator. My stuff is all still in the blue room, of course. I hear footsteps in the hall, and there she is again: Belinda Langridge.

'I want a word with you,' she says, fiercely. Her hair is damp with sweat, and there are dark patches under the arms of her frankly hideous black dress.

I spin on my Louboutin stilettos so I'm facing her, but I don't descend the stairs again, forcing her to come nearer. 'What's up, babe?' I drawl.

'Don't think I don't know what you've been doing.' She keeps her voice low, but there is plenty of venom in it, nonetheless. She glances over her shoulder, presumably to make sure her gormless husband isn't in earshot. 'You were sleeping with Hugh.'

'Not any more, obviously.' I can't resist being flippant.

Belinda's lip curls. 'You're disgusting. A disgusting, cheap little tart.'

I'm wondering how she knows. She can't know, surely? I decide to call her bluff. 'Look, I don't know where you're getting your information from, but that's bullshit.'

'You were seen,' she hisses. 'At The Crown and Cushion in the village. Pawing him shamelessly, apparently. So don't try to deny it.'

I wonder if she's told Juliet yet. Not that it matters now that a financially crippling divorce is off the table for good. I shrug and start walking up the stairs again, the points of my heels making a series of little dents in the plush carpet. But she's not done yet.

'You should leave,' she shouts furiously. 'You don't belong at Mullens End.'

Ah, but that's where you're wrong, I think. *I'm not going anywhere.*

PART THREE

HUGH

NINETEEN

21 JUNE

Carrying on an affair under your wife's nose requires a degree of skill, not to mention a brass bloody neck.

I will be the first to admit that discretion is not my strong point. But somehow – and to this day I'm not sure how – we got away with it for a long time. Maybe if something is right under your nose – staring you in the face, if you will – it's harder for the wronged party to see it. The sexy vixen once even lured me into having sex in the library, while said wife and assembled guests were in the dining room. That was pretty risky, even by my standards.

Anyway, I'm getting ahead of myself. My real problems started when Juliet reminded me of the existence of my third cousin Alexis Lambert, announcing that she had made contact out of the blue on Instagram. And only days later – wham, there she was at our front door. That's how it all began, really.

Alexis has been in the house less than forty-eight hours before I've screwed her. Then on Monday, I leave her there at Mullens End and go up to my office in Mayfair.

Or at least, that's what I tell Juliet. The fact is, my business doesn't require me to be in the office, not if I have my phone on me and can take calls. I just go there to get some breathing space. There's not a lot of movement in the Ottoman antiques trade. Business perked up when all the Russian oligarchs and Chinese billionaires arrived in London a decade or more ago, but now they've all kitted out the houses they don't bother to live in, things have gone a bit quiet. I've only sold five pieces in the last three months, although I haven't told Juliet that. My darling wife already sneers enough about it not being a proper job. Which is rich coming from her, running her little hobby business selling lampshades and cushions to rich housewives while living in a gracious home maintained by money from the Mullen Trust.

But I digress. I made sure to flirt heavily and unsubtly with Alexis as soon as she arrived, really laying it on thick. It's important she thinks I fancy her, for me to achieve what I need to. Not that I don't fancy her, in the purest animal sense. I mean, who wouldn't? Shagging her on that second night was no hardship. She's got a body to die for as well as a stunning face. The sort of prettiness that the camera just laps up. But her personality is godawful. Not my cup of tea at all.

I imagined it was going to be tricky finding an address for someone who died several years back, but I've already been through my mother's things and found what I was looking for. My parents and Avril Lambert were not exactly friendly, but they did at least exchange Christmas cards once a year, and, sure enough, I found the last one that Avril sent, six years ago. Mum used to bundle them up with ribbon when the Christmas decorations came down and stow them away in a box in the library, so that she would know who to send cards to the following year. And, conveniently, Avril was one of those people who put a prissy little gold sticker inside the card with their full name and address on it, just for this purpose.

I take the tube to Euston and catch a fast train to Hemel Hempstead, then walk the half-mile to the detached post-war house on a pleasant tree-lined street to the west of the town. Avril's been dead several years, so there's no point calling at number 41 where she used to live, but the house next door looks as though it's probably occupied by an older couple. I ring the bell of number 43.

The door is answered by a grey-haired man wearing a sleeveless sweater over a checked shirt, and flannel trousers, despite the heat.

'So sorry to disturb you.' I give him my most charming and boyish smile. 'But I'm looking for my cousin. Avril Lambert.'

The man hesitates, takes a step back. 'Marjorie!' he calls, into the carpeted hallway behind him.

A woman of similar vintage appears. She, at least, is wearing a floral summer frock.

'Marjorie, this young man is looking for Avril.'

Clearly, he wanted the difficult news of her death to be broken by his wife, as if a woman's touch would somehow soften the blow.

'Oh dear, I'm so sorry,' Marjorie says, instinctively putting her hand to her pearl necklace. 'Didn't you know? Avril passed away, about five years ago now, isn't it, Kenneth?'

Kenneth nods. 'House was sold about six months later, to a nice young family. The Pattersons. Two young kiddies.'

'Oh no!' I feign surprise. 'So what about her daughter?'

'Alexis?' Marjorie shakes her head. 'Oh, she hasn't been there in even longer. She went off to London to study acting. One of the top drama schools, wasn't it, Kenneth?'

'That's right, I believe it was, yes.'

'Ooh, now which one was it...' Marjorie gives herself a little shake, as if trying to dislodge the memory. 'Not RADA, I remember that much...'

'LAMDA?' I suggest, but she shakes her head. 'Central School of Speech and Drama?'

'No...' She's getting frustrated now. 'It was Something and Music...'

'The Guildhall School of Music and Drama?'

'Yes,' she beams with satisfaction. 'Yes, that's the one. Very proud, Avril was, when she got in. But after she started there, I don't get the impression she came back home very often. Did she, Kenneth?'

'No,' Kenneth agrees.

'And you don't have an address for her?'

'I'm afraid not,' Marjorie says sadly. 'Although colleges usually keep records of their former pupils, don't they? I suppose you could try there?'

'Thank you so much,' I say, and I'm not faking my gratitude. 'I'll do that.'

The receptionist at the Guildhall is young, pretty and – best of all – bored.

I flash a smile at her. 'Hi.'

'Hi,' she smiles back. 'Can I help you?'

'Yes, I hope so.' I affect a slightly clueless air. 'My stepson is thinking of applying to study drama, and I told him I'd pick up some information next time I was passing.'

Of course I wasn't just passing, since the place is all the way over in the Barbican.

'Here you are.' The girl dimples at me and hands me a shiny brochure. I flick through it, pretending to be interested.

'So, the students put on their own productions?'

'Absolutely. We've got three full theatre spaces, and the final-year productions are very much of a professional standard.'

I glance around at the large photos on the walls; stills of plays and musicals which must presumably feature those final-year productions. Sure enough, plaques underneath give each their year, title and cast.

'May I take a look?' I ask, waving my hand at them.

'Of course. All our major productions are on those, in date order, starting with last year's here' – the girl points to the one nearest to her desk – 'and going back along the corridor.'

I walk past them all, scrutinising each in turn. And, eventually, there it is. I'd know that face anywhere, despite the stage make-up. Chekov's 'The Seagull' in 2014, at the Milton Court Theatre. Her hair is lighter, but it's definitely her. I read the description below, and then re-read it. *Featuring (left to right): Nina – Summer Willetts, Konstantin – Noah Sweeney, Masha – Alexis Lambert.*

The blonde-haired girl playing Nina is her. Alexis. Except that she's not Alexis. According to this, she's someone called Summer Willetts. Alexis Lambert is playing Masha and is taller and more gangly, with the distinctive Mullen red hair. I shouldn't really be shocked, but for a few seconds, I confess I am.

I thank the girl on the reception desk and walk out onto Silk Street, tossing the prospectus into the nearest bin. Then I whip out my phone and google Summer Willetts. And there she is. Social media photos as well as professional headshots leave no doubt. Okay, so she's altered her hair colour, turning the blonde red, but it's definitely her. The woman who is currently in my house, pretending she has a legal claim to it.

The thing is, she could never pull off a ballsy scam like that if the real Alexis was around. So what the hell's happened to *her*?

At this point, I decide I need a little help.

Back in my office that afternoon, I phone an acquaintance of mine called Jeremy Dinsdale. He went through a really bloody divorce and had to use an investigator to get some dirt on his ex-wife.

'Jay,' I say, when he picks up. 'How are you, mate? I'm good, yes... Listen, you know that private dick you used to put the squeeze on Felicity? Can you give me his details? No, Jules and I aren't getting a divorce, nothing like that. It's a business matter.'

He gives me the details and, since the office is in Soho, I walk over there before catching the train home. This chap, Terry Brooks, says he wants a week to do the work. I tell him he can have forty-eight hours.

The following night, I sneak into Summer's room again, partly out of curiosity, partly – if I'm honest – out of horniness. She's asleep. By now, I'm sensing Juliet's eyes on us constantly, so it's probably wise to keep my distance for the time being. And until I know a little bit more.

On Wednesday, Terry Brooks comes to my office to collect his fat fee, one he's certainly earned. Summer Willetts grew up on a council estate in Bromley, South East London, showed an early talent for acting and did well to land a place at the prestigious Guildhall. Since then, her career's stalled and she's not lived up to her early promise. She received a police caution as a student for a minor credit card fraud, and her father, who left home when she was a toddler, has been in and out of prison for various financial misdealings.

'That tracks,' I tell Brooks. He's a non-descript beige man who looks like an accountant, which I suppose must be an advantage in his game. 'And what about Alexis Lambert? Have you found her?'

Brooks chews his lower lip, looks uncomfortable.

'Oh God, please don't tell me she's dead.'

'Not exactly...'

'How can someone be not exactly dead, for God's sake?'

And he tells me. Alexis Lambert has officially changed her

name – to Alex Lambert. She now prefers 'they', and has applied for and been issued with a new passport in that name. Oh, and for good measure, they are now legally a resident of the United States.

All of which makes perfect sense. It explains how Summer can be so confident in stealing her fellow student's identity; it's not an identity that's being used any more. And everything Alex Lambert stands to inherit, Summer seems to think she can now get her mitts on.

Of course, for now, I have no intention of letting on that I know who she really is. But as I watch her that evening, sipping a vodka and soda and making banal chit-chat with my wife, I can't help but admire her sheer nerve.

Nor at this point am I entirely sure what her endgame is. But whatever it is, what she's doing is not just identity theft; it's theft, pure and simple, and on the most breathtaking scale.

But two can play at that game.

TWENTY

27 JUNE

Jules' trip to Italy to see Luca gives me the perfect opportunity to find out more.

'Give him my love,' I tell her breezily as I wave her off. Her departure also coincides with a mini heatwave, and Summer and I embark on a three-day hedonism binge; drinking swimming and fucking. Keep your friends close and your enemies closer, I tell myself. And I can't pretend the physical stuff isn't fun.

Unsurprisingly, once we're alone, she's curious to know more about my marriage. She's clearly not stupid, and can see that we're mismatched. I give her vague answers, unable to explain exactly the peculiar kismet of my meeting Juliet. I was still in my twenties, and my mother had recently died, leaving me orphaned and alone at Mullens End. I'd been going through old photographs of my mother when she was young, and found one taken on her honeymoon. She was on the shores of Lake Lugano, dressed in a pink flowered dress with a full skirt, her dark brown hair cut into an angular bob. She looked beautiful, and happy, which was exactly how I liked to remember her.

My childhood had been happy too, spectacularly so. I

lacked for nothing, apart from siblings. Once my mother had grieved for the daughter who died in infancy, she focused all her attention and affection on me, her only child. And what could be a better backdrop for an idyllic childhood than Mullens End? I went to the local primary school for a while before being packed off to a boarding prep, and my local chums and I ran wild in the garden and grounds during the holidays, making dens, playing cricket and football, swimming in the newly installed pool, chasing the dogs: my father always had at least two Labs. Later, when I was in my teens, I had friends to stay, and threw parties with booze and proper DJs.

My father, who was a more distant figure, died of heart disease when I was eighteen. Mullens End was then officially mine, but Mummy went on living there, holding lunches and dinners for her friends and overseeing the upkeep of the gardens while I drifted between London in the week and the country at weekends. It was all perfectly harmonious, until she died when I was twenty-four. And then it was just me, on my own with the dogs in that large house. I'd started the art dealership by then, but my heart wasn't really in it.

Then one day I was standing looking out of the window of my gallery, wondering if I should pack it all in and go off travelling for a while, when I saw her. My mother as a young woman. Or at least for a few seconds that's what I thought. Then I realised it was someone else with glossy dark hair cut in a bob, wearing a pink fitted dress. She was petite, and slightly exotic-looking, which I later discovered was because she was part-Italian. After a few sightings it became apparent that she was working at the interiors shop next door. I got into the habit of looking out for her, and eventually contrived to bump into her.

It worked like a dream. We went out for a drink, and before long we were dating. Juliet was not like most of the girls I hung out with. She was more sensible, and more grown up. Not only because she was a few years older than me but because she'd had to grow up fast: she was a single mother with a young son. I was infatuated – temporarily – by Juliet, and her maturity, and her maternal status just lent her even more mystique in light of my recent bereavement. Yes, I was a little put off by the existence of a kid, I can't claim otherwise. But I pretended I didn't care, telling myself we would all be a proper family unit once children of our own arrived to join Luca. Except they never did.

It was only after I'd proposed and she and Luca had moved to Mullens End that I realised the presence of a child was going to be more of a problem than I'd originally anticipated. Not that he was a bad kid; he and I rubbed along all right. His natural father was still on the scene, so it wasn't like I had to assume the paternal role in his life. But I'd grown up without ever having to share, and didn't like having to share Juliet with Luca. I wanted her to devote herself solely to me, and, of course, that was never going to happen.

And then there was the question of her suitability for a place like Mullens End. She'd grown up in a suburban semi, and while she obviously has style and a good eye, she just doesn't have a feel for what's involved in running an important early-eighteenth-century house. Her tastes are very bourgeois, and she doesn't understand art. I've had to let her introduce a few touches of her own to the place, but they're all wrong.

Then there's her temperament. When we got engaged, a few of my friends tried to warn me off. They felt she was too uptight, too highly strung. And they were right.

'Are you happy with Juliet?' Summer asks, when we're lying by the pool one sweltering evening, eating ice lollies.

'What do you think?' I ask with an eyeroll. And then I explain to her why, however unsatisfactory the marriage, I can't divorce the bloody woman. That my status as a life tenant puts me in a gilded cage: one that would bankrupt me if I had to fork out for a divorce. I'd either be in crippling debt or have to move out and rent the place to some wealthy oik just so I could cover the alimony.

She nods slowly, and I can see the cogs whirring. At this point, I don't bother trying to guess what's going through her mind. Eventually, she'll tell me.

And, sure enough, later that night, she does.

'I've been thinking,' she says, trailing a long, pointed nail down the line of my spine. 'About what you told me about the trust.'

Ah, there is it is.

'Go on,' I say, keeping my face turned away from her. We're sprawled naked across her bed, after a marathon shagging session. The few clothes we were wearing are strewn across the floor, and there's an empty wine bottle on its side on the carpet. The curtains have been left open to let in what little breeze there is.

Summer sits up, propping herself against the pillows and wrapping her arms round her knees. 'You get to stay here forever, but you can never get rid of Juliet. Because if you do, you won't be able to carry on living this life.'

'Correct.'

'But what if there was another way of getting rid of Juliet.'

I twist round and stare at her, although her face is half in shadow. 'Come on now, Alexis, when I told you about my marriage, I didn't for one second mean to imply I wanted harm to come to Juliet! Not at all, I just—'

'Christ's sake, that's not what I'm saying.' There's a new sharpness in her voice, as she temporarily drops the Alexis mask. This is Summer Willetts, the actress, inadvertently revealing what a good actress she is as she lets the act slip. She softens, reaching out to touch my back again. 'What I mean is, if you're dead, the house goes to me. Juliet has to move out, and, by all accounts, she'd probably go and join her son in Italy.'

'That's true.' I try to keep my tone light as I say, 'One small problem: I'm very much alive. And fully intend to stay that way.'

'I know, but what if everyone believed you were dead. If, to all intents and purposes, you were.'

I sit up and stare at her. 'You mean, fake my death?'

'Exactly. We could do it.'

But I'm already shaking my head. 'Don't be ridiculous Alexis, there's no way I could pull that off. Even if I wanted to. If I disappeared, my assets wouldn't just be handed over to you; it doesn't work like that. For the will to be executed, you need a death certificate showing a non-suspicious cause of death. And what about the funeral, for God's sake? You can't bung an empty coffin in the mausoleum.'

'In the digital age, it's the easiest thing in the world to fake a document. And the coffin... well, it needn't be empty.'

I give a snort of disdainful laughter. 'There's no way I'm being put in there alive, if that's what you're thinking.'

'Think about it,' Summer says coolly. She jumps off the bed and roots around in her bag for a small joint, which she lights and puffs on, blowing the snoke towards the open window. 'It's already been established that this local land development consortium have a vendetta against you. Their actions have made their position clear. So if you come to a sticky end, there's an obvious culprit.'

She sounds sharp, analytical. Nothing like the ditsy airhead who first arrived at the house.

'You mean if I pretend to have come to a sticky end.' I take the joint from her and have a drag.

'Exactly.'

'Okay.' I hand it back. 'Suppose we pull it off and success-fully make people think I'm dead. Mullens End is formally transferred to you. Juliet obligingly buggers off abroad. What do I do then? If I'm dead, then I can't enjoy living here, which is the whole point. I don't want to be anywhere other than here. Ever.'

Summer hesitates. 'Okay, I know that bit wouldn't be easy. You'd have to stay away for a while obviously, so it wasn't too suspicious. But then you could alter your appearance sufficiently for people not to recognise you – dye your hair, grow a beard, wear glasses – and come back with a new identity. And live here as my new boyfriend.'

I stare at her. The weed has spaced me out a bit, but even so, I'm incredulous. 'That's utterly insane. It simply wouldn't work. I've lived round here all of my life. Everyone in the area knows me. I might be able to pull that off in London, but not here. Someone would twig, as soon as they were within a few feet of me. Our local friends and neighbours—'

'Stay away from them. I'm not inviting them over here, so they'd have no reason to see you.'

'There are still people like Pete—'

'Get rid of him. In fact, that would already have happened, right? Once you and Juliet were gone and I'd moved in.'

'But working here... it's Pete's job, for God's sake, Alexis!' In my dismay, I almost call her Summer, remembering at the last second that I'm not supposed to know she's an actress impersonating my distant relative. I grab the joint from her, take another puff.

'He'll get another one.'

She's glossed over the other obvious problem, but I feel compelled to point it out. 'Okay, so suppose faking my death works, and convincing people I'm someone else also works. But I'm still not the beneficiary of Mullens End any more. You are. I'm here on your say-so.'

Her eyes narrow slightly. 'Correct.'

'So we'll be in a relationship... what, forever?'

'Why not? The alternative is being in a relationship with Juliet forever, only with a lot less sex. So what have you got to lose? I'm sure we can muddle along all right.' She takes a final drag on her blunt and throws the butt out of the window.

I want to ask what she envisages will happen if we fall out, but I let it go because at this point picking apart the detail will achieve nothing. What she's suggesting is as nutty as squirrel shit; of course it is. There's no way I could live long term as a couple with this flagrant scam artist, even if it were possible to somehow deceive everyone around us. Including my very much alive wife and stepson, for God's sake. Eventually, something would go wrong, and I would be exposed. Even if she were the real Alexis Lambert, I wouldn't want to attempt it. As I've already said, this woman is not my cup of tea.

But I'm starting to see that there are parts of what she's prepared to do that could serve me very well. I can incorporate them into my own plan, one that admittedly I'm still working on, but could somehow play out in my favour.

And one that *she* doesn't need to know about just now.

'All right,' I lie, taking hold of her wrist and pulling her towards me again. 'You've convinced me. As you say, I have nothing to lose. Let's do it.'

TWENTY-ONE

30 JUNE

I wake up the next morning feeling pretty pleased with myself.

Until, that is, I discover Summer has poisoned the wretched dog. Dear old Pongo, who had first been my father's dog, then my mother's, then mine. He'd had a good innings – seventeen years – but even so, his death was a shock.

'What did you do that for?' I hiss at her, as I pull her into the library. I tell her that Patrick Doherty has phoned with the results of his tests and that antifreeze was used, deliberately.

'So?' She tries to act innocent.

'So it was you who gave them their breakfast. You must have done it. There were no gangsters letting themselves into the kitchen at eight in the morning. The only people around apart from me were you and Pete, and I know for a fact that Pete would never do anything so vile.'

Eventually, she admits that it was her who used the antifreeze, but insists that she hadn't meant to kill Pongo, just make him ill.

'Because we need to escalate the perceived threat from Jamie Molcan's heavies. It's important for people to think they're still out to get you for our plan to be believable. That's why I slashed the tyres.'

'You did that too?'

'Of course. I'd have thought it was obvious.'

I stare at her furiously for a few seconds, realising as I do so that it adds more authenticity to my becoming her co-conspirator if I seem less than one hundred per cent convinced to begin with.

'No,' I tell her firmly. 'No. There is no plan, Alexis. Not anymore. If you could do something as horrendous as killing my dog, then there's no way I can trust you in this. You need to forget it and clear off back to where you came from: it's not going to happen.'

So – surprise, surprise – she then tries to blackmail me, by producing some risqué photos and threatening to show them to Juliet. I pretend to back down, and agree to her demand for cash.

But I should have paid more heed to her unilateral decision to carry out poor Pongo's execution. I should have realised that if she was prepared to do that, she was prepared to do anything. Including to me.

Time is of the essence when it comes to Summer's crazy plot, and she has impressed on me that I have no time to waste carrying out my part in it.

So, that evening, I tell Juliet I've got a meeting with the PCC and head down to Nether Benfield's pub, The Crown and Cushion. You could say that I'm on a recruitment drive, and I have a particular target. The landlord's son, a hulking 6'5" gym rat called Harvey. A well-known petrolhead, with a conviction for joyriding. I've caught him giving my Range Rover the once-over when it's been parked in the Crown's car park. I've also heard rumours that he supplements his wages from helping out behind the bar with a little dealing in banned substances. Steroids, by the look of him.

The landlord, Brian Curwen, greets me with a nod and serves me a shot of single malt, which I take to a corner table and nurse for nearly an hour, scrolling through my phone mindlessly until Harvey Curwen finally appears and starts collecting glasses and emptying ashtrays. He glances frequently in the direction of the door, and, sure enough, one of his mates lopes in wearing cheap sportswear, his face hidden by his hoodie. Harvey nods in the direction of the door out to the car park, and the youth turns round and goes out the way he came in.

I drain my glass and head outside, skirting the building to the narrow passage by the door to the kitchens. Lo and behold, the little scrote in the hoodie is being handed something in a twist of paper, and pulling out a couple of ten-pound notes, which Harvey shoves in the back pocket of his jeans. I take a quick snap on my phone, then press back against the side of the building, staying out of sight until Hoodie has sloped off again. Then I step out and intercept Harvey as he's about to go back through the kitchen door.

'I don't know what was in that wrap, but I'm guessing it wasn't legal,' I say, with a grin and a shrug. 'I'm also guessing you wouldn't want your old man finding out.'

Brian Curwen is one of the church wardens at St Peter's, and his own father used to be the local police sergeant. He's straight as a die. His brother Kevin – conveniently for me, as it turns out – owns the local scrapyard.

Harvey scowls and shoves his hand into the pocket where he has just put the cash, pushing it down further. 'You're not going to tell him, right?'

'That depends.'

'On what?'

'On you doing a little job for me. And keeping this shut about it afterwards.' I mime a zipping motion across my mouth.

He shrugs. 'What kind of job?'

'Oh, don't worry, I'm pretty sure you're going to enjoy it.'

I beckon him to follow me into the car park, and point to the Range Rover, pulling out the key and waggling it in his face. 'It involves having a go at this...'

Harvey's face lights up. He has unusual light-coloured eyes that remind me of a fox.

'Oh, and we'll need your uncle's tow truck. Reckon you can manage that?'

He shrugs again. 'Yeah, whatever.'

As I've just said, timing is everything. Summer has stressed the importance of carrying out the plan to a strict timeline.

On Friday morning, I tell Juliet that I may or may not spend the night in the flat; that I'll update her later. I keep things deliberately vague because I don't want her questioning my movements too closely. I go up to London and purchase a new phone – the burner phone, Summer keeps calling it, as if we're characters in a crime drama – a portable LED work light, some fake police tape from a fancy-dress costume shop, and a cheap digital camera. I spend time in the office, but as you might imagine, I can't really concentrate on anything. I head out to buy a coffee and a sandwich, then walk down to Piccadilly and wander Green Park aimlessly.

I send Juliet a message telling her I'm on the 7.59 from Waterloo, and make sure I'm actually on it, just in case anyone checks CCTV. When I get off at Benfield Holt, I drive my Range Rover out of the station car park – again, for the sake of the cameras – but I don't drive the three miles along the twisty country lane to Mullens End. Instead, I turn in the other direction and head for Kevin Curwen's scrapyard, having first switched off my mobile. The place is locked up and in darkness, and I pull in through the metal gates, switch off my engine and wait.

From time to time, I pull out the burner phone and check it. Then a text comes through, just two words.

She knows.

This means that Summer's actor buddies have been to the house and informed her that I've driven my car off the road and been killed. I felt it would have been more realistic following a traffic accident for uniformed officers to go straight from the scene to inform the next of kin, but Summer says that they didn't have enough time to get their hands on genuine uniforms, and didn't want to risk using something that didn't look like the real deal. She's hoping that plain-clothes CID officers will reinforce the idea that Molcan and his associates might have had a hand in what happened to me.

'Don't worry,' she told me on the phone earlier that morning, 'Alan and Naomi will be very convincing.'

'Can they be trusted though?' I asked her. 'Given they're in the position to blow your whole bloody plan apart.'

'*Our* plan,' she corrected me. 'Think about it: you face a prison sentence of up to seven years for impersonating a police officer. They're not about to tell anyone. Plus, they're both out of work and just happy to get the very generous fee.'

We've agreed that it isn't good enough for them to just tell Juliet I'm dead: we need to prove it. But I couldn't run my car off the road there and then, not in daylight, with other commuters driving back from work along the same stretch of road. The last train gets into Benfield Holt at 11.40, and from midnight onwards there's no traffic to speak of on that road. I sit outside the scrapyard, increasingly stiff and bored, as rain thunders down on the roof of my car. Finally, at ten to one in the morning, I hear the sound of Harvey Curwen's scooter approaching. I'm glad to see he's followed my instructions and left his lights off.

He greets me with a grunt, before unlocking the heavy metal gates.

'Where does your uncle keep his tools?' I ask.

He points to a Portakabin, with a padlocked door.

I start to sweat slightly. 'I hope you can get in there. Otherwise, we're fucked.'

'No worries, safe, bruv,' he intones with his faux-ghetto patois, waggling another key at me.

Once the Portakabin is unlocked, I select a lump hammer. 'Right,' I say, offering it to Harvey and pointing to the Range Rover. 'You like to do the honours?'

He stares at me.

'Go on,' I prompt. 'It's got to look convincing. Like it's come off the road at speed. It can't be undamaged.'

He takes the lump hammer and aims it where I'm pointing, at the front driver's side wheel arch, smashing it down and crumpling the metalwork. I point to the driver's side door and he puts a dent in that too, then has a go at the passenger side windscreen.

'Steady,' I warn him. 'I still need to be able to drive the fucking thing.'

Once I'm satisfied that we've done enough, I drive back towards the station again, with Harvey following in his uncle's pickup truck. I stop at my selected spot: a sharp left-hand bend on a wooded stretch of the road between Benfield Holt and Mullens End, just past the entrance to the local riding school. I position the Range Rover at an angle, let off the handbrake and Harvey and I push it ten feet or more down the steep overgrown bank. I then set up the light, and take photos of the crashed car from various different angles.

Obviously, we can't leave it there, or the real cops would quickly be asking questions about it. We attach the hook and chain to the axle and winch it out of the ditch again and on to the flat bed of the tow truck. I cut my hand detaching the hook, and the blood drips onto my trousers. I wrap the wound briefly in my shirttail until the worst of the bleeding stops, then help Harvey fix the straps on the wheels to secure the Range Rover in place. We climb into the cab, and he drops me at a motel on the A3.

'That car's got to be in the crusher first thing tomorrow, all right?' I tell him.

He squints at me, shaking his head to indicate that he thinks I've got a screw loose.

'And don't you dare think about hammering out the dents and selling it on,' I tell him. 'Possession of Class A drugs with intent to supply carries a prison sentence, remember?'

He eyes me, blankly.

'Am I making myself clear?'

'Sure,' he says, starting the engine of the truck. 'Sweet, bruv.'

I shake my head slowly as I watch him drive off. I have no idea if any of this is going to work.

TWENTY-TWO

5 JULY

It's not easy being dead.

The day after my 'death', I point out to Summer that I have a perfectly good flat sitting empty in Tower Hill where I could lie low for a while. But she insists it's too risky. Juliet might decide to stay there if she makes a trip to town to sort things out with the trustees, or drop in at my Shepherd Market office to make a start on dealing with my affairs there. So I end up squatting in a studio flat just off Kilburn High Road. It belongs to a friend of Summer's currently away in Australia. It's small, pokey and depressing as hell.

Summer's the only person who I can currently have any contact with, but she won't visit because she says it would look odd if she doesn't stay around at Mullens End to support Juliet in her bereavement. So I don't even get a bit of mindless sex out of the situation.

'Just hurry up and get the funeral bit out of the way as fast as possible,' I tell her on the burner phone after I've been in Kilburn three days. 'I don't know how long I can stay cooped up in this shithole.'

'It's not that easy,' she tells me. 'The day it happens is not down to me, is it? It's down to Juliet.'

'How's she... you know, bearing up?' I can't help but feel curious about my widow's state of mind over my demise.

'Oh, well, you know Juliet!' There's a hint of scorn in her voice. 'Everything neat and tidy and under control as always.'

I'm a little taken aback by this. 'Are you saying she's not upset?'

'Well, I mean, it was a huge shock for her. Obviously. But now she's dealing with things okay.'

'As long as she believes the accident was real. That's the only important thing.'

'Oh yes, I'm sure she does.'

I'm relieved. It looks like we might have got away with our outrageous scam. But later that day, as I'm wandering aimlessly round Queen's Park, Summer phones me again.

'Juliet wants to see you.'

I feel the blood draining from my face and I stop dead in the middle of the path. 'What do you mean? How has she found out?'

Summer snorts down the line. 'No, you moron, she wants to see you dead. You know; a viewing. In your coffin.'

I press my hand against my brow. 'Shit! What the hell are we going to do about that? You can hardly tell her she can't.'

'Don't worry,' Summer says breezily, 'it's all in hand. You just need to get a train down to Woking in the morning.'

She explains that the friend who played the male detective already has two actor pals lined up as undertakers, and that the plan is to use some of the cash I gave Summer to pay for a coffin. Apparently, they're buying it from a friend of a friend whose family has a funeral directors' business, and the story they've spun is that they need it for a short film they're shooting. They've also asked these people if they can shoot a scene in one of their viewing rooms. All I have to do is show up and lie in the coffin without moving a muscle, while my grieving widow weeps over me.

Like I said, it's not easy being dead.

To give Summer credit where it's due, she's thought of everything.

Her part is to accompany Juliet, and follow my instructions to keep her as far away from me as she possibly can. Meanwhile, she's sent her pal Matt to meet me at Woking station, and he takes me to the funeral directors' premises and applies professional screen make-up to my face to make my skin look waxy and pale.

'They use this stuff for deathbed scenes in soaps,' he tells me cheerfully. 'It's very realistic.' My hair's then combed back and blasted with hairspray to make it look as though the mortician's been at me.

It's a hot, sunny day, but lighting has been kept as dim as possible in the viewing room, and Matt and his brother Tom come up with this ingenious cardboard box contraption they arrange over my torso beneath the drapes to obscure any sight of my chest rising and falling. This technique is used in TV drama too, apparently. Add some sombre dirge-like music, piped in on a sound system, and that's it. All I have to do is lie still on the cheap white satin, eyes closed and not move a muscle. I try not to think too hard about where I'm lying, and whether it's tempting fate. I just hope Summer will do her bit and keep the viewing brief.

'The eagle has landed,' Tom sticks his head round the door and whispers. 'She's coming. Don't move, okay.'

I hear two sets of footsteps come into the room, and I'm desperate to open my eyes the merest crack, but I resist. There's silence. No crying. Then Juliet asks if she can touch me. The room is air-conditioned and I feel quite cold, but I'm still not sure whether this will equate to the chill of dead flesh. Fortunately, she changes her mind, and a few seconds later they're gone.

Summer phones the next morning to let me know that my funeral is going to be on 12 July.

To wind her up, I tell her that I plan to attend, in disguise, and have to deal with her having a complete meltdown until I assure her that I'm kidding. Of course I'm not going to be there: that would be too weird. But I am planning to return to Nether Benfield. I don't tell Summer this. Of course I don't.

The night before the funeral, I pull on a beanie hat and a hoodie and catch the last train to Benfield Holt and walk the two and a half miles to the village, which takes me another forty-five minutes. So by the time I reach my destination, it's after midnight, and as I would have expected, all the lights are off. Only once I'm standing there in person, looking up at the house, do I realise the flaws in this plan.

I think about chucking gravel up at the window, but there's always the risk that the wrong person will hear it. Or the dog will start barking. Instead, I pull out a scrap of paper from my jeans and unfold it. It's a list of phone numbers I transcribed from my old mobile before I chucked it in a bin at Waterloo station. I punch in one of them on the keypad of the burner phone and press 'Call'.

She doesn't answer straight away. It takes three tries. After a few tense minutes, I get a sleepy, croaked, 'Hello?'

I hang up without speaking, aware that if she hears me speaking from beyond the grave, she will freak out, probably loudly. I send a text straightaway that says simply 'Come outside. QUIETLY.'

Two minutes later, the front door is inched open. 'Hello?' Then she sees me. 'Oh my God. Oh my God. Hugh.' Her knees give way and she clings to the door frame, as the dog, sensing the opportunity for a late walk, shoots past her. She reaches out and touches my face. 'Are you real? What the hell is happening?'

Once she has ascertained that I'm not dead, she's furious.

'Have you any idea what you've fucking well put me through? What... you've just been *pretending* to be dead?' she spits in a hoarse whisper. 'Can you imagine what it's been like these past ten days?'

'I'm sorry, darling,' I say, pulling her into a tight embrace. 'Christ knows I wanted to tell you sooner, but I just couldn't. I will explain, all of it, I promise.'

'So why are you here now?' she demands. 'When you're being buried tomorrow. Or are you?'

'I had to see you now, with the funeral tomorrow. I was worried you'd get so overwrought when you know... you saw the coffin... you'd break down and confess to Jules about our affair. And I couldn't bear the thought of what you'll have to go through at the service. It seemed so cruel; I had to let you know.'

She shakes her head. 'So I'm just to pretend? That you're actually dead?'

I take her hand in one of mine and with the other touch my fingers to her lips. 'Afraid so, my darling. But listen, it's all part of the plan. And it's not for much longer.'

'Promise?'

'I promise.'

TWENTY-THREE

9 AUGUST

Enough is enough, I conclude several weeks later, on a dank humid Monday in August.

I stayed away from my own funeral, and my coffin (filled with a couple of sandbags) is now safely installed in the vault in the Mullens End mausoleum, no questions asked. I remained in the grotty studio flat in Kilburn until I was sure that Juliet had departed for Italy, having removed some of her own belongings from the house. After that, although Summer and I had agreed that I should stay away from Benfield for a while longer, I moved back into the marital flat in Tower Bridge as Juliet was out of the country. I was comfortable there at least, with decent Wi-Fi, a Nespresso machine and Sky Sports on the plasma-screen TV. Our London neighbours are a transient lot, mostly renters and city workers, so if anyone spotted me, no alarm bells would be raised. If they don't know me, then they won't care if I'm alive or dead.

Apart from one brief, highly cloak-and-dagger visit from my beloved, I don't see a soul and, inevitably, I grow bored. Things have been quiet at work for a while, but there was always *something* to do, if only making phone calls to suppliers and prospective clients, researching available pieces, planning buying trips. Having my own little gallery in a smart part of town boosted my self-importance. It gave me a routine. Now I'm reduced to living like a bloody student, rising at midday, living on bowls of cereal and daytime TV. In addition to the hustle of running a business, I miss having a dog to walk, playing tennis, being outdoors, enjoying a drink with my friends.

There's also the issue of money I'm owed by clients. They won't be expecting to receive invoices from beyond the grave, but I'm going to have to claw back those funds somehow, especially as I can't currently access any of Jules' and my joint accounts, or the cash in the safe at Mullens End. So, one night, after all the office workers and high-class call girls have long since left Shepherd Market, I put on a baseball cap, hoodie and my reading glasses and let myself into my gallery. A security guard outside the building next door nods to me as I go in. Does he recognise me? I wonder, feeling paranoid. Then I tell myself I'm being ridiculous. Even if he does, so what? He's hardly likely to know that I'm supposed to have died. It's not like my demise has made the national news, and the people who work round here tend to keep to themselves. I doubt I've been talked about in Shepherd Market, although in Benfield my death will be a source of dinner party gossip for months to come.

I send out invoices using my work email address but signing myself 'P. Taylforth, Assistant to Mr H Mullen'. I'd once had a temp called Patricia Taylforth helping me in the office, so I reckon it seems believable. And, even when you're dead, outstanding payments are still owed, to your estate rather than to you personally.

Once I've sent out the invoices, I grab a laptop, a bottle of malt I was given by a client at Christmas and whatever bits of paperwork I think I might need. After double checking that I've not left any incriminating evidence, I slink out of the place, making sure to cover my face with my hood as I leave.

I'm like a ghost, I realise. A ghost haunting my own former life. I go back to the flat and, in the absence of any company or entertainment, set about getting rip-roaringly pissed on the whisky.

It's been several days since I've heard from Summer, so the next morning, when she's still not picking up my calls or answering my messages, I decide I'm sick of sitting around on my arse waiting for her to break cover.

I pack an overnight bag and head out to the car rental place on East Smithfield Road. I have to use my own driving licence, because it's all I have. It's still valid, at least, since I'm only deceased In an unofficial capacity and my death certificate was fake. Once I've been given the keys to a standard four-door saloon, I drive west along the embankment and over Southwark Bridge, heading for the A3 and Benfield.

The last time I was here was the day before my funeral. Astonishingly, that's only around four weeks ago. It feels like a lifetime. I pull up outside the house and wait for the sound of Jeff barking when he hears the wheels crunching over the gravel, but there's silence. I have my keys with me, but the front door is unlocked.

'Hello?' I call, as I open it.

Then I stop in my tracks and stare around in disbelief. The rugs on the stone flags are gone, as are the burr walnut oval table that stood in the centre of the space and the gilded French rococo console table. The paintings have been removed from the walls, leaving slightly darker rectangles on the paint. I hurry through into the drawing room. Instead of furniture, there's just a series of large crates, surrounded by rolls of foam and what I recognise from my own line of work as glassine paper, used in the packing of fine art and antiques.

'Summer!' I shout, enraged, then correct myself. 'Alexis!' I go back into the hall and shout up the staircase. 'Where the fuck are you?'

There's no response.

I march into the kitchen, and find her there emptying the contents of the larder into carboard boxes. She's wearing denim overalls and has her hair pushed back with a thick polka dot hairband. I notice that the roots are now blonde. The pretence of her having the Mullen red hair is clearly a thing of the past.

'What are you doing?' I ask, although the question is redundant.

'Packing up the house,' she says calmly. 'I would have thought that was obvious.'

'But why?' I demand. She avoids my eye. 'And where's it all going?' I wave my arm back in the direction of the hall.

Inwardly, I feel a sense of rising panic. Obviously, I never planned to live here at Mullens End with Summer long term. But she's not supposed to know that.

'Oh, it's going to be auctioned,' she says, with a smile that shows her Persil-white veneers. 'Don't worry, it's not some tinpot little local place; it's going to a top auction house in Mayfair. They're coming back tomorrow to finish the job.'

'You can't do that.'

'Oh, but I can.' She smiles again, self-satisfied. 'I got my lawyer to expedite probate, and it was granted last week, and the paperwork transferring this place into my name is all signed and sealed.'

I flap my arms uselessly. As the guy who controls the purse strings, Roger Banborough had to be one of the deceived parties in the plan, but now that's backfired on me. He will have had to see some formal ID before transferring anything into Alexis's name, so Summer must have produced something convincing. But when you consider what she's pulled off so far, producing a fake driving licence or passport would have been a mere detail for her.

'Alexis, *we're* supposed to be living here.'

She gives a derisive little laugh. 'Come on, Hugh, you didn't really think that was going to work, did you? You and I were never going to be long term.'

She's quoting my own justification back at me, and it sends a chill down my spine.

'You're dead now, right? So the place belongs to me. Okay, so I can't sell the house, which is annoying, since it's worth a fuck load of cash, but I can sell the contents. They're worth quite a lot. And the new tenant wants the place unfurnished, so I can't just leave it all here.'

I press my right hand over my mouth. Summer turns her back to me and continues moving bottles of oil and vinegar, all neatly organised by Juliet, into a box.

'Excuse me,' I say coldly after a few seconds. 'The tenant?'

'Yes,' she says simply. 'I'm leasing Mullens End. The trust beneficiary is entitled to rent the place out, and to do what they like with the rent money. And, thanks to its proximity to a commuter route, it'll bring in well over ten grand a month. I can get somewhere pretty nice in central London for that, and still have plenty left over. Or Paris, or New York, or LA: I haven't quite decided. And Jamie Molcan is happy to sign a long lease, which suits me.'

She seals up the box she's working on and reaches for another, starting to fill it with bags of sugar and flour.

'Molcan?' I say faintly. 'You mean...?'

'The CEO of the JM Developments, yes. He wanted to rent a local base for one of his ex-wives. And, Christ knows, he of all people can afford it. He didn't quibble about the extortionate rent I suggested. As soon as this lot is clear, and he can get an idea of what he's going to need, we'll both sign the tenancy agreement and that will be that. *I'm outta here.*' She affects an American accent as she waves her hand at the half-packed boxes.

I'm looking round the room, noticing the empty space next to the Aga where the dog bed used to be.

'Where the hell is Jeff?' I demand angrily.

'Don't worry, Patrick and Justine have taken him. He's fine. They're going to rehome him.'

It's the way she smiles when she says this that makes me lose it. I grab her arm and she spins round, her composure gone at last. 'You little bitch!' I snarl. 'You're not going to get away with stitching me up like this.'

Okay, so I had fully planned on stitching *her* up, but she doesn't know that, not yet.

She yanks her arm free. 'I already have, Hugh.' She sees the disgust on my face and wrinkles her perfect nose. 'Oh, please, you didn't really think our steamy fling was going to lead to a lifelong partnership, did you?'

'Maybe not, but I didn't think you'd turn out to be quite such a snake,' I say, disingenuously. 'I thought at least we'd come to some sort of arrangement once Juliet was gone.'

'Why would I bother?' she asks simply. 'You're dead, remember? And, as your cousin, I'm now the beneficiary of the Ernest Mullen Trust.'

It's my turn to smile. 'Oh, but you're not though, are you?'

Her grey-green eyes narrow. 'What do you mean?'

'Come on now, *Summer*. You didn't think if someone turned up out of the blue saying they had a claim on all this' – I wave my hand in the direction of the terrace doors, with the swimming pool and rose garden beyond – 'that I'd just take their word for it. How dumb do you think I am? I know you're not Alexis Lambert. Alexis Lambert is now permanently resident in the States, and known as Alex Lambert. You're Summer Willetts, out-of-work D-list actress, raised on a council estate in Kent.'

Her hand stops halfway to putting a handful of spice jars into a box. It's shaking, and she's turned pale beneath the layer of fake tan. Nevertheless, she's resolved to call my bluff. She gives an insouciant little shrug. 'And what are you going to do about it? You can't exactly report me to the authorities, not without exposing your part in it all.'

'Oh, but that's where you're wrong, Summer. You see, it's actually not a crime in this country to fake your own death, unless you do so for financial gain, like claiming on a life insurance policy. And I clearly have not gained any financial benefit.' I point to the packing cases. 'In fact, it's easy enough to prove it's quite the opposite.' She avoids my gaze, but I put a finger under her chin and lift it so that she's forced to meet my eye. 'Whereas you, *sweetie*' – I spit the word – 'have committed a major fraud in impersonating the heiress to an estate worth millions in order to take control of said estate. Not to mention paying your friends to impersonate police officers, which probably also makes you liable to a prison sentence.' I pull out the burner phone and waggle it in her face. 'I guess I should probably get on with reporting your crimes, before Molcan's ex rolls up with her removal van.'

She snatches the phone from me and pushes me hard, so I fall against the edge of the kitchen table. Before I have recovered my balance, she's raced up the back staircase to the first floor. I hurry after her, but she's already run into the master bedroom, which is the only room on that floor with a locking door. It's entirely slipped her mind that I don't share her millennial disdain for landlines. The one in my former office is still connected and I go and use it.

Not to phone the police, not yet. I'd still rather avoid their involvement, given my own, separate, agenda. But I do call for backup.

When that backup arrives about ten minutes later, it's pointed out to me that I know the house much better than Summer, so I should take advantage of this. Does she realise, for example, that the master dressing room has not only a connecting door but also its own window onto the front of the building?

My accomplice and I fetch one of Pete's ladders from the garage and lean it against the front wall. Once I'm up there, it's easy to push open the sash and climb through it into the dressing room. I throw open the door to the bedroom, and find Summer sitting on the edge of the marital four-poster, typing frantically into her phone.

She looks up in alarm, and before she has chance to react, I've unlocked the bedroom door and removed the key. But she's not stupid, and within a split second she realises that I intend to keep her in this room, only this time by locking the door from the outside. She rushes at me, aiming a kick at my right shin and using my momentary loss of balance to dart past me and out onto the landing.

I shoot after her, grabbing at the straps of her dungarees and yanking her backwards, just as she reaches the top of the staircase. She rolls her left shoulder to try to free herself and in doing so loses her balance, twists and tips over the polished balustrade, screaming as she falls over the edge of the staircase head-first. There's a sickening crunch as she hits the stone flags, exposed by her having taken up the Turkish carpet to add it to the auctioneers' haul.

I feel all the blood drain from my head, and my legs almost give way underneath me. I don't need to get any closer, or to touch her, to know that Summer is dead.

'Oh Jesus,' I whisper, clinging to the newel post of the staircase for support. I don't need to look up at my accomplice to know they will be equally appalled. 'Now what the hell are we going to do?'

PART FOUR

BELINDA

TWENTY-FOUR

15 JUNE

I'm late, of course. I always am.

I mean, how on earth am I supposed to be on time when I have to jump through so many hoops just to get out of the wretched house? As soon as I've done the school run, I race back home – via the supermarket, because who else is going to get stuff for supper? – then have a quick shower and change, before driving at top speed to Benfield Holt. By then, all the commuters have gone to work, so there's nowhere to park. I have to dump the bloody car in the lane that leads up to the station and just hope that nobody I know notices it.

It's a warm day, and by the time I'm actually on the train, I'm sweating in a very unladylike fashion, and the blow-dry I had done the day before is looking less bouncy and glossy than it did when I left the salon. It goes without saying I would rather have got my hair done this morning before heading to London, but there simply wasn't time. There never is. Rush, rush, rush: that's all I ever seem to do. I rearrange the waves as best I can, but there's nothing much I can do about the sweat patches under the arms of my linen dress. It's a pale duck-egg blue, so they really show.

Never mind, I tell myself as I take a grateful gulp of the iced coffee I grabbed at the station's coffee stand. On this occasion, it's not about the dress but what's underneath it. And underneath is the exquisite lace lingerie that I bought in Mimi's – the racy paprika red a far cry from the beige stretchy stuff I wear for Simon. A plunging balcony bra that shows off the girls to full effect, and a pair of knickers that are as skimpy as I can get away with.

Of course, Juliet, who notices everything, saw the Mimi's bag, so I had to go through the absolute bloody charade of pretending the contents were to spice up my sex life with Simon. As if! Since I was knocked up with Rufus six years ago, we've had sex about four times, and then only when we were both pissed. I know Juliet thinks of me as the mumsy, jolly hockey sticks type, so she would never imagine that the saucy undies could be for the benefit of another man. It simply won't have occurred to her.

I also had to pretend the reason we couldn't meet for coffee this morning was because of school sports day. It's not sports day today – of course it's not – but that was all I could think of off the top of my head. Fortunately, Juliet doesn't have any kids at St Hilda's, so she won't have any reason to spot the lie. Me being the unglamorous, stay-at-home mother of three sprogs is the best alibi I could ever have. Juliet likes to think of herself as my best friend, and yet she has no idea that for the past four years I've been immersed in a passionate affair. As I've said, the notion simply wouldn't cross her mind.

I manage to get to the front of the queue at the Waterloo cab rank, and the traffic between there and Tower Hill is not as awful as it sometimes is. As a result, I'm not too horribly late.

He's pacing when I arrive, impatient to get his hands on me. My lover. Hugh Mullen.

He upbraids me for my tardiness. But not for long. He's too eager to peel off the linen dress and get down to business.

'Well, well, well, you saucy little minx,' he says when he sees the red Mimi's lingerie. 'What have we got here, eh?'

He kneads my breasts over the bra, then pushes the front of it down and moves his thumbs expertly over my nipples, sending electric shock waves through the ridiculously tiny lace knickers. In only seconds they're off and he's plunging himself into me, groaning with pleasure. The sex is rampant and orgasmic, just as it always is.

'My God, you're amazing, Belle,' he groans. 'You're just so fucking irresistible.'

This is the thing, you see. Hugh finds me sexy in a way that no one else does. Simon calls me 'old girl' and treats me either like a brood mare, or like one of his buddies. Juliet, and women like her, make subtle digs about my weight. But Hugh loves my body. He loves the fact that I have boobs and hips, that my mane of hair is abundant and out of control, that I have freckles and a gap between my front teeth. 'So does Brigitte Bardot,' he informs me happily. Most of all, he loves what he calls my 'fecundity'; the fact that I produced three children in two easy pregnancies, just like shelling peas. That both times I conceived first try. 'One and done,' he said admiringly when Simon once drunkenly admitted this over the dinner table. 'You're an earth mother, Belle. A proper one, I mean, like the Greek goddess Gaia. Not some hemp-wearing hippy who doesn't wear a bra.'

We started sleeping together when Rufus was a baby, but things began even earlier, at Vik Kuchar's fortieth birthday. I was heavily pregnant with Rufus, my boobs blue-veined and huge, my belly straining against the thin fabric of my dress.

'You look gorgeous when you're in full bloom,' Hugh whispered, when we passed each other on the path between the marquee and the house. He pressed his palm over my stomach, his eyes widening as the infant squirmed under his touch. I'd just announced that we were leaving to get back for the babysitter, so when he bent to kiss me, I assumed he was just giving me a goodbye peck. His lips landed not on my cheek but at the edge of my mouth, partially covering my own lips. He pulled back and we stared at each other, me blushing furiously, like a fifteen-year-old schoolgirl. He, by contrast, looked simply amused.

Outwardly, this incident was temporarily forgotten in the arrival of Simon's longed-for son and heir, and the maelstrom of going from two children to three. But neither of us had really forgotten. It lay there, dormant, until Rufus was weaned and I returned from our annual summer holiday in Cornwall having gained a tan and finally lost the baby weight. We went for supper with the Mullens in the beer garden of The Crown and Cushion. And while Juliet bored on to Simon about her work, the girls played on the jungle gym and Rufus slept in his car seat, Hugh pulled me into the narrow ginnel behind the building, pressed me up against the wall and had mind-blowingly raunchy sex with me. It was risky in the extreme, but that was what made it so mind-blowing. And what kept me going back for the next five years.

Like many girls do as they're growing up, I used to imagine my wedding day. I imagined the marquee in the garden of my parents' house, the silk dupion dress overlaid with lace, the cadre of adorable attendants, my hair in an updo topped with my grandmother's pearl tiara. And I had all of that eventually, down to the last detail. Because it was romantic and perfect: the archetypal English country wedding and I was so excited to become Mrs Simon Langridge, I told myself I must be in love. But I'd known Hugh Mullen since we were teenagers on the same county party circuit, and I'd always had the most enormous crush on him. It was an obsession that never really left me.

And when our paths crossed years later in Nether Benfield, I realised that I had never been in love with poor Simon. Yes, I loved him in a comfortable, everyday way. But it was not the same. Not even close to the way I felt about Hugh.

I thought at first that our tryst at the pub would be a one-off, just an itch that Hugh – who everyone fancied – wanted to scratch, just to see what it was like. But it was quite the opposite. Our need for one another seemed to increase. We were both less than fulfilled by our marriages, and we found something in one another that each of us needed. And then, of course, there was the baby thing. As we got closer, and started to confide in one another, Hugh told me that he'd come to bitterly regret marrying someone who hadn't been able to give him children, and who, thanks to the nature of the family trust, he couldn't leave without risking losing every penny too. And, as so often happens in extramarital affairs, we allowed ourselves to enter the dangerous realm of 'what if'. What if he'd married me, Hugh mused. I was quite a few years younger than Juliet and capable of having several more children. What if we could have a house full of flaxen-haired children? And not just any house, but Mullens End. Who wouldn't want to live in such an amazing house? I certainly did.

After we've shagged one another senseless, Hugh opens a chilled bottle of fizz and we lie drinking it in the anonymous, neutrally decorated bedroom of the Mullens' London pied-à-terre.

Juliet rarely visits the flat, which has made it a useful location for our assignations. Sadly for me, they don't happen all that often. We have to make sure that Juliet doesn't get suspicious, but also with three little people and a completely undomesticated husband making demands on my time, these snatched moments are just that: snatched. They're exciting, but also stressful, because I'm always having to keep an eye on my phone, both to check the time and make sure there have been no child-related disasters that require my attention. Things have been a little easier since Rufus joined his sisters at St Hilda's, but we're still always on a knife-edge. Today, the children are all going on playdates after school, but I still need to get to Waterloo and catch a train back to Benfield to collect them from their various friends' houses by six.

Hugh picks up one of my specially coiffed blonde locks and twirls it between his fingers, while I stroke his bare forearm.

'I wish we didn't have to sneak around like this,' I pout, repeating a lament he's heard many times before. 'I wish we could be together all the time.' And, because my hormones are raging, making me broody as hell: 'I wish I could have a baby with you.'

He twists his head and gives me a long look. 'You're not...?'

'I'm not pregnant, no,' I say with a sigh. Because of my hyper-fertility, we've had a couple of scares over the years. 'But I wish I was.'

'One day,' he mumbles into my naked shoulder. 'One day and it will be amazing. I can't wait for you to have my baby. When the time's right, of course. Not until everything's out in the open.'

I sigh again. 'Talking of family, Juliet's asked me and Si to dinner on Saturday.'

'Yes, I know. It was my idea.'

It's my turn to twist round in his embrace so that I can look at him.

'I find it really tricky, you know: watching you and Juliet play happy couples when you're entertaining.'

He touches a lock of my hair. 'I know, I know. It's frustrating for me too, you know.'

'So when are things ever going to change?' I demand plaintively. 'When it comes to you and I getting what we want?'

'You mean being together at Mullens End, and having our own family?'

'I do.'

'I really don't know,' he says darkly. 'But, trust me, I'm working on it.'

TWENTY-FIVE
19 JUNE

I hate Alexis from the second she shows up unannounced at the dinner party.

No big surprise there. For goodness' sake, not only does she have the body of a Victoria's Secret model, but she's annoyingly pretty. And she has that vapid, girlish way of speaking that has men drooling. Hugh pays far too much attention to her. I'm fuming.

When he announces that he'll go to the kitchen in search of a vegan option for the little madam, he reaches his hand to his face and scratches his left eyebrow. This is our private signal, one we've used many times over the years to snatch a few stolen moments. Once he's out of the room, I put my napkin on my plate and push my chair back.

'I may as well just pop to the little girls' room,' I say to Patrick Doherty, who's on my right.

Once I'm in the hall, I can hear Hugh in the kitchen, opening and closing the drawers of the freezer and swearing under his breath. I daren't follow him in there in case Juliet comes after him to micromanage things, so I slip into the library, closing the door behind me. A minute or so later, there's a light tap at the door and he comes in.

'Found her some Linda McCartney sausages,' he whispers, rolling his eyes.

'Are you sure that'll be acceptable for Princess Alexis?' I ask drily. I've had a few glasses of champagne and a couple more of wine, and I realise I'm talking a bit loudly. 'She seems like she's going to be bloody hard work.'

Hugh puts his finger to his lips, moving towards me. 'We'd better be quiet.'

'Obviously.'

'Only, we don't want anyone to hear us.'

He discovers the stockings I'm wearing and calls me a tease. He loves it, though. Juliet is strictly a tights woman. There's no time for foreplay, for obvious reasons, and because we're both a little bit drunk, things get hot and heavy and a little bit rowdy.

'Shh!' Hugh puts his hand over my mouth. 'She's only across the hall!'

I grin at him and grind my hips hard against his crotch.

'I mean it. If Juliet finds out, she'll kill us both!'

'Don't worry,' I whisper back at him, 'she's got other things to worry about now.'

It didn't improve my feelings of resentment that after we'd got home, Simon went on and on and bloody on about how hot and sexy Alexis Lambert was.

And then on Monday, Juliet texts me to say that Alexis had not returned to London on Sunday but was staying on for a few days because she was 'between flats'. I compose a text to Hugh to try to glean more information. He's saved in my phone as Bethany Pritchard, a teenager who used to babysit for us from time to time. She's actually gone off to university in Newcastle now, but, of course, Simon has no idea. He never pays attention to details like that. But Hugh, usually quite good at discreet messaging, does not reply. This does even less to improve my mood. I shout at the children over supper and snap at Simon.

'What the bloody hell's got into you, old girl?' he asks after the children are in bed and I'm sitting sulking on the sofa with a glass of red in one hand and a Twix in the other. 'You going through "the change", or something?'

'*The change?*' I shriek hysterically, no doubt giving fuel to his idea. 'I'm only bloody thirty-three.'

'Plenty of life in the old brood mare yet, eh?' He pats my thigh playfully and tries to nuzzle my neck. I wriggle away. 'In fact, why don't we think about getting you up the stick again? Now that Rufe is at school and you've got more time on your hands... it would be nice to have another little ankle-biter running around the place, wouldn't it? And we do make such pretty sprogs.'

'We don't have the space,' I say coldly. 'Plus, the three of them are enough work as it is. I don't want another.'

The truth is, I want another baby very much. Just not his.

I get a few hurried texts from Hugh during the week, assuring me each time that Alexis is 'about to go' but that he can't really meet with me at the moment with her around. Naturally, this makes me despise the woman even more. To make things worse, Simon seems more randy than usual. I push him off me every time he tries to initiate a fumble, then – because I'm feeling guilty – agree to hold a party to celebrate our tenth wedding anniversary.

On Friday morning, Juliet drops round uninvited, moaning on about some damage to their expensive cars, which will easily be covered by their insurance. I pretend to be interested, but I'm not. Juliet's neuroses and self-obsession bore me, if I'm honest. I just foster our friendship so that I can see even more of

Hugh. I ply her with cake and pump her for information about what's going on between Hugh and his newly discovered cousin. I can see that she's worried about it. I'm alarmed when she says she thinks he fancies Alexis. Okay, yes, she also says there's nothing going on, but that's just Juliet and her blinkers. She doesn't believe Hugh could be unfaithful to her, but we all know that's not true, don't we?

My unease increases when I get a message from Juliet saying she's brought forward her trip to Italy, and that I'm to keep an eye on Hugh and Alexis while she's gone. Immediately, I'm driven into a frenzy of jealousy. It's the thought of the two of them messing around together at Mullens End, enjoying warm evenings on the sun-soaked terrace and downing the contents of Hugh's enviable cellar. Juliet's already told me they've been playing tennis. I keep messaging Hugh and he does reply, but whereas before it was usually within half an hour or so, now it's after a delay of hours. What's happening during those hours? All weekend, I can't think straight, so I do my best to palm the kids off on their friends, and in the evening stare blank-eyed at the TV screen to avoid talking to Simon.

Then, on Tuesday, Hannah, my cleaner, who also does the occasional shift behind the bar in The Crown and Cushion, tells me that she saw Hugh in there one evening 'with someone who's not his wife'. I press her for details and she says it was a younger woman with reddish hair and that they looked 'a bit cosy'. As if I couldn't guess.

My blood's boiling all day, and once the kids are in bed, I tell Simon that Rocket needs a walk and head on foot to Mullens End.

When I get to the end of the drive, I put Rocket's lead on and tie it to a tree stump, leaving him there as I approach the house alone. If one of their Labradors is roaming around outside, then as soon as Rocket scents him, he'll start barking like a mad thing and give the game away.

'I'll be back in a minute,' I reassure him, as he whimpers and strains frantically against the lead.

As I round the top arc of the drive, I can hear music. Some sort of late-nineties chillout stuff. This does not seem like a good omen. I round the west side of the house and head towards the rear sun terrace. Jeff appears and rushes up to me, wagging his tail frantically. I bend to pat him, and, once I'm sure he's calm, let him walk at my heel as I go to the pool area. Because that's where the music's coming from, along with sounds of splashing water and laughter.

I'm not sure what I was expecting, but it's not what I saw. Alexis and Hugh are on the pool loungers, and they're both bloody naked as jaybirds. Her tits must be fake is the first thought that comes into my head. Nobody's tits can be both that big and that perky. And she's got no pubic hair either. The effect is of an unclothed Barbie doll.

The second thought is why on earth are they sucking on ice lollies, like a couple of kids. Weirdly it's this, rather than the nudity, that confirms to me that they're shagging. There's something intimate about their licking the rapidly melting orange ices in unison. Their clothes are discarded in little puddles on the stone flags, and there's an empty wine bottle and glasses on the table. The setting sun lends their bodies a golden glow. They make a stunning-looking couple.

I push Jeff away from my knees and run back up the drive, tripping and stumbling, wiping away hot, angry tears. Rocket yaps with delight when he sees me and I fall to my knees, burying my face in his ruff. Once I'm home, I go straight upstairs and shower and get into bed. I'm still crying.

When Simon comes up and asks me what's wrong, I tell him it's just bad PMT.

'You don't get PMT when you're pregnant,' he wheedles, which just makes me feel even worse. I turn my back on him and hunch the covers over my shoulder.

And then, once the light's off and Simon's snoring like a chainsaw, it occurs to me. Hugh wants me to be pregnant, because he so desperately wants to have a child. He should have married me, I think sadly, like I fantasised he would when I was sixteen. Then we could already have a big brood of our own.

But Alexis can still give him a baby. She's several years younger than me, and she's having sex with Hugh; careless, abandoned sex. When the light of the rising sun blazes through the curtains at 4.45, I'm still lying there awake. I haven't slept a bloody wink. Because all night I've been torturing myself that Alexis is already pregnant with Hugh's child. That she might already have stolen the love of my life.

TWENTY-SIX

30TH JUNE

I'm a mess the next day.

As soon as I've dropped the kids at school and have the place to myself, I send a furious text to Hugh.

You're sleeping with Alexis. Don't deny it, because I know you are. I saw you together last night.

After an agonising five-hour wait, he replies. The reply is lengthy, at least, compared with his usual brief messages.

Look, I'm not going to deny it. I have had sex with her. But you've got to trust me, Belle, it means nothing. I'm only doing it because I need to get close to her for my plan of action to work. To get Juliet out of Mullens and pave the way for you and I to be together. Seriously, darling, have faith and know it's only you I want xxx

A second text arrives immediately afterwards, all caps this time.

YOU HAVE TO TRUST ME. I LOVE YOU.

I'm somewhat reassured by this, although I can't stop thinking about Alexis Lambert's perfect boobs.

When can I see you? I text back, but this time there's no reply. And by now I'm so drained and sleep-deprived, I barely care, dragging myself to bed as soon as the kids are in theirs.

The next morning, out of the blue, Juliet calls me from her car. It's funny, but in the midst of my meltdown over Alexis I'd more or less forgotten about Hugh having a wife. She's just heading back to Mullens End after dropping Alexis at the station, she says, and will I please come over for lunch?

Frankly, quite apart from what's going on between Hugh and I, and my subsequent sleep deprivation, I don't really have the energy. We're supposed to be heading to Cornwall in a couple of weeks when the kids have broken up, and I'd planned on going through all the drawers in their bedrooms, sorting out the shorts and swimmers they'll have outgrown. Also, to mollify Simon after being a complete bitch for the last few days, I promised I'd make a start on the party planning, draw up some lists, do some online research to get a feel for prices. I'm dressed in an old shirt of Simon's and gardening trousers, and I'm bedraggled and sweaty. I don't much fancy the contrast between my own appearance and Juliet's effortless Italian chic.

But, on the other hand, I'm bloody curious to know how much she's worked out about what's been going on between Hugh and Alexis. So I shove Rocket in the car and drive over there. I make sure I arrive late, which I know will piss off the ever-punctilious Juliet.

I offer condolences over the poisoned dog, even though the creature was on its last legs. And, having told Juliet I wasn't going to drink, I have some wine anyway. Only the best stuff at Mullens End, and if there was a time when alcohol was needed, this is it. Then I stick the knife in about Hugh and Alexis being spotted at the pub. Juliet seems genuinely upset, and I feel a bit of a bitch. Okay, so we're very different, but she's not a bad person. There are plenty of times she's been kind to me. I can't claim I've never felt guilty about my affair with Hugh.

But not for long. Because then we end up having a huge row about the anniversary party. God knows I'm stressed enough about it already, so it doesn't take much to set me off. It starts when Juliet condescendingly asks why we don't just erect a marquee. Problem solved, according to her.

'Because there isn't space in our tiny little garden for fifty people,' I tell her coldly. 'We don't all have a mini stately home to hold our events in, you know!'

Between the wine and my rage, I can feel myself turning bright pink.

'I know, I wasn't suggesting...' She loses her characteristic cool at this point. 'I just meant... I mean, why don't you and Simon have the party here? Mullens End is the perfect venue. I'm sorry, Belle, I should have suggested it earlier, I just didn't think—'

'"The perfect venue"... Have you any idea how smug you sound, Juliet? And you'd just love that, wouldn't you? Another excuse to flounce about playing the lady of the manor. When we all know you're not exactly to the manor born. God knows how, but you struck lucky when you managed to snare the most eligible man in the county.'

This has, of course, ceased to be about the party, or even Juliet. It's about my jealousy of both Alexis and Juliet, along with the mingled fury and longing I feel towards Hugh.

'Belinda, I don't understand where this is coming from,' Juliet bleats. 'I've no idea what I've done to upset, you, but if I have done something without realising, then I'm sorry.'

At this point, I've had enough, and make a swift exit, but not without knocking over the wine.

I see no sign of Alexis as I make my way back to my car, but

I feel her presence everywhere. And this confrontation leads inevitably to my first proper row with Hugh. I wasn't to know that it was also the last one we would have before our lives changed forever.

Juliet keeps trying to call me, but I ignore her. Despite the overflow of my pent-up resentment towards her, she's not my problem right now. I send Hugh endless '*Call me*' messages, but he doesn't respond. On Thursday evening, driven mad by the thoughts in my own head, I text him, '*Call me NOW or I'll tell Jules everything*'.

He calls ten minutes later.

'What's this about, Belle?' he demands. He sounds irritable, distracted. 'I thought I'd made the situation clear.'

'I need to see you. Can't we meet somewhere?' I've taken my phone out into the garden. The girls are in their room playing and Simon is bathing Rufus.

'I can't. I've got a lot of stuff to take care of.'

'Is that what you call it? Fucking that bimbo?'

'Come on now, Belle, I've told you that's not what this is about. Things are not what they seem—'

'You tell me to trust you, but how the hell can I when you've been having sex with someone else?' I'm sobbing openly now. 'Have you any idea how that makes me feel?'

Of course, he's always slept with Juliet since we've been lovers, even if infrequently. But this is different.

'I know it's not nice, darling, but listen, I had to sleep with her to get close enough to find out what's going on. And I have done.'

'What do you mean?' I sniff.

'I mean that Alexis Lambert is not all she's cracked up to be. She's a fraud. But just for a little bit longer, we have to go along with it, and pretend we don't know what we know.'

'I'm not sure I understand.' I'm suddenly thinking back to when Juliet and I looked at her Instagram account together. How the content was patchy and staged and felt inauthentic. And Juliet commented to me once that Alexis never posted anything at all when she was at Mullens End. Which, given how picturesque and Instagrammable the place is, seems odd.

'You know what we've always wanted, yes?'

'Yes,' I say quietly. I can see Simon's silhouette in one of the upstairs windows and I walk barefoot down the lawn so that he can't overhear me.

'Well, if I keep Alexis onside for just a tiny bit longer, we have a chance of getting what we want. And try to avoid talking to Jules, okay?'

'We've had a massive row, so that's not very likely.'

'Yes, I heard...' He sighs, then his voice takes on an urgent tone. 'Look, I can't tell you everything now, and things might get a bit rocky, but I'm begging you just to keep your cool and ride it out. Can you do that for me?'

'Looks like I'll have to.'

'That's my Belle. You superwoman, you. I love you.'

After the phone call, my equilibrium returns.

Honestly, I still don't really understand what's going on, but having heard Hugh's voice for myself, I believe he's absolutely sincere. On Friday, I finish sorting the kids' summer clothes and make some progress with the party planning, and although I'm still ignoring Juliet's messages and calls, I feel much calmer. The humid weather breaks finally, bringing a summer storm, which means I can face preparing a fish pie for supper: Simon's favourite. He's delighted, and dashes down to the village shop in the pouring rain to pick up a bottle of suitable white to accompany it. We finish the whole bottle and it turns out to be one of the jollier evenings we've had for a while.

After we've sunk the bottle of wine, I dig out a box of fancy chocolates that someone brought round for a supper party and we dig in to them while watching tennis on the TV. As the match comes to a close, I leave Simon watching the late news and go upstairs to soak in the bath, planning to flop straight into bed. As I go upstairs, I notice half a dozen missed calls from Juliet, but honouring my promise to Hugh, I ignore them.

What's that saying about calm and storms?

At eleven, I've just shaved my legs and spruced up my pedicure, and as I rub on some scented body lotion I'm contemplating whether I might let Simon get away with a rare bit of nookie. He's been a good husband in many ways, and I do feel horribly guilty. At the same time as this thought crosses my brain, I hear his voice in the hall, talking to someone at the front door. Who on earth can have called round so late? I wonder.

Then I hear his tread on the landing and he appears in the doorway. He's trembling, and has the strangest expression on his face.

'That was the police,' he says, and as he locks his eyes on my face, I see tears in them. 'Hugh Mullen's been in a car crash. He's been killed.'

TWENTY-SEVEN

11 JULY

How I got through the following week, I have no idea.

I'm devastated.

Well, everyone is devastated; our circle of friends are exchanging messages and phone calls where we all pronounce: 'I can't believe it; I'm just so devastated.' But I have reason to be far more distraught than everyone else. One of the hardest things about those days was experiencing my whole world being ripped apart, yet having to outwardly be no more distraught than anyone else in Hugh's friendship group. And definitely not more so than Juliet herself, although when I went over to Mullens End the next day, I felt that of the two of us I was the more upset.

I had to go over there, because it would look odd if I didn't, but my God, was it a strain! Talk about an Oscar-worthy performance. I had to be all bossy and in-charge, which was what she would be expecting. When, in reality, seeing the Susan Ryder portrait of Hugh on the wall in the front hall, painted when he was twenty-one, made me want to break down and howl. He's leaning back against a sofa, his hair swept back, looking divinely aristocratic and handsome.

I spent the morning throwing together a casserole and some other bits, partly because it would be expected, but also because having something practical to do helps soothe my reeling brain. I think Juliet was grateful, but she was so cool and in control that it was hard to tell. I apologised for having rowed with her, so at least that elephant was no longer in the room. I mean, now that Hugh is gone, I don't want to be at odds with her. And there's no point being jealous of her anymore. Neither of us mentioned it, but of course now Hugh is dead, she will no longer have Mullens End. It will belong to the ghastly Alexis. I can hardly even bear to think about that. Not least because it seems the ugliest of coincidences that so soon after her appearance, Hugh is gone.

I have to find something to wear for the funeral tomorrow.

There's my black wool crepe suit, but the fabric's thick and itchy and it will be far too hot for July. I thumb frantically through the stuff on the wardrobe rail, fighting back tears. I ought really to go into Guildford and find something new, but I can't face the shops or the crowds or the heat. I can't face any of it.

I collapse onto the side of the bed and, for about the twentieth time, try Hugh's mobile number. And, as with all the previous times, it goes straight to voicemail: the default pre-recorded one, not Hugh's voice. I make a decision. I go into 'Contacts', find Bethany Pritchard and press 'Delete Contact'. It doesn't make me feel any less wretched, but at least I can stop torturing myself.

I find an old black poplin shirt dress from years back. It's a bit too small for me now, but it's going to have to do.

Simon comes into the room as I'm running an iron over it.

'You all right, old girl?' he asks quietly.

I nod, biting my lip.

'Tomorrow's going to be rough. I suppose I should dig out the old black tie.'

Wildly irritated, I slap the dress back on the hanger and yank open his dresser drawer, pulling out his black tie and hurling it onto the bed. Then I go into the bathroom, lock the door and cry for as long as I need to, getting it all out.

Simon taps on the door, complaining that he needs to brush his teeth, but I tell him to use the kids' bathroom.

By the time I emerge, he's in bed and snoring. I climb in next to him, but I don't sleep. I lie staring at the ceiling. My tears are used up, for now at least, to be replaced by a bleak, blank emptiness. Hugh is lost to me forever. The idea is too big, too terrible, to comprehend.

About half past midnight, just as I'm finally dozing off, my phone vibrates. I answer it, thinking it will be Juliet, but it's an unknown number and the call disconnects straight away. Then I get a text.

Come outside. QUIETLY.

I stare at it for a few seconds. A cold thread runs up my spine, and my skin prickles with goosebumps. I slide off the bed and descend the stairs like a sleepwalker. Rocket's in his basket in the kitchen, and when he sees me, his gets out and trots after me. I open the front door as quietly as I can, and walk out onto the step.

'Hello?'

I'm so exhausted that I'm now hallucinating. Because I see Hugh, standing in the shadows.

He puts a finger to his lips, and beckons me towards him. But I can't move; my muscles in my legs are like liquid. I clutch the open door, while Rocket recognises the intruder and scrabbles to get past me, wagging his tail furiously. So, not an apparition then.

'Oh my God. Oh my God. Hugh.' My voice sounds strange, otherworldly to my own ears.

He comes closer and I reach out and touch his face. He's wearing a beanie hat and has a beard, but it's still Hugh. Oblivious and joyful, Rocket has run past me and out into the freedom of the moonlit garden.

'Are you real? What the hell is happening?'

For a few seconds I feel as though I'm about to faint. But then, as my pounding heart steadies, fury at the agony I've endured surges through me. 'What... you've just been *pretending* to be dead? Have you *any* idea what you've fucking well put me through?' I snarl. 'Can you imagine what it's been like these past ten days?'

'I'm sorry, darling.' He pulls me into a hug, as my tears start afresh. 'Christ knows I wanted to tell you sooner, but I just couldn't. I will explain, all of it, I promise.'

'So why are you here now?' I demand.

'I had to see you now, with the funeral tomorrow. I was worried you'd get so overwrought when you know... you saw the coffin... you'd break down and confess to Jules about our affair. And I couldn't bear the thought of what you'll have to go through at the service. It seemed so cruel; I had to let you know.'

I shake my head, uncomprehending. Why have a funeral if he's not dead? And where the hell has he been?

'So I'm just to pretend? That you're actually dead?'

He takes my hand in one of his and with the other presses his fingers to my lips. 'Afraid so, my darling. But listen, it's all part of the plan. And it's not for much longer.'

'Promise?'

'I promise.'

But as I say the words, I'm still shaking my head dumbly, unable to decode what's happening. Rocket gives a little bark and I shush him, aware of Simon and the children asleep upstairs.

'But why, Hugh? *Why?*' I sound like one of the twins when they're whining. 'Why would you pretend to everyone that you'd been killed when you crashed your car?'

'Because if I'm dead, Juliet has to give up the house.'

I'm still uncomprehending. 'But... but you can't have it either, if you're dead. Alexis gets it. So how does that help us?'

Rocket scents a fox and starts to yap.

Hugh glances around nervously. 'Look, there's not time to explain it all now. I will do, as soon as I can.'

'So Jules... she doesn't know you're alive?'

He shakes his head. 'No, she really thinks I'm dead. And whatever you do, you mustn't let on you know. Not to a living soul. It would ruin everything, obviously.'

'But Alexis knows?'

'Yes, but she's... Look, I'll fill in all the details later. You can use the number I called you on tonight, but not until a few days after the funeral, okay? And probably best not to save it.'

I nod, but I'm not smiling. The range of emotions I'm feeling is just too complex: relief, fury, fear, confusion.

Hugh bends and kisses me on the centre of my forehead. 'We just need to hang on a bit longer, and then we can start making plans for our life together.'

After that, the funeral turns out very differently from the day I was originally dreading. It's really rather fascinating. Knowing the truth and yet going along with the charade.

For a start, I manage to feel genuinely sorry for Juliet. At the end of the day, she still lost her husband, even if it's not in the way she believes. I help out by taking charge of the catering, and as I get busy in the kitchen, I can't help feeling a little thrill that the place might indeed be mine one day soon. Although I can't work out exactly how Hugh is going to pull this off. I picture a high chair at one end of the huge table, and a playpen on the rug near the Aga. I start to think about how I'll rearrange things. This image of my perfect new life distracts me from wondering how on earth I'm going to break the news to Simon.

What else can you say about a funeral for someone who's not really dead? It was boiling hot and I regretted wearing tights, but otherwise it was a strange rehearsal for something which will – as I'm now hyper-aware – take place for real one day. The mass in the mausoleum, the placing of the coffin in the crypt (there must have been something in it, because it looked genuinely heavy), the eulogy and tributes from friends... it was like a rehearsal. A practice run for a death that hadn't yet happened. How is he going to come back? I wonder over and over. How on earth will that work? Will it be under a different name, a different identity?

And, of course, that little cow Alexis was there. Or whoever she really is. I made sure I didn't betray the fact that I know she's a fraud, but also I couldn't help but mark her card. *She* doesn't belong at Mullens End, and I told her as much.

'You should leave,' I hissed at her. 'You don't belong at Mullens End.'

TWENTY-EIGHT

20 JULY

A week after the funeral, I get a WhatsApp from Juliet, telling me she's about to fly back to Italy with Luca. She says she's found a lovely apartment to rent, and will probably buy a place over there eventually. I am, she assures me, very welcome to visit her out there if I'd like a break. The fact is, I'm relieved she'll be gone. The burden of having to support her through the charade of her husband's 'death' has been hugely stressful.

The next morning, I get a text from the unsaved number Hugh used to contact me the night before the funeral.

Will be at the flat for a while, now J gone abroad. Try and come to see me xx

I don't reply for a while, trying to decide exactly how I can possibly manage it, this week of all weeks. The children are breaking up for the summer in a couple of days, and we're heading down to Cornwall, as we do every year, to stay in a borrowed holiday house that belongs to friends of my parents. We like to give the children a traditional bucket-and- spade holiday, featuring rockpools, crabbing and ice-cream cones.

We're leaving on Thursday night to avoid the mass exodus to the coast on Friday, and the next two days are completely crammed with holiday preparations and end-of-school activities. And yes, I'm aware that I'm lucky to have this lovely life with Simon. That being Hugh's lover brings nothing but stress and complication. On the other hand, I can't not go and see him. I'm like a drug addict in withdrawal when it comes to his touch.

When Simon gets back from work, I fake a bad toothache, which by Wednesday morning has become so bad that it requires me to visit a dental hospital in London.

'But what about Daisy's dance recital this afternoon?' Simon demands. 'You know how hard she's been practising.'

'I'll be back in time,' I tell him, though I'm absolutely not certain that's the case. 'And, anyway, you'll be there.'

Then, of course, Simon discovers he has a meeting in town and hits on the brilliant idea of picking me up at the dental hospital and travelling back to Nether Benfield with me.

'Let's not overcomplicate things,' I say, not meeting his eye. 'They're fitting me in as a last-minute thing, so I'm not sure exactly what time I'll be seen. You head to St Hilda's and I'll meet you there.'

He agrees, but still hovers over me for a while before leaving for work, which means I can only give my hair a cursory wash and style and can't put on the sexy Mimi's undies. I only just make the 9.53, hurtling down the station platform as if I'm competing in an Olympic sprint. I collapse onto a seat in a pool of sweat, just as the train's wheels start to move.

Fortunately, we remove our clothes so fast, there's no time for Hugh to take in either my sweaty hair or the much-washed beige bra and granny pants. We're desperate for a fix of each other and have some gloriously abandoned nookie.

But as much as I need the intimacy with Hugh, I also need answers. I have so many questions.

'How are you going to get rid of Alexis?' is the first and most obvious one.

'That's the relatively easy part,' Hugh says confidently. 'I mean, come on now, I did my bloody homework when she pitched up. And she's not my long-lost cousin Alexis. Alexis is in the States, going under the name Alex Lambert. The woman who's currently in my house is an actress and con artist called Summer Willetts. And when I tell her that I'm on to her, she'll have no choice but to leave or face a hefty prison sentence.'

I prop myself on an elbow and look at him. He pulls an unruly lock of hair away from my face, twirling it in his fingers. 'But the two of you have planned this together?'

'Correct. It was her idea, and I just went along with it, pretending not to know who she really is. She organised the actors to play the police officers and undertakers, I took care of the crashing the car bit.'

'So you'll both get into trouble then.' I frown. 'I'm sorry, Hugh, but I just don't see how this is going to work.'

'Because, darling, Summer may be bright, but she's not bright enough. She didn't reckon on the financial gain part of the plan being entirely hers. If she impersonates someone else to get money – or in this case a house – that's a serious fraud. Pretending to be dead for no material benefit is not actually a crime. And the Range Rover was mine to do what I wanted with. If I let it roll into a ditch and then got a local firm to tow it away and scrap it, so be it. Thus far, I haven't actually done anything wrong in the eyes of the law.'

I think about this for a while. 'Okay, supposing you do get Summer to leave quietly. There's still the issue of Juliet. She's left the house because she believes you're dead and she has no choice. But if you're not dead, and you're back at Mullens End... how the hell is that going to work?'

Hugh reaches over to the nightstand for a glass of Scotch he poured, even though it's only eleven thirty in the morning. 'That is the part that's a gamble,' he admits. 'I'm relying on Jules wanting to stay away. To stay in Italy. Once she's accepted that our marriage is over, I'm pretty sure that's what will happen.'

I frown. 'But, still, if she divorces you, how will you afford to keep Mullens End?'

'Fortunately, there's nothing in the trust's conditions that gives her the half value of the house in the event we simply separate. So I can stay there, and she can live elsewhere, as long as we're still legally married. I'll have to bung her some money, of course, but we'll cross that bridge when we get to it.'

I'm both confused and exasperated. 'But you're relying on her being okay for you to stay married and just lead separate lives. I know Juliet, she likes things clean and tidy. She'll want a divorce. Of course she will. Especially once she knows about you and me.'

'Then it's up to me to persuade her against it.'

'And where does that leave us?' I sit bolt up in bed and reach for my bra. 'We're supposed to be together. To have children together. I'm not going to do that without divorcing Simon... but you'd still be married to Juliet?'

He takes hold of my arm, and pulls me back to the bed. 'Darling, I know it's not ideal, but does us being legally married really matter that much? If we're finally living together at Mullens End?'

'Not to me, no. But surely if we're not married, any child we might have can't then inherit the place. So what then?'

Hugh shakes his head. 'Any natural child of mine would be a Mullen, and would be eligible to inherit, as long as paternity was established.'

I'm still staring at him in confusion. 'But if you're not going to divorce Juliet, why bother with all this risky "faking your death" stuff? It surely makes everything needlessly complicated.

Couldn't you just have asked for a separation? This is...' I wave my hands. 'Way too big, too crazy.'

'Because she'd never, ever have agreed to it, especially if you were involved. Do you think if I announced to Jules: "Hey, I want us to split up because I'm having an affair with your best mate," she'd just shrug and walk away? Of course not! She'd dig her heels in and I'd never get her out of Mullens End. And then where would you and I be? My playing dead was the only way to get her to pack up and leave of her own accord. It was Summer, with her criminal bloody scheme, that came up with the idea. I just capitalised on her greed and used her to take care of the practical details. All that stuff with the actors and the coffin... I could never have set that up without her. And her playing "Alexis" forced Juliet out. Don't you see?' He waves his arms wildly. He seems unhinged, manic, as he clings to the notion that there was a rational basis to his actions. 'She had no choice but to leave and start a new life elsewhere. And I always knew that if she did it would be Italy. Because of Luca, and her ties to the place. As soon as I twigged that Alexis was really Summer and had no legal claim, I saw her as an opportunity. The ideal device to get Juliet away from here.'

'Surely you didn't think you could trust her?' I ask, as gently as I can. Inside I'm starting to feel a rising exasperation.

'Of course I bloody didn't!' he scoffs. 'And I tried to back out of the whole thing, at least once. But she'd taken photos... of me in her bed...'

I flinch, as I'm forced to imagine them.

'And she threatened to show them to Jules. Which would have meant divorce. And you and I would be back to square one.'

'Would she have done it, though?' I wonder out loud. 'If doing so would have put her scheme to get her own hands on Mullens End in jeopardy?'

He closes his eyes briefly. 'She said something that made me think she might have found out about you and me. And obviously we couldn't risk that coming out.'

I sigh heavily. 'Even so, we're still relying on Juliet not wanting to come back once she knows the full truth. As you said, it's a massive gamble.'

'Look, I'll admit, I don't have all the answers just yet. I just know if *we*' – he points at himself and then at me – 'want to be together, *there*' – he points out of the window in the direction of Surrey – 'then this is the best I've got.'

I think about this for a few seconds. 'So how are you going to explain away the death bit? Everyone still thinks you're dead. How are you going to suddenly reappear?'

Hugh waves a hand airily before taking another gulp of his Scotch. 'Oh, that bit's easy. I'll just blame Molcan's gang. Say they faked the crash and kidnapped me, kept me captive to make sure they could push their development plan through. You and I will have to keep what's been going on between us quiet for a while longer, obviously. We'll need to give people some time to adjust before we drop that massive bombshell.'

I pull a face. 'Wouldn't that mean the real police getting involved?'

'If they do, I'll just fake amnesia.'

Afterwards, when I've made it to Waterloo just in time to get the 13.48, I sit on the train and think about Hugh's plan. I want it to work, of course I do. Since we became lovers, all I've ever wanted was to be with Hugh Mullen and live at Mullens End. But nothing about this convoluted plot is reassuring me: quite the opposite. It's absolute madness.

And it can only go wrong.

TWENTY-NINE

10 AUGUST

The day after my visit to Hugh's flat in Tower Hill, Simon and I load bodyboards and wetsuits into the car's roof box, fill bags and cases with flip-flops, beach towels, sun cream, raincoats and favourite teddies and drive down to the holiday cottage on the north Cornish coast.

In all honesty, at this point it's a relief to be away from Benfield and all the craziness and stress of the previous two weeks. Not just a relief but an absolute necessity. Bereavement is physically and mentally exhausting, and although I now know that Hugh is not actually dead, for an entire week I grieved him and our potential life together with every atom of my being. By the time we reach Treyarnon, I'm absolutely on my last nerve, my last atom of energy. I am utterly drained.

In the past, the lack of mobile signal down here has driven me crazy, but this time it's rather nice. I have no choice but to forget about Hugh and Summer Willetts and their dangerous shenanigans. The weather is good and the children frolic happily on the golden sands of Treyarnon Bay, making sandcastles, collecting God knows what in their plastic buckets, pestering us for chips and Mr Whippy ice cream. The fresh air and exercise ensure we all sleep better than we have done in months, and my tiredness starts to ease. I'm able to relax.

The kids are happy to crash out early after being on the beach for hours, and Simon and I can sit in the tiny garden overlooking the bay with a gin and tonic and a packet of crisps and talk about the day. We start getting on well again, like we used to. Because of what we have just been through with Hugh's 'death', he doesn't pester me for sex or go on about us having another baby. He also takes up a lot more of the slack when it comes to dealing with the children, making them breakfast while I have a lie-in and playing with them while I sunbathe or read a book in a deckchair. This is a quieter, kinder, more considerate Simon. I remember why I liked him in the first place, why I agreed to marry him, how I thought – for a while at least – that he was 'the one'.

The holiday is bittersweet, because I realise that it's probably our last. There will be no stopping Hugh now his juggernaut of a plan is underway. Even though it seems doomed to fail, things will never be the same.

We return to Benfield two weeks later, properly rested and sporting impressive sun tans, and, for once, I'm not desperate to contact Hugh. Given everything he was dealing with, it can wait, I reason.

We've only been back a couple of days when I get an incoming call from a number stored as 'Mullens Landline'.

'I'm at Mullens End,' is the first thing he says. Then: 'Belle: you've got to help me.'

I hesitate a few seconds. 'What do you mean?'

'I need you to come over here. Right now.' There's something unfamiliar in his voice, desperation, or even fear. I've never known Hugh Mullen be afraid of anything.

'I can't,' I say, putting down the basket of post-holiday ironing I was about to start. 'Simon's at work and the children are all here.'

'Please. It's urgent. Really, really urgent. Come as quick as you can.'

He hangs up.

I look out of the window and see my neighbour, a retired teacher called Barbara, in the garden of the cottage next door. She occasionally babysits for me when I can't book one of the village teenagers.

I race downstairs and shout to her over the garden fence. 'Barbara, can you be an angel and keep an eye on the children for half an hour? Something's come up. Bit of an emergency.'

She blinks in surprise, more at my frazzled state than the request. 'Yes, I expect so, dear, as long as it's not too long. I've got a dentist's appointment at four thirty.'

I'm already running back to the kitchen to grab my car keys, yelling goodbye to the children and calling back over my shoulder to my startled neighbour.

'There's some sandwich stuff in the fridge, and packets of crisps in the larder; they can have one packet each. And if Rufus gets tired, the girls know how to find one of his cartoon channels on the TV.'

As I open the driver's door of the car, I hesitate. I felt the usual Pavlovian reaction when I first heard Hugh's voice on the line. My pulse quickened and there was the familiar fizz of excitement. I think of all the times I've been desperate to see him, how I've rushed giddy as a schoolgirl to our meetings. But this tense, frightened Hugh is a completely different proposition. Now, after I've been away and enjoyed a welcome interval of peace and domestic harmony, do I actually still want this drama, this pressure? I'm not sure.

When I get to Mullens End five minutes later, the front door is open.

I'm shocked when I see the state of the place. All the beautiful paintings are down, and half the furniture crated or covered.

Hugh appears, looking stressed. He doesn't even embrace me.

'She's only gone and rented the place out,' he says, raking his fingers through his hair. 'Which being the trust beneficiary entitles her to do. Or entitles Alexis Lambert to do, I should say,' he adds bitterly.

'Where is she?'

'She's locked herself in our bedroom. Mine and Jules' bedroom,' he qualifies. 'And she's got my bloody phone. We've got to get her out somehow. I suppose between us we could break the door down?'

'Doesn't the master dressing room have a connecting door?'

He nods.

'And if I remember rightly...' Ironically, few people know the Mullens End floorplan better than me. 'The dressing room has its own window onto the front of the building.'

Hugh slaps his forehead. 'Oh God, of course! Let's get a ladder.'

We fetch an enormous ladder from where it's stored at the back of the garage and lean it against the front of the house. I hold the bottom while Hugh climbs up and opens the sash window to the dressing room.

'Once I'm in, go back inside to give me backup,' he calls down. This is bloody ridiculous, I'm thinking. It's like something out of a farcical *Carry On* movie.

Once he's disappeared through the window, I go back into the front hall, just in time to see Summer racing out onto the landing with Hugh behind her. As she reaches the top of the stairs, he grabs at her dungarees and pulls her back towards him, but she ducks and wriggles free and in doing so loses her footing and falls.

I hear the scream, then the thud. It all happens so quickly. I stare in disbelief.

'Oh Jesus,' Hugh says, clutching on to the banisters. 'Now what the hell are we going to do?'

We stare at each other in silence for a few seconds. Then my brain kicks into gear. My reaction when something shocking or tragic happens is to go into practical, capable mode. Maybe it's an instinct that mothers have, I don't know. But within seconds I find myself making a mental list of what needs to be done.

'We have to be sure she's...' I can hardly bear to say it. 'She's actually dead.'

Hugh has come down the stairs, his face white and waxy with shock, his jaw clenched so tight, I barely recognise him. 'Oh, come on,' he says with a slightly sneering note. 'It's pretty fucking obvious. Look at her: she's broken her neck.'

I don't want to look at her: I want her gone. That's the next objective. 'We need to call an ambulance then. They're used to dealing with these sorts of things.'

He stares at me in horror. 'No, no, no. We're not going to do that.'

'But it was an accident,' I protest.

Hugh puts his hands on my shoulders and looks right into my eyes. 'I know, but I can't prove it. I can't prove I didn't push her. They'd have to involve the police.'

'But I saw it. I'd tell them what happened.'

'And then they'd go digging into our lives and find we've been having an affair. Which would discredit your testimony. It would look like we conspired to kill her. We've got a big fat motive: having the house for ourselves, now Juliet has left to live abroad.'

I stare at him. The shock's kicking in, making my feet and hands feel completely numb.

'Not to mention the whole pretending to be dead thing coming out, and adding a whole heap of fuel to the fire. It would be one enormous fucking mess.'

We look at one another for a long moment.

I take a deep breath, let my logical side kick in again. 'Then we need to get rid of her. Bury her or something...' My mind races wildly to the police dramas Simon likes to watch.

'No call for that. We've got the mausoleum. And luckily it happens to have an empty coffin in it.' Relief washes the colour back into his face. 'Thank God for that. We can just put her in my coffin and no one will be any the wiser.'

'Okay, but we need to be quick,' I urge, 'I can't be here for long. I've got someone minding the children, but if I'm late back, then questions are going to be asked. And we can't afford that.' I snap back into practical mode. 'We need to wrap her in something.'

I take one of the dust sheets that the removal company have conveniently provided, and together we encase Summer's body in it. I avoid looking at her face, once so pretty and now broken and bruised.

'Where are the keys for the mausoleum?' I demand.

'There's a lockbox outside. The combination's my birthday.'

'And we're quite sure Pete's not here?'

'His truck isn't. I think Summer let him and the cleaners go, in readiness for me coming back from the dead.'

'Good. That's good. I guess we just take one end each?' It feels all wrong, but off the top of my head I can't think of any suitable conveyance. I know there's a wheeled trolley in the utility room, but it wouldn't be long enough.

They say that dead bodies feel heavier than live ones, and I can now confirm this is true. Hugh and I struggle to get Summer's corpse to the mausoleum. Rigor mortis has not yet set in, and although we had wrapped her as tightly as we could, the centre section of her torso still sags. It's a relief to reach the mausoleum and set her down on the floor inside while Hugh opens up the crypt. It's still a shock to see the engraved sign on the vault.

Hugh Ernest Douglas Mullen
1985–2021

It's only when we slide open the vault, which is like a huge drawer set in the marble wall, that we remember the coffin lid is screwed down. Hugh has to race back to the house to find a suitable screwdriver, leaving me alone with the body. I check my phone to avoid looking at it. It's 3.22 and there are several WhatsApps from Simon, which after I've failed to respond culminate in: *Where TF are you??*

As I'm reading it, Hugh returns and we get the lid off the empty coffin, remove the sandbags and place Summer inside, screwing the lid back down and replacing the coffin inside 'Hugh's' vault.

'What do we do with these?' I point to the sandbags.

'Let's take them back to the house, and I'll bung them down in the cellar,' Hugh says. 'We keep some down there in case of flooding.'

'We need to clean the hall floor,' I tell him, as we trudge back to the house carrying a sandbag each. 'And then we need to find Summer's phone.'

He leaves me scrubbing the hall flagstones with a solution of white vinegar and caustic soda while he goes off in search of the phone. 'Got it,' he says, coming back down from the first floor. 'It was by her bed. Shall I cut up the SIM and get rid of it?'

'No!' I say sharply. 'Or at least not yet. We may need the information that's on there, and we need to know who's trying to contact her and why. And, as long as you've got it, it means you can always pretend to be her.' I glance at my watch. 'Look, I'm going to have to go.'

'We need to phone the estate agent first,' Hugh says, jabbing in numbers, as he tries in vain to unlock the phone. 'And you're

going to have to do it, because you can pretend to be Summer. I
saw some paperwork from them in the kitchen, I think.'

We find a copy of the as yet unsigned tenancy agreement on
the kitchen counter and I phone the agent, telling them my
circumstances have changed and will they please tell Mr
Molcan that Mullens End is no longer available to rent. The
next call I make as Summer is to the auction house, cancelling
the removal of the house contents and planned sale.

'Good,' says Hugh, relieved. 'That at least buys us some
time. Although God knows how I'm going to get this stuff
unpacked alone.'

'It's going to have to wait until you've staged your comeback
from the dead,' I tell him. 'At least she'd only done the ground
floor so far.' My shoulders slump and I let out a long breath.
'And now I really am going to have to leave.'

I get back to Birch Cottage at 4.19 pm. Barbara is clearly
not best pleased, since I've been gone longer than an hour and
made her late for the dentist, but she lets it go. I text Simon and
say I had to pop out and do some shopping for the imminent
visit of his cousin and her husband, and he asks no more
questions.

We've got away with it. For now.

THIRTY

12 AUGUST

But, of course, things are never that simple.

I get a phone call from Hugh's new, unsaved number two days after we put Summer Willetts' body in the mausoleum, but I'm forced to ignore it. Simon's cousin, Jilly Dormer, and her husband, Gareth, have come to stay with their two children, and although it's one hell of a squeeze to get us all into the house, the children get on fantastically and Jilly and Gareth are easy company.

'Enjoying yourself, old girl?' Simon asks, filling gin and tonic glasses as I put out a bowl of nuts for the adults and twiglets for the children. He puts the gin bottle down and gives me a playful squeeze on the left buttock. 'It's been jolly, hasn't it?'

'Yes,' I say, and I mean it. We've had fun, and like the trip to Cornwall, it's taken my mind off the fraught goings-on at Mullens End. Then my mobile vibrates with a message from Hugh.

Need to speak to you ASAP

I nip to the downstairs loo and message back.

Got people here, can't talk right now

Ten seconds later, there's a second message.

Call me when everyone asleep

My initial reaction is one of irritation. Doesn't Hugh realise that it's not that easy? The kids are overexcited and disinclined to sleep, constantly hopping out of bed and giggling with their visitors, and Jilly, Gareth and Simon are laying into first wine and then Scotch, also showing little inclination to end the evening.

At around one, they head upstairs and I use the excuse of needing to clean the kitchen to remain downstairs. I creep out into the garden and call Hugh.

The second he answers, I can tell he was asleep.

'Finally,' he says gruffly.

'I told you, Si and I have got people staying. His cousin's family.'

There's an impatient grunt at the other end of the line. 'Listen, you know I've kept Summer's phone? Well, she got a text from Jules this morning. She wants to come over sometime in the next few days and get some more of her stuff.'

'And is that bad?'

'Of course it is!' he snaps. 'I'm not supposed to be here. I'm not even supposed to be alive. Not yet at least. I can't have her arrive and find me here, and just say, "Surprise, darling! I'm actually not dead after all!"'

I'm tired, and I've got a headache from the red wine, and my patience is running thin.

'But I thought that was the plan? To come back and tell everyone you were abducted.'

'Yes, Belle, but not yet, for God's sake! Summer's idea was that I would come back as another Mullen relative. But there's no need for that pantomime now she's...' He lets this go unsaid. 'I can just come back as myself. For the time being, there's the Alexis problem. As far as Jules knows, she's still in residence here. She'll be expecting to see her when she arrives. We have to come up with a new story for what's happened to her.'

The layers of deceit are piling up, and I'm grappling with this latest twist in the narrative. 'So just text her from Summer's phone, pretending to be Alexis, and say you won't be there, then make yourself scarce. I doubt Juliet will want to hang around long, not given everything that's happened.'

'That's the thing, I can read incoming messages when they're displayed as a notification, but I don't know Summer's passcode, remember? I can't reply, and that's going to make her suspicious.'

I look up at the darkened windows of Birch Cottage. I just want to be in there, tucked up next to Simon's familiar snoring form. I let out a long, heavy sigh. 'I don't know what to suggest, Hugh. Can we talk tomorrow? I could try to pop over.'

'That's the thing, Belle, I've already come up with a plan. You need to go to Italy, right now, and head Juliet off at the pass. Not for long, just so I can sort out getting this phone unlocked and reply to Jules so that she doesn't get suspicious about Summer's whereabouts. And it won't do any harm for you to talk to her anyway; get a feel for what her longer-term plans are, going forward. We have a chance of making this all come together, but only if she stays out there once I'm back from the dead.'

'Italy?' I wail, temporarily forgetting the need to keep my voice down, 'I can't, Hugh! The kids are still on their school holidays, Simon's family are staying and—'

He cuts across me. 'Didn't she invite you over there for a visit?'

'Yes, but—'

'Well, there you are then, my darling. You need to get your-self to Italy tomorrow.'

I WhatsApp Juliet as early as I can the next morning.

Hugh and I have agreed we need to present my trip as a fait accompli, and not something to be negotiated. That's going to necessitate some pretty major lying, but having just covered up a death, this seems relatively trivial. I'm still not happy about this latest twist in the tale. Not at all. For the first time, I start to feel resentment towards Hugh.

I google flight availability before messaging Juliet. *Surprise!* I type, after locking myself in the bathroom and leaving Jilly and Simon to deal with the children. *I'm going to be in northern Italy for a few days without Si and the kids – been granted a mummy break! Thought I could come and see you xx*

Blue ticks appear on the message a few minutes later, but frustratingly it's over half an hour before she replies. I turn on the taps in the shower and pretend to be taking ages, forcing Simon to go and shave in the kids' bathroom.

It would be lovely to see you. When?

I look out of the window. Rufus and Primmy are taking it in turns to push little Eloise Dormer on the swing, while Charlie races round and round with Rocket. The sun's rising in a pale blue sky, promising a lovely day. I really don't feel like fighting my way through an airport during the summer's peak travel period. And that's even assuming I manage to book a seat on a flight.

Leaving UK today

I add a wide-eyed emoji.

Juliet is typing... says the script at the top of the screen.

Okay, I suppose that would work

Not exactly enthusiastic, but I can't really blame her after I've dumped myself on her like this.

I was planning a trip to Benfield actually, but I guess I can put it off for a bit longer.

I send a smiley face.

Juliet, organised to the nth degree as always, then sends me a map with a pin where her apartment is. It's in central Bologna rather than Modena, but I can see from the map that the two cities are close together.

Let me know when you land. Will you need to stay here? There's only one bedroom, but I have a sofa bed.

Too much proximity might be risky, I decide. Better to keep a distance.

Don't worry, Jules, I don't want to crowd you out! I'll get a hotel. It'll be a treat for me xx

So far, so good. But selling this mad plan to my husband is going to be more difficult. Once again, I decide to present a fait accompli. I go online and book the only flight available: one leaving from Stansted early that same evening. Because it's such short notice, it's ridiculously expensive, but I bite the bullet and stick it on the credit card.

Simon is in the kitchen shoving papers into his briefcase.

'I need to talk to you about something,' I tell him.

He glances at his watch. 'Make it quick, old girl, I want to get the 8.42.'

'Can you work from home today?'

He frowns. 'Not really, why?'

'I'm going to Italy to see Juliet. This afternoon.'

His shoots me a startled look, which quickly morphs into irritation. 'Don't be ridiculous, darling, no you're not.'

'Actually I am.' I attempt a devil-may-care smile. 'It's all arranged. Jules is really struggling at the moment after... you know, Hugh... and she asked if I could go and visit. So I said I would. It'll only be for a couple of days.'

'It's out of the question, Belinda. Not at such short notice. What about the kids?'

We both have our hands on our hips staring at each other, like a Mexican stand-off.

Jilly has just come into the kitchen and overheard our exchange. And, bless her heart, she now chips in. 'Gareth and I can take the children with us for a couple of days, and you can pick them up at the weekend, Si. We'll just be pottering around at home, but we'll have the paddling pool and the water slide out; they'll be fine.'

The Dormers live in a large suburban house between Esher and Kingston, with a lovely big garden and lots of bedrooms. They also have a people carrier with enough seats for our three.

'Perfect,' I say, beaming. 'I'll go and pack some clothes for them, then I'll get my own stuff together, and work out how I'm going to get to Stansted in time for check-in.'

'Suit yourself,' sighs Simon, grabbing his car keys and heading for the door, kissing Jilly on the way. 'Great to see you two.' He gives a little nod of disgust in my direction, and I feel my flesh chill. 'I'll talk to *you* later.'

THIRTY-ONE

13 AUGUST

There are many, many opportunities for me to regret this part of Hugh's grand plan.

Once I've rushed to pack a carry-on case, and got myself as far as London, the tube train gets stuck for nearly fifteen minutes between Waterloo and Embankment, meaning that as I finally arrive at Liverpool Street, I've just missed the wretched train to Stansted Airport and have to wait for another one. I'm rushing once I get to the airport, which is heaving with screaming children and lager-soused yobs, and then it's just queue after queue after bloody queue.

When I finally stumble up the steps of the plane, my face bright pink and my hair damp with sweat, a stony-faced member of the cabin crew wrestles my carry-on bag from my hands, telling me that the overhead lockers are already completely full and that it will have to be put in the hold. It's dumped unceremoniously at the top of the jetway and I'm almost pushed along the aisle to my seat. In the back row, next to the toilets, naturally.

During the two-hour flight, passengers queuing to use the increasingly stinky facilities stand with their backsides in the space occupied by my tray table, while the toddler in the row in front drops half-sucked pieces of bread over the back of the seat and onto my lap.

I messaged Juliet just before boarding, and once we've landed at Bologna airport and I've been released from this hellhole, I'm hoping she might be there to meet me, but I only get a brief WhatsApp.

Jump in a taxi: only about fifteen minutes to me

More queuing; this time at the baggage claim carousel. The baggage hall is crowded, noisy and airless, and I can feel the sweat soaking through the back of my shirt as I wait. People drag their cases and rucksacks off the moving belt and melt away one by one in the direction of the 'Nothing to Declare' exit, but I'm still standing there. There's nothing on the belt but a broken cardboard box and a folded baby buggy. My case is missing.

It takes me nearly half an hour to find an airport rep who speaks enough English to decipher what I'm saying and another twenty for them to track my case's barcode. It's still at Stansted. Somehow it got left off the loading of the last-minute hold items. I picture it standing at the end of the walkway, where the plane once was, and I could weep. But there's nothing I can do except hope their assurances that it will be put on the next flight are true. I text Hugh a running commentary of what's happening, my tone becoming more and more desperate.

Come on now, Belle, it's not that bad, he replies eventually. *An excuse to go shopping for some lovely new stuff x*

I don't want to, I type wanly. *And anyway I can't afford it.*

It'll show up. Try and think of the big picture xx

The big picture. In that same picture I see myself at Mullens End. I resolve to apply myself to my mission.

Bologna is about 40 degrees, dusty, airless and crowded.

I fail to be seduced by the fourteenth-century porticoes and the vibrant terracotta roofscape. At this point, I just want to be at home lying in the hammock in my small but pretty garden, sipping a glass of something icy while the children play around me. Once I'm at my hotel, I can take a shower at least, but I have nothing clean to change into. Juliet, who has invited me to go over to her apartment for supper, promises to lend me what I need until my own things show up, but we both know this is grasping at straws. I'm at least two sizes bigger and three inches taller than she is, and our feet aren't the same size either.

I text Hugh.

Going to visit J at her apartment. Will update you later xx

I send Simon a brief message telling him I've arrived safely, but not mentioning the ghastly journey or the loss of my luggage. I'm definitely not in the mood for an 'I told you so'. Then I set off on foot – and still wearing my travel-stained clothes – to Juliet's address on Via Santa Caterina. The street has no pavements and is super-narrow – far too narrow for cars, in my opinion – but, of course, that doesn't stop the Italians whizzing down it on their scooters and in their cars, honking crazily.

Juliet's apartment is on the top floor of a block with pale ochre walls and dark green shutters. She gives me a quick embrace at the door, but doesn't seem thrilled to see me, and to be honest, I can't really blame her. I mean, I've pretty much dumped myself on her.

She leads me into an open-plan living room which has dark

wood floors and filmy white drapes at the window, lifted by the air from a ceiling fan. It's blissfully cool after the street, and I accept a glass of the local white wine gratefully.

'I'm confused,' I tell her. 'I thought Massimo and Luca were in Modena?'

'They are,' Juliet says, giving me a little nod of acknowledgement for remembering this. 'But they need their space, and I wanted the facilities of a bigger city. It's only twenty minutes on the train and about half an hour in a car.' She shrugs. 'I can see them as often as I like.'

I scrutinise her as discreetly as I can. She looks better than when I last saw her. She's got a nice tan, and her hair is shiny. She's wearing a white linen shirt with the sleeves rolled up and a pair of skimpy khaki shorts that show off her neat little figure.

'Well, it certainly seems to be agreeing with you, Jules,' I enthuse. 'You look great.'

I just get a little shrug by way of reply. 'Has your luggage shown up yet?'

'No, it bloody well hasn't. That's why I look such a sweaty wreck.'

'Bring your wine through and I'll see if I can find you something to borrow.'

She leads me into a sparsely furnished bedroom that has the same dark floors and floaty drapes. There's just a bed with plain white linen, a large rattan chair and a few arty prints on the white walls. She roots through her wardrobe and finds a pale blue linen man's shirt which I suspect must once have been Hugh's, and a maxi skirt with an elasticated waist which she has clearly alighted on as the only thing that will fit me.

'I'm afraid I don't think I can do underwear,' she sighs, looking from her own tiny torso to my ample bosom, 'But if you walk up to Via San Felice in the morning, there are several lingerie stores. I'll leave you here to get changed, then. If you like, I can pop what you've got on now into the washing machine. If I put it outside on the balcony, it'll be dry in no time in these temperatures.' She takes in the frizzy state of my mane, which I've just washed and dried with an inadequate hotel hairdryer. 'And do help yourself to any beauty products and hair styling stuff. I know it's hard when you don't have your own with you.'

I emerge from the bedroom about ten minutes later wearing the blue shirt and the skirt, which is far too tight round the waist, and with my hair somewhat tamed by Juliet's hot brush and styling tongs. She tops up our wine glasses, puts my grimy trousers and T-shirt in the washing machine and then sets about making us something to eat.

'I'm doing *tortellini al brodo*,' she explains as she sets a pan of water to boil. 'It's a local speciality. I get the pasta from this divine little place in Via Saragozza. The ladies who make it have been doing it for decades.'

To be honest, I'd rather have a salad than something hot to eat, but it does smell delicious. I watch the deft way she handles the pasta, remembering as I do that she's part-Italian. 'Did one of your relatives teach you to do that?' I ask.

'My grandmother,' Juliet takes a block of parmesan from the fridge and starts to grate it, then sets about making a green salad. 'My mother's mother. She went over to London as a young woman in the 1950s, when her parents moved there to find work. Nonna Carmelita, as we always called her. I used to love hearing her talk about growing up in this part of the world, and when I had a chance to study in Perugia, I grabbed it.'

She hasn't mentioned Hugh, I realise. I wonder if I should.

'How are things back in Benfield?' she asks, as though reading my mind. 'Have you seen anything of Alexis?'

I shake my head vigorously. This, after all, is the truth. I may have been present at Mullens End in time to be trauma-tised by the death of Summer Willetts, but I've never laid eyes on the real Alexis Lambert in my life. 'No, Simon and I haven't been asked over, and to be honest, I wouldn't want to go.'

By now we're at the round table in the kitchen corner, which has cornflower blue units and Eames dining chairs in funky colours. All very different from the sleek designer kitchen in Mullens End. Which is a place I want to steer the conversation away from.

'So, you're settling in all right, after... after everything that's happened?'

Juliet thinks about her answer for a few seconds. 'It's good to be here,' she says eventually. 'I suppose it's been...' She chooses the next word with care. 'Healing.'

'And have you been out much? Have you met new people?'

She sighs. 'I mean, it's only been a few weeks.' She catches my eye and colour creeps into her cheeks. 'But actually, Belle, I have met someone.'

'Really?' My mouth falls open with genuine surprise. 'My goodness, Jules! Tell me more.'

'His name's Stefano,' she says, her mouth curling up at the corners with pleasure as she pronounces his name. 'He's a friend of Massimo's. Another engineer: this part of Italy is full of them.' She gives a self-conscious little laugh. 'And, obviously, it's very, very early days, but I do really like him.'

I clasp my hands together, as Juliet refills our glasses yet again. 'Well, that's fantastic, Jules. Good for you: you deserve it.'

Of course, I'm privately thinking about the implications of this news for Hugh and I, when he eventually reveals that he was alive all along, and decide it can only be a good thing. If Jules falls in love with some dishy Italian, then she's not going to be too worried about what's going on back in Surrey. She might agree to Hugh's mad scheme to hang on to Mullens End without paying her half after all.

I start to relax a little, and actually enjoy myself. Granted, I originally only ever befriended Juliet to be close to Hugh, and apart from living in the same village, we had little in common, but it turns out it is quite nice to see her. I prefer this Italian version of Juliet: she's less uptight.

'So, how come you've got time away on your own without the children?' she asks, eyeing me over the rim of her glass. 'I wouldn't have thought Simon would be able to cope, to be honest.'

'Oh, he can't,' I say, and we both giggle. 'His cousin, Jilly, has got the children for a few days, so all he has to do is get himself to work every day. He's probably thrilled to be able to watch porn on his own.'

Juliet snorts with laughter at this, and reaches for another bottle of white wine, pouring generously. I'm pretty tipsy by now, but I don't really care. It's not like I have to get up early and deal with three children. Which actually makes a pleasant change.

'But things are all right between you and Simon?' she asks in a more serious tone.

I shrug. 'Oh, you know. Same old Simon. He never changes.'

'He adores you though, Belle.'

Another shrug. 'In his own way, I suppose.' I knock back a generous gulp of wine.

'Come on, you know he does!'

'I suppose so. But whose marriage ever turns out how they expect it to? I mean, nobody gets married expecting to have an affair, do they? When I married Si, I assumed that he would be the last man I'd ever sleep with. But he was not.'

This time, it's Juliet's turn to look astonished. 'Belinda! Are you saying what I think you're saying?'

'What d'you think I'm saying?' I slur.

'Well, that you've been unfaithful to Simon.'

I cross one leg over the other – difficult in Juliet's tiny skirt – and raise my glass to my lips again, raising my eyebrows in what

I'm hoping will be a suggestive manner, but which probably just makes me look mad.

'So have you?'

I don't answer.

'Come on, you can't just drop a bomb like that and not tell the whole story. Who with?'

It's dawning on me that I'm straying into dangerous territory. 'I'll tell you about it another time,' I say, though I sure as hell won't. She'll find out eventually what I'm talking about, but not till I'm miles away from here and it's all too late. I push my chair back, panicking now. 'Look, Jules, I've got a thumping head from the travelling and the heat... I think I'll take myself back to the hotel.'

Once I'm back there – with my travelling clothes neatly washed and folded and placed in a bag and a plan to meet for coffee the following morning – I phone Hugh. He's delighted with the news that Juliet has an Italian love interest.

'Wow!' He seems nonplussed. 'I didn't see that one coming. But it's brilliant for us, isn't it? I mean, this is what we needed.'

'That's what I was thinking.'

'And I went up to town this morning and took Summer's mobile to one of those dodgy phone shops on the Commercial Road. Cost me a couple of hundred quid, but I've got it unlocked. I can reply to Jules' message now and tell her I'm probably going to be away when she gets here, but to give me the heads-up when she wants to come to Mullens End. That way, we've got all bases covered, and I can just lie low in the flat for a bit.'

'What if Juliet goes to the flat?'

Hugh gives a derisive snort. 'She won't, don't worry. I expect she'll think about selling it at some point, but not yet.'

'Okay, so what if someone comes looking for Summer?'

'From what she's told me, she's not close to her family, so

that's hardly likely. And why would they look for her at Mullens End?'

'I suppose so.'

'Anyway, you've done brilliantly, buying us that extra time, but there's nothing to keep you in Italy now.'

'Good. It's far too flipping hot for my liking.'

'Oh, Belle,' Hugh laughs. 'You are so wonderfully English. It's one of the things I love about you.'

I hang up and then text Simon to reassure him that I will be back at the weekend as promised, before flopping gratefully onto the bed with the fan directed at my sweating face. I should be feeling a massive sense of relief, firstly that I managed to get to Italy at short notice and without my husband smelling a rat, and secondly that I have successfully avoided Juliet's suspicions being aroused about what's happened to Summer. But instead, all I feel is a deep sense of unease.

No, worse than unease, downright dread.

PART FIVE
JULIET

On the morning after Belinda's arrival, I finally get a response from Alexis.

> *Hi! Sorry, been busy! Sure, fine for you to come whenever but I probably won't be around. Off to Ibiza! xx*

I still have a set of keys for Mullens End, but Alexis doesn't know this, and I have no intention of telling her.

> *How will I get in if you're not at home?*

There's quite an interval between the first text and the second, but eventually she messages again.

> *Will leave a set of keys with Belinda and Simon L, because I expect you'll be going to see them anyway xx*

Does Alexis know that Belinda is actually here in Bologna at the moment? It seems unlikely. But I don't mention it, nor do I mention keys to Belinda later, when I meet up with her for coffee. And, trust me, I have good reason to withhold such a recent piece of news from her.

I arrange to meet Belinda at one of my favourite cafés on Strada Maggiore. It's about a twenty-minute walk from her hotel, and when she arrives, she's pink-faced and damp with sweat.

Instead of my borrowed clothes, she's now wearing the yellow sundress which I know is a favourite of hers, handing me a carrier bag containing the shirt and skirt I lent her. 'Did your luggage arrive?'

'Yes, thank God, it was dropped off at the hotel while I was with you yesterday evening.'

I order us each a 'shakerato' – an espresso shaken with a generous amount of ice – and Belinda gulps greedily at the cold, foamy liquid. 'So, what's next?' I ask. 'Now you've seen Bologna, what's the next stop on your itinerary?'

'I was thinking Verona,' she muses, dabbing her top lip with her napkin. 'I've always fancied seeing where *Romeo and Juliet* is set.'

'Verona's lovely.' My tone is neutral. 'And it's only about an hour away.'

But I know that she's not going to visit Verona. She doesn't have time. What makes me so sure of this? Well, she left her phone in the sitting room while she was in my bedroom last night. It was unlocked, and I opened the email with her e-ticket attached. She's flying back to London first thing tomorrow, after being in Italy for less than forty-eight hours. I know that she has three young children, but even so, if her objective is a relaxing solo trip, she'd surely be in the country a bit longer. I'm still not one hundred per cent sure of her real agenda, but one thing's clear: this 'mummy break' story is pure nonsense.

The conversation switches to Stefano. How old is he, Belinda demands to know, and what does he look like? Does he have any children of his own? Does he want to get married? I fill her in on all the details, smiling dreamily at the mention of his name and giggling coyly every so often, as she would expect. But it's all bullshit. There is no Stefano, no Italian boyfriend. Quite apart from the fact that it's the last thing I want right now, in Italian culture widows have something of a sacred status, and no man would look at me a mere six weeks after my husband has died. No, he's a fictional creation to throw Belinda off the scent.

And there's another very good reason why I can't get hitched to some Italian, real or invented.

My own husband is still alive.

How do I know this? How can I even think something so outrageous could be true, when I saw his dead body with my own eyes and witnessed him being buried in the family crypt? There are quite a lot of reasons actually. Little things, that appeared one after the other in a macabre breadcrumb trail.

At first, I believed it. That was down to sheer shock. I would have believed anything anyone told me during the first twenty-four hours or so. But then the questions started to creep in. If Hugh had been the victim of a criminal gang, surely the case would have been passed to some sort of serious crime unit. Hightower and Carter said something vague about it being looked into, but nothing further happened. There was never any update on the inquest date. The house was never searched, statements were never taken, Hugh's computer wasn't examined, nor was anything more ever said about Hugh's car. From the photos, it was damaged but didn't look a complete write-off. So where was it? After it had been examined, wouldn't it have been returned to me?

Then there was the business of the undertakers. The premises where the viewing took place seemed completely legitimate, and when I later looked up Ellesmere and Daughters online, they checked out all right. And Hugh... well, yes, the fact is that when I was there, in the room with him, I thought he was dead. But Alexis gave me some elaborate excuse as to why his body had been moved there, which didn't add up to me. So, after the viewing, I phoned Donald Drewer, the senior funeral director at Drewers'. His company has had a long association with the Mullen family and he dealt with the funerals of both Hugh's parents. He was surprised, to say the least, by what I told him; upset even. He said that normal practice was for the staff at the hospital or sometimes a police family liaison officer to consult the next of kin about where they would like their loved one's body taken. He offered the services of his firm and said he would happily collect the coffin from Ellesmere's and take over the arrangements. I thanked him for his help but told him that wouldn't be necessary. Because by now, I wanted to see how this was going to unfold.

Then there were the two police officers: DS Hightower and DC Carter. On the surface, they could have been plain-clothes detectives. But there was something about her, in particular, that didn't ring true. On my second visit, I noticed that her glasses had clear lenses: the sort of prop glasses that you can buy on an online fast fashion site for £5.99. She was not really short-sighted: just affecting short sight. I know Instagram influencers sometimes wear them to try to look brainy or serious, but why would a police detective do that? It made it look as though this woman was merely playing a police detective. Then, on the afternoon of the funeral itself, I tried googling their names and found nothing. I phoned Surrey Police and discovered that they did not have either a Sergeant Derek Hightower or a Constable Niamh Carter on the force. Alexis mentioning the inquest also prompted me to phone the coroner's court, who had no record of an upcoming inquest into the death of one Hugh Ernest Douglas Mullen.

This did not necessarily mean that my husband had not been killed. But a false narrative was being presented to me and my mind was like a rat in a trap at this point, desperately trying to sift through what was real and what was not. I tried to cling on to what I knew for sure: the police weren't genuine, the Mullen family undertakers had deliberately been cut out of the picture, and there was no inquest. I like to watch crime shows and read thrillers, and the first thing that's always asked when trying to solve a mystery is *Cui bono?* Who benefits? And the answer to that was blindingly obvious. Alexis Lambert.

She was right there at the centre of this web that I'd been unravelling, like a black widow spider. It's more than obvious what she stands to gain from Hugh's death: she gets Mullens End. And in order to avoid awkward questions from the authorities, an elaborate accident had to be staged. It was Alexis, after all, who took me to the wrong undertakers, who took control of organising what she called 'the paperwork', who liaised with the police, presumably knowing they weren't genuine police officers. The false narrative was being created by her.

I know people will be wondering why I didn't confide all of this to anyone, or at the very least go to the real police with my suspicions. There was enough there for them to investigate. And why on earth would I want to walk away, leaving someone to get away with murdering my own husband and taking our home? There's no easy answer to this question. I just had a strong hunch, a gut feeling that there was more of this to play out, and if I let it happen, then Alexis would mess up at some point. The scheme was too huge, too fantastical, for her not to. But, in the meantime, the last thing I wanted was her thinking I was suspicious and running scared, disappearing. So I played along all through that awful period between the accident and the funeral, keeping it together and never appearing to question the information that was put in front of me. If I went abroad and let her get on with taking over Mullens End, then at least I could keep watch on her. At least I would know exactly where she was, and why.

Also, I really, really needed to get away, and to be near my son. I wanted to be in Italy, where I could feel a little more relaxed. It sounds facile, but what I needed most was time to think. And while I haven't been dating a Stefano or any other handsome Italian lotharios, I have enjoyed being here. Having some breathing space. Thinking about what it would be like if my marriage was over forever, my former home gone. Thinking about what I want my future to look like.

And then Belinda turned up.

When Hugh 'died', at first it didn't occur to me to be suspicious of her.

Good old Belinda, maternal and capable, offering practical help as always. I was more than happy to overlook the row we had in the garden of Mullens End, when she revealed her jealousy and resentment.

But now I'm wary of everyone and everything, and her awkward, last-minute decision to fly out to Italy seemed odd. The Langridges don't travel much, and everything they do is planned ages in advance, as it has to be with three young children. And once she'd arrived here in Bologna, she was very reticent about the reason for the impromptu trip or what her itinerary was. When she came round to the apartment for supper, she clearly didn't want to talk about it, and her answers were vague and inconsistent. So while she was in my room changing into my spare clothes and sorting her hair out, I looked in her bag. Her phone was unlocked, and it didn't take me long to find the email flight confirmation. Sure enough, she was due to fly back to Stansted on Saturday morning, less than forty-eight hours after getting here. That made no sense.

While the phone was still in my hand, it bleeped with a text from an unsaved number.

Okay, darling, speak later tonight. Try and find out if J suspicious at all xx

I stared at it for at least twenty seconds. 'Darling'? Who on earth was this from? And 'J' had to refer to me, surely? An icy chill gripped my heart and snaked its way down my spine, making my legs shake.

From the bedroom, I could now hear the sound of the hairdryer. I went into Belinda's messages and found a text thread from the same unstored mobile number. There were dozens and dozens of messages, some brief, some intimate, dating back weeks. Some of them discussed mundane arrangements, others were more cryptic, but of one thing I was sure: these were messages from a lover. And then, finally, I read one from earlier that day and felt myself growing light-headed, as though blood was no longer reaching my brain. My hand started to shake so violently, I dropped the phone. For a few seconds, I thought I was about to pass out.

Come on now, Belle, it's not that bad. An excuse to go shopping for some lovely new stuff x

'Come on now' was Hugh's signature phrase. He was always saying it to me in that vaguely patronising manner he had: 'Come on now, darling,' 'Come on now, sweetie.'

These texts were from Hugh; there was absolutely no doubt about it. He was still alive.

With shaking hands, I poured myself more wine. When Belinda emerged from the bedroom, I plied her with it too, not knowing what else to do.

In my mind's eye, I kept seeing dead Hugh in his coffin. But one of the many odd things about the viewing had been how dim the lighting was in the room. It was definitely him, but now I was sure that he had been – literally – playing dead. I wanted to time-travel, to go back and look harder, to touch him as I'd planned to.

Even more shocking than the confirmation that Hugh was alive, was him apparently being in a relationship. Not with Alexis Lambert, but with Belinda Langridge. I knew he'd always had a soft spot for her, but now so many little things fell into place. The two of them falling silent when I walked into a room. Him 'bumping into' Belinda constantly. Her buying saucy undies allegedly aimed at titillating the hapless Simon. Her ill-disguised jealousy of Alexis. How long had it been going on? Years possibly. And here she was now, in my apartment, tipsily confessing to having been unfaithful during her marriage. And with no idea that I already knew the identity of her lover.

Belinda knowing that Hugh hasn't been killed in a car crash, but still pretending he has, clearly changes everything.

I lie awake in bed the night after our meeting at the café, trying to work it out, but my increasingly tired brain just goes round in circles. And how on earth does Alexis fit into this dynamic? Was Hugh really making a play for her, or was Belinda just saying that to throw me off the scent of her own betrayal? What about Hugh himself? Why would he go along with a deception that only leads to him losing ownership of his beloved home? Was he being blackmailed by someone? By Jamie Molcan? It makes no sense.

One thing is glaringly obvious, and I take steps to make it happen as soon as I've said goodbye to that viper Belinda. I can't afford to waste any time.

I'm going to have to go back to Mullens End.

THIRTY-THREE

15 AUGUST

I only phone Justine Doherty once my flight has landed on Sunday morning. I want to minimise any chatter about my return by not giving her too much notice.

'Justine, it's Juliet,' I say, when she picks up, trying to keep my tone as calm and unemotional as I can. Which is difficult, given everything that's running through my head.

There's that tiny, tight pause that happens when people are shocked to hear from you but trying to hide it. 'Juliet! My goodness. Hi! How are you doing?'

'I'm at Heathrow... I need to come back to Benfield, but obviously I don't want to go to Mullens End... is it okay if I stay with you guys? Just for a few days?'

'That's fine,' Justine reassures me. 'Patrick and I will be working though. Will you be okay to fend for yourself?'

'Of course.'

'It's perfect timing, because the kids are in Galway with Patrick's folks and Daciana has gone back to Romania to visit her family, so you can stay in the nanny's flat.'

'Thanks, Justine, I'm so grateful. And there's one other thing...'

'Go on.'

'Please don't mention my being here to anyone. Not yet anyway. Look, I'll explain as soon as I can, I promise.'

On the day of Hugh's funeral, I came very close to confiding my suspicions that things didn't add up when Justine came into the library looking for me. I thought better of it, because although I'm pretty certain I can trust her, it's a different story with Patrick. After a few drinks, he tends to become a bit lairy, and if Justine were to repeat what I'd told her, I couldn't be sure it would remain within the sanctity of the Doherty marriage. For the same reason, I don't plan to tell her everything now.

When I departed for Italy, I left my car at my parents' house, knowing my father would keep the battery charged and maintain it for me until I needed it again. But I can't really go and fetch it without being coerced into staying with them, so instead I rent a car. I put classical music on the radio to try to help me relax, but it doesn't work. Underneath my tan, my knuckles turn pale as I grip the steering wheel for the entire twenty-five miles to Nether Benfield.

As I come into the village on the approach road from the A24, I'm held up behind a couple of heavy tipper trucks, blowing dirt all over my windscreen. They turn off down a track, and as I pass, I see excavators, rollers and other earth-moving equipment on a cleared patch of land. 'Welcome to Meadowcroft' proclaims a large poster depicting an artist's sketch of idealised houses in green surroundings. 'Call to reserve your plot.'

So it's happening. Whatever the depth of the entanglement between Hugh and Jamie Molcan, he has clearly failed to stop the development.

The Dohertys live in Glebe Farmhouse, a rambling red-brick place on the opposite edge of the village to the Langridges.

Justine greets me warmly and shows me into the nanny's 'flat', a self-contained studio over one of the outbuildings. Daciana's belongings have been discreetly tidied away, fresh flowers arranged and the best guest bedlinen put to use.

'Will you be joining us for supper?' Justine asks. 'Just us obviously, since the kids are away.'

I'm extremely grateful that they are, because the Doherty children are friends with the Langridge children and too young to be entrusted with keeping my presence a secret.

'I've got a few things to take care of, so can we play it by ear? Eat when you would have eaten anyway and if I can, I'd love to join you.' I place a hand on Justine's shoulder. 'Look, sorry about all the cloak-and-dagger stuff, but there are some things to do with... with the estate... that need sorting out without attention being drawn. If that makes sense.'

Justine, ever shrewd, narrows her eyes slightly. 'Are you all right, Juliet? You're not in some kind of trouble?'

I shake my head. 'I will explain soon, I promise.'

'All right then, but before you go, come into the kitchen and have a quick cup of tea. There's someone there who'll want to see you.'

And there, curled up on the rug next to the range, is Jeff. He whimpers and squirms with delight when he sees me.

'We couldn't bear to rehome him, so he's become a fixture. The kids adore him, of course.'

I feel a rush of emotion at this flesh-and-blood reminder of my former life, and tears prick at the back of my eyes as I bend to pet him. 'Oh, thank you, Justine. I'm so glad. I didn't like leaving him with Alexis, even though she said she'd take care of him.'

'She was straight on the phone to us the minute you left,' says Justine drily, handing me a mug of tea. 'Didn't waste any time at all. But don't worry,' she adds briskly, seeing my worried look. 'He fits in here just fine. Couldn't imagine life without him, in fact.'

As soon as I've finished my tea, I get into the hire car and drive to Mullens End. The first thing I notice is that the garden looks unkempt. The grass hasn't been cut, the bins are overflowing, the pool in need of cleaning and the rose bushes tarnished with dead blooms. I had assumed that Alexis would want to keep Pete on, but he would never allow the place to look like this.

I unlock the back door and let myself in. The place smells as neglected as the garden looks. There's a mug on the draining board, rinsed but not properly washed. Instinctively, I pick it up and put it in the dishwasher. I open the fridge. There's a dried-out hunk of cheddar, some salami, a few yoghurts and half a pint of milk. I take out the milk and examine it. The expiry date's still several days away, so it can't have been here all that long.

Upstairs, my former bedroom looks pretty much as it was when I last slept there, except that the bed has been made rather sloppily, and in the bathroom the toothpaste is on the vanity counter rather than in the tooth mug, and the cap is off, with chalky white smudges on the marble. The towels hang untidily from the rail, rather than being folded neatly as I would have left them. I reach out and touch them, the slight dampness under my fingers confirming my suspicion that at least one of them has been used recently. Most of my clothes are now in Italy, but all of Hugh's things still hang in the wardrobes in the dressing room. I go in there and take out a jacket, putting it to my face to inhale the familiar sandalwood and leather of his aftershave. The scent of betrayal. My stomach contracts, painfully.

In the blue room, the bed is unmade and Alexis's perfume still hangs in the air, even though her belongings are gone. Back on the principal landing again, some instinct drives me up the stairs to the top floor. There are a couple of guest rooms up there, but it's mostly used for storage. I open every door until eventually I find it, shoved to the back of the smallest guest room's wardrobe. Alexis's large silver suitcase.

I drag it out onto the carpet and open it. Her clothes, shoes, make-up and accessories are all in there, but shoved in roughly and haphazardly in one huge tangle, the clothes unfolded, tufts of fake hair from her extensions visible here and there. This was all the stuff she had here at Mullens End, so if she went away on a trip, wouldn't she need to take at least some of it with her? I disentangle the neon-green bikini she wore when she swam in the pool. If she's gone to Ibiza, surely she'll need swimwear, and the bottle of factor thirty that's still here in the case? A cold, sick feeling runs through my body, and I run down both flights of stairs, through the kitchen and down the path to the mausoleum, retrieving the keys from the lockbox on the exterior wall. I unlock the door of the building and then – once inside – the door to the crypt.

I open the vault door and stare at the coffin, the one with Hugh's name on the brass plate, the same one that he lay in alive, to trick me. The lid is screwed down, of course. I look at the brass fixings, unsure what sort of tool I would need to remove them. Unsure if I even dare do it. Instead, I place a hand on the edge of the oak rim and push it hard. It's not empty, that's clear from the resistance I meet. If it were empty, it would slide easily on its shelf. But no, there's something in there. Something heavy: as heavy as a dead body. Goosebumps prickle on my arms and I turn and run back to the car, not even stopping to return the bunch of keys to the lockbox. I don't want to be in the place a second longer.

A couple of minutes later, I'm pulling up outside a late-1970s semi in a cul-de-sac just off the village high street.

I'm welcomed warmly by Pete's wife, June, who insists on making tea, even though I've only just had some at Glebe Farmhouse.

'So where are you working now, Pete?' I ask, perched on the edge of a chintz-covered sofa.

'He's not,' says June briskly, proffering a plate of chocolate biscuits. 'He's finally retired, and about time too.'

Pete nods in a resigned way that makes me suspect he misses the excuse to leave the house every day.

'Well, I'm sure you have plenty of wonderful things to fill your time with...Listen, Pete, I need your help with something a little... sensitive.'

'I expect it's to do with poor Hugh's death,' June sighs. She picks up the empty teapot. 'I'll leave you both to it.'

Once we're alone, I ask Pete about the security camera he installed just after the incident where the car tyres were slashed. Discreetly, as Hugh was insistent they shouldn't be obvious. 'D'you know what happened to the recorded footage? I assume there were digital files of some sort?'

'Yep,' Pete confirms gruffly. 'I do know, as it goes. I downloaded it all every few days and backed it up to my own PC.'

He falls silent again, looking at me expectantly. I feel my cheeks flush slightly as I ask, 'The night of Hugh's accident... do you think you could show me what was recorded on that night?'

He leads me into the dining room, where a desk in the corner has a computer terminal, a printer and various pieces of equipment that I don't recognise. I'm a little surprised at first, but remind myself that security and surveillance were once the major component of his day job. We watch the footage from the night of the second of July, and there it is: the silver car driven by 'DI Hightower', entering the gates of Mullens End. I get Pete to pause the playback and take a photo of the car registration plate.

'Do you think if I took this to the police, they'd look up the car's owner on their database for me?'

Pete shakes his head firmly. 'Not unless it was part of an ongoing investigation, and even then, they wouldn't disclose the owner's details to a member of the public such as yourself. There are strict rules about that.'

My shoulders slump, and I let out my breath in a little sigh of frustration.

'The only other way is to get the information off the dark web. I take it you've heard of it?' He's looking at me directly now.

I nod. 'Yes, but I wouldn't have a clue how.'

'I could do it for you,' Pete offers. 'We had to learn how to access it when I was in the Specials.'

I stare at him, wide-eyed. 'You'd do that?'

'If it helps you find out what happened to Mr M, of course.'

Dear Pete, so devoted to his former employer. *If only he knew the truth.*

'How long do you think it would take you? I'm staying with the Dohertys for now, but I'm not sure how long I'll be around.'

'Leave it with me, Mrs M.'

Four hours later, just as Justine and I are clearing up after the evening meal, Pete appears on the doorstep of Glebe Farm-house. Without saying a word, he hands me a folded-up piece of paper and touches his right hand to his forehead in a salute, before driving off into the night.

THIRTY-FOUR

16 AUGUST

The silver car is registered to an address in Bracknell, around thirty miles away.

I drive there as soon as I'm out of bed the next morning, and find myself on a modern housing estate on the south-west side of the town. There's no car parked on the driveway or by the kerb outside. I check my lipstick and smooth my hair in the driver's mirror of the hire car before walking up the path of 32 Moorhead Drive and ringing the doorbell.

A trim, neatly dressed woman in her seventies opens the door and points to a sign in the hall window that reads 'POLITE NOTICE: *No* junk mail. *No* cold callers. *No* canvassers.'

'I'm sorry,' I say, giving as winning a smile as I can muster. 'Are you Mrs Golding? Mrs Audrey Golding?'

She frowns impatiently. 'Can I ask what this is regarding?'

'You're the registered owner of a silver Vauxhall Vectra, is that right?'

'Yes, but—'

'Are you the only person who drives the car? Only it was

recorded on camera entering my property on the night of the second of July.'

Audrey Golding presses her hand to her cheek, looking concerned now. 'I hardly use it myself. My son, Alan, he borrows it from time to time, when he needs a car for something. He's got it now, as it happens.'

'So it would have been Alan driving it on that night in July?'

'I suppose it must have been, but, look, what's this about? Are you from the police? Is he in some sort of trouble?'

I shake my head. 'No, no, he's not in trouble, please don't worry.'

He might be, I think. *He might well be.*

'Oh good.' She sags a little with relief, clutching the door frame.

'But I do need to speak to him, if you can tell me where he is?'

'He's working at the moment. He's an actor.'

Of course he is. That makes total sense. An acting pal of Alexis's.

'He's doing summer rep at the Connaught Theatre in Worthing. *Noises Off.*' She smiles proudly. 'He's Lloyd Dallas. It's the lead role.'

'Thank you,' I say sincerely. 'And sorry to disturb you.'

Back in the car, I consult the satnav, then head back towards the M25 for the hour and a half's drive to Worthing. I arrive just before midday, as it's starting to rain. Marine Parade is crowded with miserable-looking holidaymakers with the hoods of their cagoules up, battling with umbrellas being turned inside out by the strong sea breeze. Should bring punters into the theatre, I think, checking the performance times on my phone. As anticipated, there's a matinee, starting at 2.30.

I park in the multistorey on the high street, and position myself at the stage door of the theatre, my face hidden by my own umbrella. Sure enough, just after one, I recognise a familiar figure approaching. The sandy goatee is gone, but there's no doubt it's him.

I step into his path. 'DS Hightower?'

He stops in his tracks, blinking at me, and his pale skin colours faintly. 'I'm sorry—'

'Or is it Alan Golding? You remember me, I take it? Juliet Mullen?'

He's very pale now. 'What do you want?'

'I would have thought that was obvious.'

He runs his fingers through his damp hair, turning his face up towards the sky, as though avoiding looking at me will make me go away.

'It needn't take long,' I tell him.

'Look, I've got to be on stage in just over an hour, and we always do a technical run through before the performance. Can you come back later?'

'No.' I'm just about managing to remain polite, but my voice is firm.

Realising I won't be deterred, Golding leads me through the stage door, along a narrow passageway and into a windowless dressing room. There's a small, grimy sofa and a messy dressing table, every square inch of its surface taken up with greetings cards, takeaway coffee cups, an empty wine bottle, an overflowing ashtray. A couple of wilting helium balloons hang next to it.

'I'm the lead, so I get this to myself.' He moves some clothes off the sofa so I can sit down before sitting at his dressing table. I remain standing.

'I'm guessing it was Alexis who arranged for you and that woman to impersonate police detectives?' I ask, coming straight to the point. 'Only it doesn't really seem like my husband's style.'

Golding exhales heavily and rubs his forehead with his fingertips.

'I take it you know my husband is alive?'

As he nods, I feel a fresh reverberation of shock at the confirmation of what has only been supposition so far.

'Have you no shame?' I spit. 'Or did it at least occur to you that what you were doing – impersonating a police officer – was illegal. Did you think about that?'

He picks up a tube of panstick and turns it over and over, his fingers trembling slightly. 'Of course I did.'

'And you were okay with that? With letting a woman believe her spouse of ten years had just been killed? You could surely see that I believed it, and that I was suffering. Because I don't know what Alexis told you about our marriage, but it wasn't all bad. I did love him.'

'I'm sorry,' he mumbles. 'I can see now that it was wrong. But I hadn't worked in a long time and I was up to my neck in debt. And I was being offered a very substantial sum in cash. I felt I had no choice.'

'How much?'

'Ten grand for me, seven for Naomi... DC Carter. That was for our expenses too, and I saved a bit by using my mum's car instead of hiring one. Is that how you found me?'

'Yes.'

He clearly has more to say, so I wait for him to go on.

'Listen, there's something else you need to know.' He lets out a long sound that's half groan, half howl. It comes off as melodramatic, but then he is an actor. 'Oh God... where do I start? The woman you refer to as Alexis; she's not.'

I stare blankly. 'Not what?'

'She's not really Alexis Lambert. She's called Summer Willetts, and we met when we were in a play together.'

The sensation that hits me is that of a bucket of ice-cold water being tipped over my head. 'What d'you mean... you mean the real Alexis Lambert knows about this, or—'

'No,' Golding shakes his head. 'Alex – that's what she likes to be known as now...' He frowns, remembering. 'Sorry – she is "they" now, I believe. Anyway, Alex is a friend of Summer's from drama school, but they now live in California permanently.'

So not only is Golding not really a police officer, but 'Alexis' is not really my husband's cousin and the heiress to Mullens End. I think back to the Instagram account that didn't seem quite real, the vagueness of the stories about her upbringing. The scale of the deception I've been subjected to is only just starting to sink in. The back of my neck prickles. I'm unable to formulate more questions, or even speak.

'I appreciate that's a hell of a shock, but since you're here, can you tell me where Summer is now?' Golding asks. 'Only I've been trying to get in touch with her for the past week. She's not replied to any of my texts and her phone seems to be switched off. And that's not like her; she's always on the bloody thing.'

I shake my head slowly. 'She told me a couple of days ago that she was going to Ibiza. She's certainly not at Mullens End.'

'Maybe that's it then. Maybe she's partied off her tits.' He gives a dry laugh.

I picture the silver suitcase, hidden in the attic wardrobe. *Maybe not.*

'So, apart from paying you, what exactly did she tell you about this job? About why?'

'Not a whole lot. The bare bones, really. She said she was fucking this married guy, Alexis Lambert's cousin, and that she'd let him think she *was* Alexis...' He has the good grace to look embarrassed at his choice of words. 'And that they had this plan to be together, but it involved him going away for a while and pretending to be dead. Look, I'm sorry, but for me and Naomi it was just another acting job. We played a part and got paid for it. But I mean it when I say I am genuinely sorry. I realise this must be awful for you.'

There's a knock on the door and a disembodied voice says, 'Principles to stage in five, please.'

I get to my feet, picking up my damp umbrella and shaking it. 'And apart from you and your actor pal, who knows about... all this?'

Golding shrugs. 'I really have no idea. Listen, are you planning to go to the police?'

But I turn and walk out of the room without answering him.

THIRTY-FIVE

17 AUGUST

It's perfectly pleasant staying in the Dohertys' annexe, but the absurdity and sheer wrongness of my situation is starting to chafe after two nights.

I'm also aware that the children will be back in a couple of days, followed by Daciana. So the morning after my trip to Worthing, I tell Justine that I'm going to visit my parents before flying back to Bologna.

But there's just one thing I need to do in Benfield first.

When I arrive at Birch Cottage, Belinda is in the garden, hanging washing on the line. She's wearing denim cut-offs under a loose white linen shirt, and her thick blonde hair is swept up in a ponytail. She caught the sun on her brief foray abroad and looks healthy, glowing.

I stand watching her for a few seconds before she realises I'm there. Yes, I'm showing a degree of sensitivity in confronting her while Simon is out at work, but this is for the children's sake rather than for hers. She doesn't deserve this consideration for herself.

Inevitably, Rocket scents me and runs yapping to my side, alerting Belinda to my presence. Rufus is playing with a miniature cricket bat and ball and the angelic blonde twin girls have a doll's tea set spread out on a rug on the lawn. It's an idyllic scene.

'Jules!' Belinda shrieks and claps her hands together. 'What are you doing here? I thought you were still in Italy! I've only just got back myself.'

She seems flustered, but throws her arms round me and envelops me in a warm hug. I don't return it, remaining rigid with my arms by my sides.

Now she looks nervous. 'Is something wrong?'

I stare at her for a long time, trying to decide where to begin. What's worse, I'm wondering – sleeping with someone's husband while pretending to be their friend, or pretending to believe that husband is dead when you know damn well they're alive?

'You tell me,' I say coldly.

'It's not Luca, I hope? Everything's all right with him?'

'Cut the crap, Belinda. You know exactly what's wrong.'

She tries to lead me over to the garden chairs, but I stay stiff as a statue, my arms folded across the front of my body. That broad smile, the one that exposes the charming gap in her front teeth, melts away. 'What is it? I swear I have no idea what—'

'You know Hugh's not dead, don't you?'

She startles, and the colour drains from her face.

'I... I didn't...' She's stammering now.

'How long, Belinda? How long have you known he was faking it?'

There is a moment's hesitation, before she speaks in a rush. 'I didn't know at first, I swear. I thought he'd been killed in his car, just like everybody did.'

'So when did you find out?'

'The night before the funeral. Hugh told me then.'

Disbelief and fury course through my body; though at this moment it's mostly fury. 'You knew at the funeral?' I spit. 'And you let me suffer through the whole bloody business of saying mass for the dead and interring the coffin. Which was presumably empty.'

She avoids my gaze, turning towards the children, who are looking at us quizzically now. 'It's all right, kids, I'm just having a chat with Auntie Juliet,' she calls.

'Even if we ignore the question of why the two of you were putting me through that sham, there's still the small matter of you having an affair with him for God knows how long.'

Her mouth opens and shuts soundlessly like a fish.

'And please don't insult me by denying it, Belinda. If you have any feeling for me at all, then don't do that.'

Her shoulders slump and she looks down at her bare feet. The polish on her toes is chipped, as always, I note. 'How did you find out?' she asks, her voice barely above a whisper.

'I'm not going to tell you that.' My own voice is hard, so hard I barely recognise it. 'It's time you started telling *me* some things. Starting with how long it was going on.'

'Since Rufus was tiny.' She has the grace to look shame-faced.

I glance over at the little boy with his white-blonde hair, now swinging his bat around happily.

'So what? The two of you just fancied each other and thought you may as well start screwing?'

Belinda's freckled face colours an even deeper pink. 'No... I mean yes, sort of. He started flirting with me when I was pregnant. Said he found it sexy.'

I don't even try to hide my shudder of disgust.

'And then after I'd had Rufe, we just sort of gravitated towards each other, and then—'

I hold up a hand. 'I don't need a blow-by-blow account of the affair,' I hiss. 'Bad enough having to imagine it. But I do need you to tell me how it all fits into the business of Alexis Lambert showing up and taking over Mullens End... Did you know that the woman claiming to be her, isn't really Alexis? Isn't Hugh's cousin?'

She nods, her mouth twisted with discomfort. 'Hugh told me, yes. She's really called Summer.'

'Exactly. And now she's mysteriously disappeared.'

That's when I see the expression on Belinda's face change, registering not discomfort but outright fear.

I feel the return of the same goosebumps I felt when I was in the mausoleum crypt, despite now being outside in the warmth of the sun. 'Has something happened to her? Has Hugh...? Please don't tell me he's—'

'It was an accident!' Belinda blurts out, her voice breaking. 'He didn't mean to hurt her.'

We stare at each other, my heart is beating so hard that I can hear a thundering sound in my ears.

'You're going to have to tell me, Belinda.' When I eventually speak, it's with a calm that I really don't feel at this moment. 'If all of this outrageous scheming is some sort of scam to get me away from Mullens End so that you and Hugh can enjoy it, that's not going to work. You can be quite sure I'm not going to divorce him, not if it means you moving into my home.'

Belinda presses her palms to her flushed cheeks. 'But we... I thought Italy was where you wanted to be. You've got Stefano...'

'There is no Stefano. I made him up.' In response to her frown of confusion, I go on. 'Yes, believe it or not, you and Hugh and Summer are not the only ones who can be deceitful.' I soften my tone the merest fraction, because I need this to be over with. 'Look, I'm going to go to the police anyway, but if you tell me the truth now, I'm prepared to convince them it was nothing to do with you. But you have to tell me exactly what happened.'

She's white as a sheet now. 'All right,' she says with a nod.

And then she tells me, keeping it as concise as she can, because the children, bored now, are beginning to gravitate in our direction.

When she gets to the end, I simply nod, and say, 'Thank you.'

'Are you going to tell Simon about me and Hugh? Please, Jules—'

I shake my head. 'No, I'm not. You are.'

I drive from Birch Cottage to the Surrey Police headquarters just south of Guildford, and after a lot of explaining and insisting and waiting, I eventually get to speak to a member of CID responsible for dealing with serious crime. The whole business takes over two hours and leaves me feeling completely drained.

Back at Glebe Farmhouse, I go straight to the nanny's flat and start to fold my clothes into my case. Just as I'm emptying the bathroom shelves, there's a thundering of feet on the staircase and Justine flies into the room.

'Oh my God, Juliet, oh my God!' She stares at me wild-eyed. 'Sit down, you've got to sit down.'

I do so.

'I'm afraid this is going to come as a terrible shock, but something's happened! Something unbelievable! Vikram just phoned to tell me.'

I look back at her calmly, already knowing what she's about to say.

'Hugh's back! Apparently, he wasn't dead, he was abducted. He's alive.'

PART SIX

HUGH

THIRTY-SIX

15 AUGUST

The way I see it, none of this was really my idea.

All right, yes, I did choose to enter into an extramarital relationship with Belinda Langridge. And yes, I did confide to her that I was less than fulfilled in my marriage to Juliet, and that I still longed for children of my own. But I wasn't necessarily planning to act on it. I hadn't spent the years before all this happened looking for a way to get my wife out of the picture while still holding on to my family home. Quite the opposite really; I'd accepted that the terms of the trust made it impossible.

But Summer Willetts changed all that by pushing her convoluted little plan onto me, and then calling my bluff. Would things have been different if she had really been my distant cousin Alexis and not some jumped-up little actress turned big-time con artist? I think they probably would.

After Belinda has raced off to Italy, to try to stall Juliet long enough for me to get into Summer's phone and explain her absence, I remain at Mullens End. I clear out the blue guest room and bathroom and hide Summer's case up in the attic so it looks like she has indeed gone away. Among the stuff in her bathroom, I find the stage make-up that she and her friends used to make me look dead and I hang on to it, having thought of a way it might come in useful.

Then, on Sunday afternoon, as I'm wondering whether I can risk going out to the pool for a swim, I hear the sound of car tyres on the gravel. I look out of the bedroom window and see Juliet climbing out of a metallic grey SUV, cool as you like, red lipstick in place, hair as immaculate as always. So, she didn't waste any time. Swearing under my breath, I shoot down the stairs, and run out of the back door, just as I can hear her coming into the hall through the unlocked front door. There's no time to take anything with me, but I'm counting on her not hanging around long.

While she's inside the house – presumably snooping about – I jog past the rose maze and the tennis court and out to the beech copse at the edge of the grounds. These days, the peace of the woods is ruined by the sound of earth-breaking machinery on the Meadowcroft construction site, but since it's Sunday, for once the place is silent. I'm too far from the house to hear Juliet's car leaving, so I'll have to hide out for a bit before heading back to the house and just bloody hope it's long enough.

I find a felled branch robust enough to sit on and perch there, distracting myself by scrolling through stuff on my phone. As I sit waiting for my wife to leave, you might assume that it's she – Juliet – who is uppermost in my mind. But it's not Juliet that I'm thinking of in that moment. It's Belinda.

I couldn't honestly tell you the moment that I first wanted her.

There was no *coup de foudre*, no instant moment of falling for her. I'd met her a couple of times as a teenager, but it was only after I was married that I remember noting the contrast between her appearance and Juliet's. Juliet petite and precise as a Dutch doll, always elegant, but in a rather rigid and predictable fashion. Belinda on the other hand was curvy and voluptuous, with long hair the colour of ripe corn and an outdoorsy, slightly retro style. A countrified English style. She always looked as though she had just come from a sailing regatta or – if she was dressed up – a garden party. Once we'd spoken a few times, it quickly became obvious that we'd had similar upbringings. Her father was a minor landowner and she'd been to a posh girls' boarding school. We knew some of the same people, understood the same public-school shorthand and references. Juliet, despite her Italian heritage making her look slightly exotic, had led a very mundane lower middle-class existence.

And, my God, was Belinda sexy. She'd been a bit wild, something of a party girl, in her teens and early twenties, and although by the time we met she was a married woman and a mother, she still had that dirty laugh, and a very naughty sense of humour. When our eyes met, there was a distinct twinkle in hers. For me, it all came to a head when she was pregnant with Rufus. To use the popular cliché, she bloomed. Her hair was thick and radiant with health, her skin luminous, her boobs even bigger and more voluptuous than usual. The point of no return was when I saw her breastfeeding Rufus at a lunch party somewhere. She was as lush and serene as a Madonna and I found it spell-binding. I had also recently started to bitterly regret marrying someone who'd failed to give me any children of my own. Forget about the heir and spare, there wasn't even an heir.

Our affair started soon after that, and to my delight Belinda turned out to be as much fun in the sack as she had been in my frequent fantasies about her. She was a lot freer sexually than Juliet, whose approach was always a bit buttoned-up and unimaginative. I loved fucking Belinda, and as I did so, I desperately wished it was me who could make her pregnant, not the likeable but rather gormless Simon. But how on earth could we ever make that happen if to do so would mean losing Mullens End? No wonder I was so quick to fall in with Summer Willetts' foolish plan.

As I sit waiting in the woods, all I can think about is that I need to see Belinda. I try her number for the third time that day, and for the third time she fails to pick up. This is not too unusual, since she rarely gets much time alone, especially during the school holidays. I whizz off a text asking if she's okay.

After about half an hour, I venture back down the path towards the house, and I'm relieved to see that the grey SUV has gone. But Juliet's reappearance has brought things to a head, and I know that I have to put the final part of the plan into operation. I have to pre-empt discovery by re-emerging into the world like a Cold War spy. But I can't be at Mullens End when this happens; that would raise far too many questions. Temporarily at least, I need to get clear.

Giving a fake name over the phone, I book a room at the same motel where I was dropped after the staging of my car crash, catching a bus part of the way and walking the rest, since the local taxi drivers all know me. I take a hoodie from home and keep the hood pulled up when I check in, paying with cash. The place is busy, with plenty of holiday visitors wanting easy access to London, and the distracted young receptionist barely glances up as she pushes a key card towards me.

Once I'm there, I spread out the things I've brought with me on the second of the twin beds. There are cable ties I found among Pete's tools and DIY stuff in the garage, and the stage make-up I found in Summer's bathroom.

It's time to come back from the dead.

THIRTY-SEVEN

16 AUGUST

As I said earlier, I've been living like a student for the past six weeks, with no routine and no access to proper home-cooked meals. As a result, I've dropped quite a lot of weight, which is going to reinforce my backstory perfectly. I haven't shaved for some time either, and I'm sporting an untidy reddish beard. Before I got into bed on Sunday night, I fixed a cable tie tightly around each wrist and each ankle, and this morning the result is an impressive set of red weals. Almost as if I've been held captive for some time.

When my car 'crashed' back at the beginning of July, I made sure I kept the same clothes with me at all times: a pair of light-weight chinos and a blue button-down shirt. I've worn them frequently in the meantime and not washed them, so they look convincingly grimy. I omitted to bring the same pair of loafers with me from the flat in London, but there's an easy way around that: I'll just leave off shoes altogether. The last stage of the process will be to apply some of the make-up – very subtly, of course – so that I look paler than usual. As though I haven't seen daylight for six weeks, in fact.

I put the tiny plastic kettle to boil, fish around in the collection of dusty-looking sachets for a teabag and peel open some of the miniature pots of rancid milk. Once I've made a very unsatisfactory mug of tea, I set about practising with the make-up in the tiny, airless bathroom of the motel room when there's a knock on the door. I'd been non-committal about the length of my stay when I checked in, so my guess is that it will be one of the management staff asking for an update on my plans.

'Hi,' I say briskly as I yank open the door. But the words die on my lips. Facing me is a tall, unnaturally muscular figure with a thick neck and arms bulging through a fitted sports top.

Harvey Curwen.

'All right, man?' he says with a slight upward jerk of his head.

I glance into the corridor before ushering him in. 'What the fuck are you doing here? How did you even know where I was?'

'Saw you getting off the bus,' he says nonchalantly. 'I knew right away it was you.' He looks down at my brogues, 'Recognised those, innit. No one else round here wears them.' He's still talking in his customary gangster patois. I find it wildly irritating.

'Cut the chat, Harvey,' I say grimly. 'Tell me why you're here.'

Because whatever it is, it sure as hell can't be good.

'Thing is, I need some lucci.'

I stare at him.

'Some bands, some racks. Some bag.'

'You mean money,' I say coldly.

He nods. 'Thing is, everyone thinks you're dead. Only, I know that's some bullshit.'

Ah, so this is a blackmail attempt.

I pull the bathroom door to, so that he won't see the stage make-up or the discarded cable ties. 'No, *this* is the thing, Harvey. We had an agreement. You'd keep quiet about the car and in return I'd keep quiet about your dealing in Class A's.'

'Thing is though, you ain't got no proof.'

Unfortunately he's right, although he doesn't know this. The photo I took is gone, when I disposed of my former phone.

'And I have.' He's pulling out his phone from the pocket of his tracksuit top and holding up a picture of my Range Rover in Kevin Curwen's crusher, the numberplate still clearly legible.

'The people who are supposed to have taken me could have got rid of the car,' I reason.

'Yeah, but I've got this.' He shows another photo, this time of me standing at the side of the road next to the crashed car, looking perfectly safe and well. 'And these.' He pulls up screenshots of the messages we exchanged about meeting that night.

I give a little snort of exasperation. I need this sorted quickly. 'How much?'

'Ten grand.'

I'm not surprised by the amount; I'm only surprised it's not higher. On the other hand, to a small-time provincial lowlife like Harvey Curwen, that probably seems a lot.

'Obviously I can't give it to you now.' I'm thinking, fast. I can't risk going into a bank and drawing on one of the Mullen Trust accounts. Not at such a critical stage of operations. That only leaves the cash in the safe at Mullens End. I'm not even sure how much is in there, but I'll just have to worry about that later.

'When, then?'

'Meet me back at the house, this evening. At Mullens End. Probably best leave it till after it's gone dark. And come on foot: I don't want to risk anyone recognising your scooter.'

This is going to delay my return from captivity for some hours, but there's not much I can do about that now. The Harvey problem has to be dealt with.

.   .   .

Once I'm alone again, I decide that I still can't risk being dropped off at Mullens End in a taxi. Not with the Curwen family being in the business. I avail myself of the motel's shuttle bus service into the centre of Woking and find a car rental place, where I pick up an unremarkable Korean hatchback: a Hyundai, or a Kia; I don't recall which. I drive it back to the motel and just before eight, as the light is starting to fade, I go down to the front desk to tell them I'll be staying one more night. I'm still wearing the dark hoodie and pull up the hood to prevent my face from being identified by any cameras I might pass. I couldn't really tell you why I'm doing this, it just strikes me as a good idea.

Once I'm at the house, I go straight to my study and check the safe. I used a lot of cash to hire Summer's associates, so I'm already aware there's not going to be much left. I place the bundles of notes on my desk and count them carefully. Six grand. It's still a lot of money for a teenager, I reason. Surely he'll be happy with that? Or I can offer to give him a second instalment later.

I make sure the recording on the security cameras is disabled, then pace around between the drawing room and the front hall, unable to settle. I should have stipulated an exact time to meet Harvey, I realise, rather than just 'after dark'. I could still be here at midnight.

At around nine thirty, I make out footsteps on the gravel and the beam of the security light bathes the transom window on the front door. I open it and peer out. There is Harvey Curwen, his own face also shrouded by a grey hoodie. He's come alone at least, and left his scooter behind.

'Listen,' I say, as he follows me wordlessly into the study. 'Slight issue with the cash.' I affect a casual, chummy tone. 'I haven't quite got the ten K, because obviously there's a problem with me withdrawing cash right now, but I can get it for you in the next couple of days.'

His pale eyes narrow. 'Nah,' he says simply. 'That won't do.'

'Well, I'm afraid it'll have to.' My agreeable act is dropped. 'You've not given me much notice; this is the best I can do. Take it or leave it.'

'Fink I'll leave it,' he says with a shrug. 'I'll take those photos to the cops instead.'

'Look, Harvey, I'm not making this up!' My voice rises in exasperation. I pick up the bundles of notes and thrust them in his direction. 'This is all I've got for now.' I stamp over to the safe and swing the door open to show him that it's empty. 'But, like I said, it won't take me long to get you the other four grand. I can probably get it tomorrow.'

He sucks his teeth, as if he's thinking about this. 'Bang-up,' he says after a suitably dramatic pause. 'But make it fourteen.'

I stare at him. 'What the fuck do you mean?'

'I mean the price has just gone up. It's gunna cost you twenty now.'

'What – twenty thousand pounds?'

Harvey grins his fox-like grin. 'That's it. You catch on quick.' He steps forward and prods me hard in the chest, making me lose my balance as I stagger backwards.

At that point, I snap. Something surges through me: white-hot rage mixed with the frustration and helplessness I've been feeling for the past month or more. Once I've regained my balance, I shove him back and he stumbles, losing his balance and falling to his knees. Then, while he's still down, I grab the brass doorstop; a Victorian piece in the shape of a hunting dog. Without even thinking, I bring the thing down hard on the back of his head. He tips forward, then, very slowly, a dark wet patch appears on the back of his hood, before seeping into a puddle on the carpet. He makes a strange gurgling sound.

Then there's silence.

THIRTY-EIGHT

16 AUGUST

When faced with the reality of Harvey Curwen's dead body, I don't panic.

I don't panic, because – let's face it – I've been here before. I've had a dress rehearsal in the shape of Summer Willetts. Looking back, I wonder if at some subliminal level, I meant to kill him all along. That I went there to meet him at Mullens End with that in my mind. It certainly wasn't a conscious plan. Consciously, I intended to resolve the problem by paying him off, but when he pushed me, I went into self-defence mode. I just saw red and lost it. And now... well, here we are.

Another reason for not panicking is the convenient existence of the family mausoleum. If I had to find a shovel, drag a body the considerable distance into the woods and dig a six-foot hole I would no doubt be considerably more stressed. But thanks to Ernest Mullen's rank snobbery and grandiose ideas, I'm in possession of a purpose-built corpse storage facility right here in the grounds.

Even so, what I have to do is far from easy. Harvey is tall, muscular and therefore heavy. The term 'dead weight' makes so much sense all of a sudden. At least when I moved Summer's body, I had someone on hand to help me. I hit on the idea of fetching Pete's wheelbarrow from one of the sheds and using that to wheel Harvey from the back door and along the path to the mausoleum.

Once in the crypt, I have another decision to make. I have to choose which of the existing coffins to use. I remember my father telling me at my grandfather's internment that it takes between eighty and a hundred years for skeletal remains to turn to dust. So the older, the better. My great-grandmother's coffin has been here the longest, but she was a tiny woman no more than five feet tall, so size is an issue. In the end, I decide on the coffin of Ernest himself. It seems weirdly fitting, and he has been dead since 1937.

I fetch a wrench from the garage to prize open the lid of the dusty mahogany casket. There are what look like some teeth inside, and a few shreds of fabric, but – to my huge relief – that's all. With some difficulty, I heave Harvey Curwen inside, keeping his hood arranged so that I'm not forced to look at his face.

After the lid has closed, I jump out of my skin at a sound coming from inside the coffin. Then I realise it is the vibrating of Harvey's phone, still inside one of his pockets. It would almost be funny if it wasn't so grim. I decide it's safest to leave it where it is rather than be caught with it on me. I wonder how many more times the silence of the crypt will be shattered by the buzz of a teenager's phone before the battery dies.

Once the heavy casket has been slid back into its vault, I lean against the wall. My heart is hammering against my ribs and I'm shaking. Within seconds, I'm also gasping for breath as if a ten-pound weight is pressing down on my sternum. For a few seconds, I think it must be a coronary brought on by the physical exertions, but slowly it dawns that I am – for the very first time in my life – experiencing a panic attack. I breathe slowly and deeply and eventually the searing suffocation recedes, although my blood is still thudding through my vessels.

After a couple of minutes, I gather myself sufficiently to return the wheelbarrow and the wrench and set about cleaning up the traces of Harvey's blood from the carpet in my study and the stretch of floor between there and the back door and, most importantly, the brass doorstop. It's tedious work which takes me until about one in the morning. Then I drive back to the motel, reattach cable ties to my wrists and ankles and fall into a heavy, oblivious sleep on top of the bed.

The next morning, I don't shower or shave, dressing in the chinos and shirt from the night of my staged accident. They're grimy from the effort of pushing a large car into a ditch and blood-stained from when I cut my hand getting the car onto the Curwens' tow truck. In my mind's eye, I see Harvey Curwen: first, brash and confident as he handled the recovery truck, and then lifeless and broken, in my great-grandfather's coffin. I push the image away, telling myself yet again that this wasn't my fault. He turned greedy, and it would never have stopped. He'd have gone on and on demanding money. Besides, he was a lowlife drug dealer. If I'm going to get through this, I'm just going to have to forget about him. And, trust me, one way or another, I'm going to come through this mess.

Once I've given myself a sickly pallor with the make-up, I bin everything else I brought with me, check out of the room and return the car. It's only when I'm walking away from the rental office that I remember the need not to show up in a different pair of shoes. I throw my perfectly good brogues into a bin and go barefoot. The lack of footwear will surely lend credibility to my story. Hell, even *I'm* starting to believe my story.

I hobble to the police station in Woking and position myself outside the gated entrance. Then, having first withheld my number, I look up the number of the village surgery online and dial the contact number.

'Hi, can you put me through to Dr Vikram Kuchar? Yes, it's extremely urgent! Vik, it's me. It's Hugh... Hugh Mullen.'

I wait for the shocked silence, then the inevitable question.

'Yes, yes, I swear. It really is me.'

Vikram abandons the patients waiting in his surgery to come and collect me in person. He embraces me tightly and keeps repeating. 'I can't believe it. I can't bloody believe it.'

I tell him that I have just come out of the police station after being interviewed and giving a lengthy statement. That I went straight there after being dropped from a car in a layby on Chertsey Road in the early hours of the morning. Of course, in reality, I haven't been inside the cop shop, nor do I have any intention of doing so. The last thing I need right now is law enforcement anywhere near me.

'So, let me get this straight,' Vik says as he drives me back to his house in Nether Benfield, glancing at me constantly in his driver's mirror. 'You say these local property developer thugs ran your car off the road, then abducted you from the scene and kept you locked up somewhere?'

I hold up my wrists, bony from my recent weight loss and scored with red marks from the ties.

Vik flinches at the sight of them. 'And you don't know where?'

'No idea. I was kept blindfolded, in some basement somewhere. From the distance I was driven, I'd say it was in London: probably in one of the buildings JM Developments owns. They kept me out of the way long enough to get the planning permission passed on the Meadowcroft site. Presumably they knew that as long as I was around, I was going to do my utmost to block it.'

'But I don't understand!' Vik exclaims. He slaps the steering wheel as the car comes to a halt at some lights. 'Police officers came to the house and told Juliet you were dead. And there must have been a body, because she held a funeral for you.'

'They can't have been real police, can they?' I reason. 'They must have been people on Molcan's payroll. Same goes for the undertakers. Easy enough for them to produce an empty coffin.'

I'm hoping to God that Summer was right when she said Juliet hadn't mentioned going to view my body to anyone.

'That's... well, frankly that's just bizarre. Why on earth would they go to such lengths?' As he asks the question, Vik is still looking at my reflection in the mirror. An expression crosses his face that chills my blood.

He doesn't believe me.

Whatever his private doubts, for the time being, Vikram goes along with my story.

I chose him to 'come out' to because as a doctor he's going to be making an assessment of my physical condition, and that should lend some weight to my story. After all, I do look as if I've been living rough for a while.

He and Faith accommodate me in their comfortable spare room at the Old Rectory, and sure enough, he insists on giving me a physical, once I've had a bath and eaten the homemade soup and toast that Faith has made.

'Hmmm,' he says, as he puts a stethoscope to my ribs 'You've definitely lost some weight.'

'They fed me,' I tell Vik. 'But pretty much the bare minimum.'

'Hmmm,' he says again, putting on a blood pressure cuff. 'Everything seems okay, but your heart rate's a bit high. You should probably get a panel of bloods done, just to be sure there's no kidney damage. I can arrange for you to come into the surgery if you like?'

He says this without meeting my eye. I'd decided him being

a doctor was a plus, but the trouble is, he's also a highly intelligent and shrewd man. Perhaps I misjudged the situation and I should have phoned Patrick Doherty, who's more interested in whisky and the craic.

As it is, Vikram now phones Patrick and Justine, who will probably then tell the Langridges. I'm hoping Belinda will see my reappearance as a sign that I'm serious about moving our plan forward. By now, I'm desperate for contact with her, but I've heard nothing. And, of course, I have to pretend that it's Juliet I can't wait to see. I tell Vik and Faith that I've phoned her. I haven't. Fortunately, although I saw her with my own eyes at Mullens End, everyone else seems to think she's still in Italy. But the way this small community works, wherever Juliet is now, it won't be long before she hears the news.

That evening, I tell Faith and Vik that I need to stretch my legs and that I'm going to have a walk. They seem doubtful, but I assure them I feel fine.

'You'll be keen to go up to the house and sort things out with your cousin,' Faith observes. 'Has anyone told her what's going on?'

'I've no idea,' I lie.

'Maybe leave that until tomorrow,' she suggests. 'Get a decent night's sleep first.'

'Good idea,' I agree. 'I won't go very far.'

I will go to Mullens End soon, of course I will. I can't wait to be living back there openly, and for everything to be normal. But as I set off, dressed in borrowed clothes and shoes that are all slightly too small, there's somewhere else I need to go first. I walk from the Old Rectory to Birch Cottage and ring the doorbell.

Simon answers the door, and for a few seconds he doesn't

recognise me. Once he's seen past the beard and the longer hair and the too-short linen trousers, his face darkens.

'I need to speak to Belinda,' I tell him.

'She's not here.' This is clearly a lie. From the top of the staircase, I can hear one of the Langridge children shouting 'Mummy!' What's also apparent is that Simon knows about my affair with his wife. Rather than being delighted at his old friend returning from the dead, his expression is stony.

'Simon, mate, we both know she is. And I really need to talk to her. It needn't take long.'

'Don't "mate" me!' It's almost a snarl. I've never seen this side of him before: Simon, who is affable, almost to the point of cluelessness. 'Frankly, you've got a bloody nerve showing up here.'

I try to pass him, but he blocks me with, 'Pity we didn't get to bury you for real.'

The door is slammed hard in my face.

There's no way I'm going to give up now. I mean, I can't, not after the terrible price that's been paid for me to get to this point. I go on thumping on the door, making the frame shake as the deadlock puts pressure on it. After about ten minutes, it's opened and Belinda herself appears. She's wearing a cotton smock dress and her hair is loose. She's a little pale, but to me she's still ravishing: ripe and womanly.

'Darling!'

She wriggles free of my embrace and steps out onto the porch, letting the door close behind her. 'You've got to stop this; you're upsetting the children,' she admonishes me in a low whisper.

'Come on now, Belle, don't pretend you're not pleased to see me.'

She still doesn't smile, and takes a few steps back when I reach for her. Unease ripples through me.

'I'm back now: no more lying doggo while I pretend to be

dead. We can finally be together, and have that family of our own, like we—'

She interrupts me. 'Juliet knows everything.'

I feel the knot tighten in the pit of my stomach. 'What do you mean?' I run my hand through my hair. It's clean now but still unkempt and in need of a cut.

'I mean she's back in Benfield. She came straight back from Italy after I did, and she came to see me.'

'Wait, wait...' I hold up a hand. 'You mean she knows about Summer?'

Belinda's face contracts with anguish. 'Look, she already knew half of it, and I had to fill in the gaps for her. She was threatening me with the police.'

The chill inside extends through my whole body, turning my hands and feet quite numb. 'You mean... she knows Summer's dead?'

She nods, tears appearing in the corner of her eyes.

'Come on now, it was an accident,' I bluster. 'We both know that, and I'm sure we can convince the police of it, given our stories will match up. All right, so we should have told the authorities at the time, but that's a minor offence. My lawyers will have a quiet word with the chief constable and we'll get away with a rap on the knuckles. The thing is, we've got Mullens, and we can be together.'

She's shaking her head vigorously, frustrated now. 'But we haven't though! Juliet's going to divorce you as soon as possible, but after Summer, she's going to make that as difficult and expensive as she can. You'll never be able to afford to stay at Mullens End. And you told me you're not allowed to sell it, so presumably that means you'll have to rent it out.' She lowers her voice. 'With Summer's body still hidden there... what will happen if it's found? Hugh, when will you accept that this whole thing has gone horribly wrong?'

I ignore her objections and continue. 'Come on, Belle, I still think there's a chance we can salvage this. Okay, so I expect Jules is pretty furious with me now, but I'm sure she and I can come to some agreement. She's got her life in Italy, she's got this new Italian chap – what's his name? Why would she want to come back? And if she stays away, then we're home free.'

But Belinda is still shaking her head. 'There is no Italian man. She made that up. She intends to come back, and whatever happens... about the other stuff... she's going to make sure you lose the house.'

I pause, trying to refocus. 'She says that now, but I bet you she won't go through with it. Besides, you're still young enough to have more children, like we planned. You'll be the lady of the house, and we can—'

'Hugh, there is no "we". Not anymore.'

She's weeping now, and she looks so helpless, I just want to sweep her into my arms.

'You and I aren't going to get Mullens End: it didn't work. I've told Simon everything, and I'm hoping he and I will be able to fix things.' As I stand there frozen with disbelief, she turns and walks back towards the front door. 'It's over Hugh; I'm sorry.'

And with that, I've lost the woman I probably loved more than anyone else in my life. The woman all of this was for.

I'm thinking hard as I walk through the village and back up the lane to Mullens End. The tight shoes are giving me a painful blister and it's starting to bleed.

I force myself to stay calm, and focus on damage limitation. Okay, so things haven't worked out with Belinda. The dream of a house full of little blonde children is over. But, hell, there's no reason I can't patch things up with Juliet. We've lived together for years at Mullens End, after all, and mostly it's been fine. We can muddle along all right together without divorcing: she can spend more time out in Italy if she wants. And perhaps, in time, Belinda will get bored of that oaf Simon again, and find her way back to my bed. The main thing is that I'll still be living at Mullens End. That's what's important, after all. Mullens End is in my blood. It's where I belong. What else has all this drama been for?

My spirits lift as I round the drive and see that beautiful neoclassical façade, the large sash windows glinting gold and pink in the warm late summer twilight. The last of the linden blossoms hit my nostrils with their sweet, pungent smell. The smell of home.

And then as well as the light refracted by the windows of the façade, I pick up the gleam of a blue light, coming and going. A flashing blue light. As I limp the last hundred yards to reach the arc of gravel at the front of the house, I see not one but two police cars parked there, and several uniformed officers. They have dogs with them, so there's no point attempting to run. I stay rooted to the spot: head up, shoulders back.

One of the policemen approaches me, holding out a piece of official-looking paper. 'Mr Mullen? Mr Hugh Mullen?'

'Yes.'

'We've got a warrant to search your property.'

It's as though I've been thumped in the solar plexus. I can only watch helplessly as the lead officer gives a hand signal to the dog handlers and they set off in the direction of the mausoleum.

PART SEVEN

BELINDA

THIRTY-NINE

25 OCTOBER

The item appeared on the BBC website yesterday.

> *Art dealer and landowner Hugh Mullen, 36, was at Guildford Crown Court for sentencing today for the manslaughter of Harvey Curwen, 19. Mullen, who pleaded guilty to all charges, expressed remorse for what he termed 'two tragic accidents'. He was sentenced to fourteen years, to run concurrently with a five-year sentence for perverting the course of justice, thirty months for preventing the lawful burial of Summer Willetts, 29, and ten months for the offence of obstructing the coroner.*
>
> *'Our entire family is devastated at the loss of a son, brother and nephew,' said Brian Curwen, 47, speaking outside the court afterwards, 'but at least we can now grieve knowing justice has been done.*

'"Tragic accident", my arse,' Simon sneered when he saw it. 'His brief obviously did a deal with the CPS.' He was referring to the fact that at his arrest in August Hugh was charged with Harvey Curwen's murder, but the secondary charge of manslaughter was also added to the indictment. 'Hedging their bets with the two charges. He claims it was self-defence, but what it boils down to is the local plod didn't have enough evidence to make the murder charge stick.'

I don't respond. My mind is elsewhere, calculating that if he's released on licence after serving half his sentence, Hugh will be out in seven years. And then he'll be straight back to Nether Benfield, I'm sure of it. Despite me breaking things off with him, he's proved his loyalty to me by never mentioning me being at Mullens End the day Summer fell down the stairs. Juliet stayed silent too, as she promised. As far as the authorities were concerned, that would have been it, but, oh no, when Simon read about the details of Summer's death, he worked out that it was the afternoon just before my trip to Italy when I suddenly disappeared and left the children with a neighbour. He banged on and on about it until I confessed that, yes, I had been there and helped Hugh put Summer's body in the crypt.

And Simon being Simon, he then insisted that I go to the police and confess. All part of his punishing me for the affair, I suppose. So I went voluntarily to speak to a very nice detective at Surrey Police headquarters in Guildford, and they took a statement from me. I was held there for several hours, which was hellish enough in itself, but, in the end, after consulting with the CPS, it was decided that I had been subject to coercion and that I wouldn't be charged with preventing lawful burial. Instead, I received a police caution, which stays on my record for six years. I could tell Simon was a bit disappointed. 'You were lucky,' he said, as though he wanted the mother of his children to go to prison. But given what I've put him through, I can't really blame him. Him being able to forgive *me* is what really matters.

· · ·

Hugh may not have been a major story on the national news, but here in Benfield it's been the scandal of the century. So much gossip, you wouldn't believe. Of course, my years' long affair with Hugh has been part of it. It may not be public knowledge, but our inner circle of friends all know. None of them are talking to me now. And at the St Hilda's school gates, there's been constant staring and whispering whenever I go to pick up the kids. It's been pretty hellish, actually.

Things with Simon have been difficult – he's allowed me to stay in the house, but he's been sleeping in the spare room for the past two months. But now at least, something has happened that could take our lives in a whole different direction. Things are about to change, at last.

He gets back late this evening. The children have had their supper and gone to bed, but Daisy is still awake and when she hears their father coming in, she calls down for him to tuck her in.

After a while, he appears in the kitchen and pours himself a glass of red wine. He holds up the bottle at me, but I shake my head, trying to discern his mood from his expression. It's calm, but also rather grim.

'I need to talk to you about something,' he says.

'So do I.' My heart pounding, I open my mouth to launch into my speech, but Simon interrupts me.

'Me first,' he says, forcefully. 'I've been asked to head up our office in Bristol, and I'm going to accept.'

My face registers an 'Oh' of surprise.

'Thing is, Belinda, I'll be going alone. I've had plenty of time to consider my position, but as far as I'm concerned, our marriage is over.' His delivery of these words is stiff and formal. 'I'm sorry, but I'm afraid I can't get past what's happened. I'm sure you understand.'

I stare at him helplessly. He's speaking to me as if he's addressing a business meeting.

'I'll be filing for divorce, and this place will need to be sold and the proceeds divided.'

'But this place is our home,' I stammer. 'The children—'

'They'll just have to get used to the idea that they'll be living somewhere else. I'm going to go for full custody. And since they'll be spending most of their time in the West Country with me, you might want to consider basing yourself somewhere nearer there.'

'In the West Country?' I say faintly, as though he's suggested moving to the moon.

He turns down his mouth in a slightly sneering expression. 'Well, I can't see why on earth you'd want to stay in Nether Benfield. Your name is mud here. And it's not like you can hang out with your *friend* Juliet.' He gives a bitter edge to the word 'friend'. 'Even if she were speaking to you, I doubt she'll want to stay at Mullens End. The place will probably be rented out. Probably at least till *he* gets out, given there are no other family members around.' He reaches for the bottle of Malbec and tops up his glass. 'What was it you were going to tell me?'

'Nothing.' I shake my head. 'There's some lasagne in the Aga, if you want it. I'm going to go up and have a bath.'

I sit on the edge of the bath, waiting for it to fill. Once the blanket of scented foam is high enough, I pull off my robe and step into the water. I'm shaking slightly as I do so. Full custody of the children? Surely he won't be able to do that? Not if I have anything to do with it, anyway. I'll fight him all the way.

Then I catch sight of my body reflected in the vanity mirror. My stomach curves gently outwards. Wearing loose clothes, I can still hide it, but when I'm naked, it's very obvious that I'm pregnant. With everything that's been going on, I initially put the tiredness and lack of appetite down to stress. By the time I twigged, it was fairly late in the day and I turned out to be about fifteen weeks gone. My first scan, which I arranged to have done privately and attended alone, showed that it's a boy.

Now that my heart rate is returning to normal, I realise it's probably for the best that Simon's bombshell interrupted what was to have been my announcement that I'm in the club. He'll find out sooner or later; that much is certain. And I'm still hopeful that this pregnancy will signal a change for the better. It has to.

Lying back in the bath, I stroke the fleshy mound of my stomach, protruding through a clearing in the forest of bubbles. 'Don't worry, little one,' I whisper to my son. 'It's all going to be all right.'

EPILOGUE

11 JUNE

Juliet Mullen stands on the gravelled forecourt and looks around her with satisfaction.

Pete and his team of extra gardeners have been working flat out, and the place is looking perfect just in time for the Open Day. There's been a fantastic crop of damask roses this year, and their scent is so heady that she can smell it from a hundred yards away. Also, unlike last year, the weather forecast is for it to remain dry.

She thought long and hard about the decision to open Mullens End to the public again, eventually deciding to go ahead with the annual fixture in the Benfield calendar because she doesn't want people to think she's hiding. She's done nothing wrong, and she intends to prove it.

She's made some minor changes to the place, but they're changes that make her feel more comfortable, more confident. The heavy old oil paintings in the hall are gone, including the Gerald Brockhurst portrait of Ernest Mullen and Susan Ryder's of Hugh at twenty-one. They're packed up and stored in the attic, their places now taken by some contemporary canvasses that she has painstakingly sourced. She's replaced some of the stuffier antique furniture in the drawing room and dining room with modern pieces from Heal's. And instead of Labradors, she has a little Bichon Frise called Tinkerbell, Jeff having been permanently re-homed with the Dohertys. Hugh would despise this last change most of all, saying the only proper dog was a gun dog. But this is not Hugh's house any more.

Since his sentencing and incarceration, the board of trustees has met and decided to invoke a clause in the trust allowing them to formally revoke his life tenancy. And this not only cancels his own right of occupation, but that of his direct heirs. They also contacted the next in line: Alex Mullen; still resident in California, but tiring of the LA life and apparently planning a return to the UK. They claim they have met 'someone special' and hope to start a family. Alex has agreed with Roger Banborough that they will take over the house either on Juliet's death or sooner if she voluntarily gives up the responsibility at some point. If Luca settles permanently in Italy and has a family of his own there, for example.

The Langridges will not be visiting today either. Simon is now living in Somerset with the three children and Belinda has moved to a small house in Chiddingfold following the sale of their former marital home. Juliet has not heard a word from her former friend since that day last August when she confronted her in the garden of Birch Cottage.

The Kuchars and the Dohertys won't be there either. They've taken Juliet's side, of course; appalled by what Hugh put her through. But the house now has unpleasant associations for them. It was the site of two murders, after all. Or, depending who you believe, an unintentional homicide and an accidental death.

But the infamy of Mullens End locally will bring even more visitors, Juliet is sure of it. They'll be keener than ever to roam around the place, particularly to gawp at the mausoleum. Which will remain firmly locked.

The gates are now open, and members of the public start to stream down the drive. Luca and a couple of his friends from his primary school days are on hand to direct cars and hand out leaflets. Now that he's finished his Baccalaureate, Luca has returned to the UK permanently, and is applying for universities in London. He's enjoying reconnecting with local friends and enjoying a new social life. Juliet is happy that he will have a home to come to forty minutes from London, once he's started his degree course. He'll be able to bring his university friends back to swim and play tennis. It will be fun, she thinks with satisfaction. And then, when he's a lot older, she can create a separate annexe for herself and let Luca and his partner have the run of the main house. With any luck, eventually there will be children – her grandchildren – being raised at Mullens End. The Mullen portraits can stay in the attic, and bit by bit she will wipe out all traces of her former husband. There'll be nothing of him left in the place that he loved more than he loved her. The thought fills her with satisfaction.

A visiting teen carelessly drops a sweet wrapper as he barrels along the path towards the rose maze. It drifts to a stop at Juliet's feet and, without thinking, she bends down to pick it up, thrusting it into the pocket of her linen trousers.

A woman in sturdy shoes and a canvas bucket hat watches her curiously, then points to the handsome façade of the house and asks, 'Is this *your* home?'

'Yes,' says Juliet, smiling at her graciously, 'Yes, it is.'

Her phone pings with a message, and she's instantly taken back to that June afternoon twelve months ago, when she discovered the Instagram message from the person claiming to be Alexis Lambert. This one is from Justine Doherty. *'Thought you ought to see this,'* it says simply, with the addition of a shocked face emoji.

'This' is a screenshot from Belinda Langridge's Facebook page. The photo is of a beatific Belinda, her skin rosy and glowing, her eyes luminous. Juliet takes in the caption – *'The future'* – but it's not this that holds her attention. It's the baby she's holding in her arms.

A baby with the Mullen red hair.

Juliet smiles, shaking her head slowly at the image. Because the child might be a Mullen by blood, but he will never inherit Mullens End.

And nor will Hugh Mullen ever set foot in the place again.

A LETTER FROM ALISON

Dear reader,

Thank you so much for choosing to read *The House Guest*. If you enjoyed it and want to get news of future releases, you can sign up at the following link:

www.bookouture.com/alison-james

We're all familiar with the old saying 'An Englishman's home is his castle,' and even in our modern lives, we like to think of our homes as our safe spaces, as inviolable. What would happen then, if somebody arrived at your door who threatened that safety and security? Who threatened your entire existence? That's the scenario I set out to explore in *The House Guest*.

I really hope you loved reading it as much as I enjoyed writing it, and if you did, it would be wonderful if you could write a review and help other readers discover my books. I'm always happy to hear from readers on social media using the links below.

Alison James

KEEP IN TOUCH WITH ALISON

goodreads.com/author/show/17361567.Alison_James

facebook.com/Alison-James-books

x.com/AlisonJbooks

tiktok.com/@allyjay855